Bolan dropped and rolled, letting the shrapnel swarm above him

Some bits came too damned close for comfort. Then, almost before the screaming started, he was up and charging off along the right-hand corridor.

He didn't want to use a third grenade yet—had gone in hoping he might extract a prisoner for questioning. That wouldn't happen if he kept on blowing them to bloody tatters, but he couldn't very well pick one out of a skirmish line and bag him, either.

Once he had engaged the enemy, inflicting damage was Bolan's top priority, with personal survival running neck-and-neck. He'd never undertaken any action meant to be a suicide attack, and while he recognized the danger waiting for him every time he hit the field, he always planned to make it out on the other side alive, intact.

Which, at the moment, meant another rude surprise for his approaching enemies.

Don Pendleton's Mack Bolan®

Jungle Firestorm

A GOLD EAGLE BOOK FROM

W❂RLDWIDE®

TORONTO • NEW YORK • LONDON
AMSTERDAM • PARIS • SYDNEY • HAMBURG
STOCKHOLM • ATHENS • TOKYO • MILAN
MADRID • WARSAW • BUDAPEST • AUCKLAND

First edition January 2014

ISBN-13: 978-0-373-61566-7

Special thanks and acknowledgment to
Mike Newton for his contribution to this work.

JUNGLE FIRESTORM

Printed in U.S.A.

Liberty and democracy become unholy when their hands are dyed red with innocent blood.

—Mahatma K. Gandhi,
Non-Violence in Peace and War (1948)

I don't dictate morality. I use the force required to stop atrocities.

—Mack Bolan,
"The Executioner"

For Abdul Ghani Lone.

PROLOGUE

Mumbai, India

By daybreak, the devotees had begun to gather. Scores at first, then hundreds, winding their way on foot or bicycles toward Babulnath, the ancient temple of Shiva that stood in the very heart of Mumbai. Built in 1780, vastly enlarged in 1890, the temple rose one thousand feet above sea level, and until the 1980s ranked among the tallest buildings in Mumbai. The faithful climbed to seek their blessings, if their legs would bear them; otherwise, they were carried aloft. They came each day, but most particularly on this morning once a year, to celebrate the rites of Maha Shivaratri.

Celebrations of Maha Shivaratri began on the thirteenth night of Phalguna, the twelfth month of the calendar that ran from February 20 to March 21. That fell in the middle of India's winter, but seasons were relative. In Mumbai, on the Arabian Sea, the temperature on winter nights rarely dropped below sixty degrees, while days simmered in the high eighties and nineties. No one bundled into parkas on their way to celebrate the year's most holy day.

In preparation for the ritual, Shaivas drew three horizontal lines of holy ash across their foreheads, symbolizing spiritual knowledge, purity and penance. Many donned rosaries made from seeds of the rudraksha tree, said to have sprung from the tears of Lord Shiva himself.

Thus prepared, worshippers approached the Shiv Lingam, a stone representation of Shiva interpreted by some as depicting the mighty god's phallus. The rite of Maha Shivaratri included six steps: first bathing the lingam with water, milk and honey, adding betel leaves to represent purification of the soul; second, applying vermilion paste to represent virtue; third, offering fruit to secure longevity and gratification of desires; fourth, burning incense to yield wealth; fifth, lighting a lamp, deemed conducive to gaining knowledge; and finally, offering more betel leaves to claim satisfaction with worldly pleasures.

All that, beginning at the crack of dawn and going on throughout the day, as thousands dedicated themselves to Hinduism's most powerful god, the Creator, Preserver, Destroyer, Concealer and Revealer. Maha Shivaratri was a day of both solemnity and festivity, climaxed by a grand procession with percussion and wind instruments. It was a day of consecration and renewal.

Or it would be, if allowed to run its normal course.

"Did you set the charges?" Kiram Kulkharni asked.

"They're set," Gopal Pawar confirmed.

"And are the others in position?"

"Ready for the signal."

"Take your place," Kulkharni ordered, and received a brisk nod in return. Pawar jogged off toward the position assigned to him, the fourth corner of what would soon become a killing pen.

Kulkharni wore traditional Indian garb: a long *sherwani* coat over a light, loose-fitting *kurta* shirt and *shalwar kameez* trousers. The coat concealed an AK-101 assault rifle chambered for 5.5 mm NATO rounds, stock folded, slung beneath his right arm on a swivel strap, and four Australian F1 fragmentation grenades, each weighing thirteen ounces, packed with sixty-two grams of RDX explosive compound and four thousand steel spheres, with a killing radius of thirty meters.

Bahrat Gunaji, stationed closest to the temple, had the detonator that would set off seven pounds of Semtex plastic explosive, wreaking havoc on the pilgrims closest to the Shiv Lingam, perhaps with force enough to bring the roof down on their heads. It hardly mattered, though. The goal was simple: start them running for their lives, into the gauntlet that Kulkharni had prepared for them, with automatic weapons and grenades to scourge their ranks along the way.

Each year in India, hundreds were killed in the bizarre phenomenon of temple stampedes—a crush of humanity fueled in equal parts by hysterical zeal and panic. One such stampede, at Sabarimala, had killed a hundred worshippers in January 2011. Another, two months later, had killed sixty-three in Uttar Pradesh. The record, Kulkharni believed, stood at 265 deaths in Maharashtra state during January 2005.

He planned to beat that body count this morning.

Starting any second now.

The first explosion barely had a chance to register before the second followed. Pawar saw a roiling cloud of smoke and dust burst from the pillared entryway to Babulnath, enveloping the pilgrims who were trudging toward communion with their god. Immediately, automatic weapons opened fire and Pawar joined them, spraying the stunned crowd before him with his Chinese Type 81 assault rifle.

Shouts and wails rose from the masses as converging streams of fire ripped through the press of bodies, striking men, women and children with complete impartiality. The magazine of Pawar's rifle held thirty 7.62 mm rounds, spent in under three seconds of steady firing at the weapon's cyclic rate of 650 rounds per minute. He swapped it out quickly for a fresh one, wishing that he could have brought the larger 75-round drums instead.

A grenade exploded in the crowd, and Pawar saw the tattered remnants of a woman's sari flutter skyward, stained with blood. Reaching under his *sherwani,* Pawar palmed one of his own grenades and pulled the pin, then lofted the bomb above the jostling sea of heads, watching it tumble, strike a pilgrim's skull with force enough to knock him down then drop from sight.

The blast was nothing next to the preceding Semtex charges, but it still tore flesh and shattered bone, killing and maiming, amplifying mass hysteria. The mob was running now, downhill from Babulnath, fleeing to save their lives.

They trampled one another by the dozen, by the score, while bullets snapped and sang among them, smacking into bodies, bursting skulls like melons struck with hammers. Pawar was exhilarated by the mayhem, emptying another magazine into the jostling, screaming mass with no attempt to aim at any given target.

"You want Shiva the Destroyer?" he called after them. "I'm right here! Worship *me!*"

Kulkharni rattled off a third and final magazine from his AK-101, chasing the massacre survivors with a swarm of bullets, dropping more as they fled limping and lurching from the killing ground. Behind those who had managed to escape, the ground was littered—heaped—with bodies. Some of them were moving, whimpering, while many more lay deathly still.

It was enough.

His orders to the others had been simple: once the temple charges blew, each man would fire three magazines into the crowd, ensuring a stampede of catastrophic proportions. Deaths and injuries from trampling would match, and possibly exceed, the damage done by Kulkharni and his two soldiers. He reckoned two hundred were dead or disabled, and probably more.

There was no doubt his master would be pleased.

And it was time to go now, while the mindless mob ran wild, and officers of the elite National Security Guard were still trying to reach Babulnath, battling their way upstream against a tidal wave of fear.

Kulkharni left the others to their own devices. He had laid out their escape routes in advance, rehearsed them, and if any of his soldiers happened to forget their orders, they were on their own. If cornered by police, their oath demanded physical resistance to the death—or, failing that, the quickest suicide that they could manage once in custody.

To live, to spill their secrets, meant annihilation for their families.

No one, Kulkharni thought as he retreated, was beyond their master's reach.

CHAPTER ONE

Dana Bandar, Mumbai

Mack Bolan, aka the Executioner, navigated Mumbai's teeming streets in his rented Maruti Suzuki Ritz—known as the Splash, outside India—handling the five-speed manual transmission, the right-hand drive and crush of city life surrounding him on every side while searching out his target. It was claustrophobic chaos, an agoraphobe's worst nightmare, but the soldier was making progress.

For a start, his flight had been only an hour and fifteen minutes late arriving at Chhatrapati Shivaji International Airport, South Asia's second busiest hub for passenger traffic, and one of only a handful on Earth located within a major city's municipal limits. Expansion of the airport was impossible, under the circumstances, but from what he'd seen inside the terminal, construction still proceeded as if there was room to grow.

Bolan had checked no luggage through, stuck with a single carry-on, but Customs, Immigration and retrieval of his rented car still took the best part of another hour. He had no specific deadline, but his mission—as was normal—called for all deliberate speed, and it required a sniper's patience to keep smiling at officials who, it seemed, were hired specifically to clog the wheels of progress.

That was the way of life in Asia, something he'd learned early as a soldier barely out of high school, on his own for the first time in a world nearly beyond imagining. One of Bolan's recent passes through the Indian subcontinent had been a flying visit on the trail of a revived assassin's cult, evoking grisly echoes from the thirteenth century. This day, his endless war had brought him back again, proving the rule that evil, though defeated in the short-term, always found a way to rise again.

His destination was a factory on Kalyan Street, inland from Princes Dock. The good news: he had found it, and he was making decent time on the approach. The bad news: Bolan didn't know how many shooters he would find inside the place, and it stood three blocks from the Mandvi police station, a quick run south on Frere Road.

That meant no time to mess around once he was on-site, taking care of business. A little shock and awe to introduce himself, rattle the opposition's cage and launch himself into the blitz he'd planned during the flight from LAX that had consumed the best part of a long and tiring day. Twenty-two hours overall, and if he didn't have it down by now, he never would.

Bolan was prepped for anything—including, so he hoped, the kind of unexpected glitches that were part and parcel of a combat soldier's life. His first stop after he had cleared the airport was a visit to an arms supplier known for his willingness to deal with anyone who met his asking price. Bankrolled with a donation from the Crips in Compton, mid-six figures from their earnings in the crack cocaine trade, Bolan found he could afford the best hardware on offer in Mumbai.

He'd started with the basics: an INSAS assault rifle chambered in 5.56 mm NATO, and a modified Kalashnikov currently the standard infantry weapon of India's armed forces. Bolan backed that up with a 9 mm Mini-Uzi submachine gun, for concealment, with a sound suppressor tooled to fit its threaded muzzle. For long-distance work, he backed that up with a Vidhwansak bolt-action sniper rifle in 14.5×114 mm, the equivalent of .57 caliber. The dealer told him that the big gun's name in Sanskrit meant *Destroyer*—fitting for a piece that sent its sixty-gram projectiles smoking downrange at 3,300 feet per second, striking with twenty-two thousand foot-pounds of shattering energy. To feed the beast, Bolan chose a selection of high-explosive incendiary rounds and armor-piercing full-metal-jacket rounds with steel cores.

For his sidearm, Bolan stayed domestic, going with a clone of the venerable Browning Hi-Power semiautomatic, manufactured by the Indian government's Ordnance Factories Board as the 9 mm Pistol Auto A1. The name change notwithstanding, it preserved the Browning's magazine capacity of thirteen rounds in 9 mm Parabellum, single-action on the first shot, carried cocked and locked for fast-draw capability. Its muzzle, also threaded, would accommodate the second sound suppressor he chose. In passing, he picked up a tantō dagger with a sheath that let it nestle horizontally, across the small of Bolan's back.

Finally, he bought two dozen RGO fragmentation grenades, imported from Russia, each weighing just over one pound. The RGOs featured an impact fuse, activated after a pyrotechnic delay of 1.5 seconds, backed up with a secondary fuse to trigger detonation within four seconds if the first one failed. Less worry, that way, for the pitcher, while an enemy on the receiving end still had no time to duck.

Nearing his target, Bolan figured he was good to go—or, anyway, as good as he could be, without a head count on the enemy. The penetration was a gamble, but what else was new? He started taking chances from the moment that a mission was accepted, and there'd been no thought of turning this one down.

Not with disaster riding on the line.

His first view of the factory from ground level made Bolan reassess the target. He had known it was around a quarter of a block in length, but now saw that it stood three stories tall—and that, from all appearances, it wasn't even any kind of working factory. The name printed across its brick facade was what he had expected—Pandit Saraf Ltd.—but it had faded almost to a ghostly afterimage, and the building clearly hadn't been producing anything for years. Weeds sprouted through the broken asphalt of the parking lot out front, some kind of oily-looking creeper had a death grip on the loading dock.

The building could well have been abandoned if it wasn't for the well-worn path that led to the back, along a driveway nobody had ever taken time to pave.

Bolan made out the tire tracks there, fresh ones, in soil dampened by recent rain. They overlapped and were of several sizes, telling him that multiple vehicles had been in and out of there the day before—or two days, max. And they had done their best to hide that fact from prying eyes.

The sun was setting at his back, casting a long shadow over the brickwork of the former factory. Its windows, long since boarded over, were blind eyes that couldn't watch him circle to his left and move along the unpaved driveway toward whatever lay in wait for him behind the hulking structure. Bolan watched his step, remained alert for lookouts hiding in the shadows there, and thought about response times from the nearby police station.

He had researched Mumbai's police en route to India. The force's motto—"to protect the good and to punish the evil"—had a noble ring to it, but media reports disclosed the same corruption scandals and brutality complaints that every police department in the world confronted constantly. On the practical side, he'd learned that officers carried a variety of sidearms, including Glocks, Smith & Wesson M&P semiautomatics and Browning knockoffs like the one he carried slung beneath his left armpit. Their long guns varied widely, from the venerable Short Magazine Lee-Enfield Mk III rifle, introduced in 1907, to AK-47s, Heckler & Koch MP-5 submachine guns and 37 mm Milkor Stopper riot guns.

In short, they could be packing damn near anything.

The force was big on motorcycles—with more than fourteen hundred of them on the street—and short on prowl cars, with 155 available if all of them were roadworthy. Toss in nine hundred Jeeps and some five hundred other vehicles, categorized as "special," "big" and "light," and Mumbai's finest had mobility.

But how long would it take them to respond, once shots were fired?

First, someone in the neighborhood would have to call in a disturbance. Given Mumbai's crowding, Bolan would have been reluctant to call any street unoccupied, but what he saw of Kalyan Street at sundown did a decent imitation of evacuation. Granting that there had to be squatters huddled in some of the older buildings that surrounded him, he questioned whether they'd have phones or would be likely to contact police for anything except a personal emergency.

He had considered exit strategies for when police arrived, bearing in mind his private vow that he would never kill a cop for any reason, even if it meant his own imprisonment and death. Evasion and escape would have to be accomplished without spilling blood of any law enforcement officer. All were soldiers of the same side in Mack Bolan's eyes, and thus immune to lethal action from the Executioner.

He reached the north end of the driveway-alley, leading with the muzzle of his INSAS rifle as he eased around the corner. Half a dozen cars were parked back there, ranging from a dwarfish Tata Nano compact to a jet-black SUV, the popular Mahindra Scorpio. A back door to the former factory stood open, with some kind of music that sounded like mutant hip-hop blaring from somewhere inside.

Enough racket to cover him on his approach, he hoped. At least to get him through the door.

THE SONG WAS a recent hit from Machas With Attitude, off their *Death Punch* album, Sumukh "Smokey" Mysore belting out the lead. Rajesh Singh kept time, tapping one foot under his desk, while listening to Ajit Benipuri make excuses for his failure to collect a debt the syndicate was owed.

"He only had eight thousand rupees, so I took it all and warned him—"

"*Warned* him?" Singh cut in. "The bastard is always short, with some excuse. You've pampered him for weeks, Ajit."

"Excuse me, but—"

"I don't excuse you. When I send you to collect one hundred thousand rupees, I expect to see the money on my desk, and not a rupee less."

"But if he doesn't have it—"

"Then you take one of his children. Make a clear example of the brat. Stop acting like a *chutia* yourself!"

Benipuri was fuming, but he dared not say whatever came to mind as a retort. Instead, he ducked his head, a jerky nod of acquiescence and submission, muttering, "I will go back tomorrow and collect the full amount."

"And think twice, next time," Singh advised him, "before interrupting me when I am busy with important work."

The work—interrogation of a spy his men had captured—was frustrating Rajesh Singh. The man was proving tougher than expected, making noise, but not divulging any of the information Singh required. His name, to start, and the identity of his employer. He did not have the bearing of a rival gangster, clearly was not an Afghani or a tattooed member of the Mudaliar crime family.

Some kind of a policeman, then, but that still left a world of possibilities to choose from. If local, was he from the Crime Branch, Special Branch, Narcotics Cell or the Economic Offenses Wing? If federal, was he an agent of the National Investigation Agency? Perhaps the Directorate of Revenue Intelligence, assigned to investigate smuggling? Or the broader-based Central Bureau of Investigation?

Singh had to know what he was dealing with, before he killed the pig and sank his weighted corpse in Back Bay. Otherwise, how could he make a sensible report to his superiors?

And failing that, what good was he? No more than Ajit Benipuri, with his whining and excuses.

The spy had been detected lurking near a lab where tablets of methamphetamine mixed with caffeine were turned out by the tens of thousands weekly. He was lucky that the guards there had not killed him outright, though considering the treatment he'd received since then, he might not say his luck was good.

Singh had reported the capture to his boss, requesting that he be allowed to conduct the interrogation himself, rather than handing the prisoner over to specialists. If he cracked the pig, it would be to his credit, perhaps justify a promotion.

But if he should fail…

Dismissing Benipuri from his office and his thoughts, Singh rose and moved back toward the room devoid of windows, where his captive had been duct-taped naked to a metal folding chair. The concrete floor around his modest throne was marked with bloodstains, smeared by footprints. As Singh entered, Tabish Khan was fastening a pair of alligator clips to two legs of the chair. Their cable trailed away to a hand-crank generator mounted on a nearby rolling dolly.

"Are we ready?" Singh inquired.

"Good to go," Khan said.

"You can control the voltage?"

"Absolutely."

"I want no mistakes. Kill him before I have the answers I require, and you will take his place," Singh warned.

Khan blinked at that, then said, "I guarantee the charge won't kill him. Not unless you want it to."

"Then let's begin," Singh said.

The crack of an explosion rocked the factory.

WHEN BOLAN REACHED the door, he peered around the corner and saw four men seated at a card table, playing a board game that resembled chess, but with pieces in four colors, starting from opposite corners. All four were packing handguns, while a couple of Kalashnikovs were propped against a nearby wall. The players didn't notice him, and Bolan took a moment to decide the best way of announcing his arrival.

Why not with a bang?

He palmed one of the Russian grenades, removed its pin and lobbed the bomb through the doorway with a side-arm pitch, lofting it just enough to drop it in the middle of the gaming table. It bounced once, scattering pieces every which way, while the players lurched back in their chairs, one of them toppling over on his back. The blast, a second later, sprayed the inner room with shrapnel, shredding flesh and chipping cinder blocks. Its hot wind wafted cries of pain into the night.

He followed through, found one man worth a mercy round and stroked the INSAS autorifle's trigger once, drilling a hole between the fallen shooter's eyes. The rest were either dead or close to dying, and he left them to it, moving on. Farther inside the one-time factory, a din of voices told him that he'd kicked a hornet's nest.

So be it.

Bolan's guiding rule of thumb was to eliminate as many adversaries as he could in any given firefight. Predators he killed today wouldn't commit a fresh atrocity tomorrow, when he had a fresh batch to contend with. Twenty, thirty, it was all the same to Bolan if he had a chance to work the odds and turn them in his favor.

The soldier cleared the game room slaughterhouse, paused in an empty corridor that led away to left and right, with doors offset on either side. None of the doors were opening, but the excited voices yelling in what he took for Hindi came from both directions simultaneously: danger played in stereo. The babble on his left sounded a little closer, and the sound of running feet was louder there, so Bolan turned in that direction as he primed a second frag grenade.

If they were any good, they would begin to fire as soon as he was visible. Cutting it close, he let the point man of the left-hand reinforcements show himself, then pitched the grenade downrange, trying to put it somewhere in the shooter's strike zone. When his target ducked aside, it only helped the Executioner, as his grenade flew on to strike a wall behind the rolling man and detonate on impact.

Bolan dropped and rolled as well, letting the shrapnel swarm above him, some bits coming too close for comfort. Then, almost before the screaming started, he was up and charging off along the right-hand corridor, heading to meet the other half of what had been a pincers movement—now a broken weapon, but still dangerous.

He didn't want to use a third grenade just yet, hoping that he might extract a prisoner for questioning. That wouldn't happen if he kept on blowing them to bloody tatters, but he couldn't very well pick one out of a skirmish line and bag him, either. Someone stunned or wounded, maybe, but with life and wits enough remaining for the two of them to have a private chat when they were safely off the firing line.

Not yet, though. Once he had engaged the enemy, inflicting damage was his top priority, with personal survival running neck and neck. Bolan had never undertaken any action meant to be a suicide attack, and while he recognized the danger waiting for him every time he hit the field, he always planned to make it out the other side alive, intact.

Which, at the moment, meant another rude surprise for his approaching enemies.

He reached the corner where he either had to turn left and move on to meet the fast-approaching gunmen, or continue straight ahead and through a door in front of him that stood slightly ajar. Reluctant as he was to let a quirk of architecture dictate strategy, Bolan decided he would try a bit of both.

A long dive first, sliding and rolling on the concrete floor that countless feet had polished over time. As soon as he had cleared the corner, Bolan started firing with his INSAS, 3-round bursts that angled upward from floor level toward his startled targets, 5.56 mm manglers ripping into groins and abdomens and chests. Emerging from the roll, he hit the door in a crouch, burst through and wound up in a claustrophobic room that smelled like suffering.

There was no other way to say it. Turning swiftly, Bolan's first impression was confirmed by what he saw: a naked man secured with duct tape to a metal folding chair, his face and body mottled with the telltale evidence of cruel abuse. Interrogation, he surmised, seeing the hand-crank generator on its dolly, cables fastened to the chair's front legs with alligator clips.

He closed and locked the door behind him, crossed the room and kicked those cables free. They snaked across the bloodstained floor. The lock, he knew, would not buy them much time. He knelt before the captive, saw a pair of dulled eyes focus on his face, and went to work cutting the duct tape free with clean strokes of his blade.

"Can you stand up and walk?" he asked.

"I think so," the prisoner said. And then added with greater confidence, "I can."

"You ready to get out of here?"

"I am, indeed."

"You come in here with clothes?"

He nodded. "I don't know where they've gone."

"All right, we'll have to get you some," the Executioner replied.

And turned back toward the small room's door.

It stood to reason that survivors from the hallway shooting moments earlier would have their weapons aimed and holding steady on that door. Shooters familiar with the layout of the former factory would recognize the one and only exit from the torture room where Bolan and his naked prisoner were penned. They hadn't started shooting yet, but likely would at the first sign of movement.

Bolan crouched to one side of the door, reached out and turned its knob. A heartbeat later, he had flung it open, braced for seven kinds of hell to hammer through and rake the walls beyond.

But nothing happened.

Cautiously, he risked a glance outside and counted five men down, three of them still alive enough to twitch. He stepped into the open, scanned the corridor in both directions, then turned back and beckoned to the nude man who was edging up behind him.

"Grab whatever seems to fit the best, and make it quick," he said. "Don't mind the blood. We'll get you something cleaner when we're clear."

Making it *when,* not *if.* A mix of confidence and wishful thinking.

Bolan stood guard while the captive dressed in haste—shirt, slacks and shoes, without going for socks or underwear. Call it five minutes, which was decent time, including grappling with the former owners of his new wardrobe.

And just in time, based on the sound of new voices approaching, somewhere from the cold heart of the building.

"Time to go," Bolan growled.

"I am ready, sir," his new companion said.

"No need to 'sir' me," Bolan replied, already moving back the way he'd come, in the direction of the game room and its exit on the night. "We'll do the introductions later."

"As you say, sir."

The hostile voices were advancing as the pair moved away, somebody shouting orders to the others, likely barking at them to shut up, since silence fell after the second repetition. Bolan only heard the sound of running feet now, trying to judge distance as the gap was closed, relieved to see the game room with its twisted bodies lying in their pools of crimson on the concrete floor.

"Outside," he said, and led the way.

The liberated prisoner wasn't exactly steady on his feet, but he was keeping up, lurching along in clothing torn by Bolan's bullets, soaked with blood so that the shirt and trousers stuck in places to his own bruised flesh. A passing stranger might have thought he was the ultimate in walking wounded, and that still might prove to be the case. Besides the obvious—the beating, burns from cigarettes and the electric shocks he had received—there might be serious internal injuries. If he could just keep moving until they cleared the killing zone and reached Bolan's Suzuki Ritz, at least he had a fighting chance.

As they neared the driveway that had granted Bolan access to the factory, the men faced a glare of headlights rolling toward them. Two vehicles at least—no, three, he saw now—and to play it safe, he had to calculate that each contained two shooters on their way to reinforce the home team.

But they didn't seem to know that anything was wrong, so far. To break the news, Bolan held down the trigger of his INSAS autorifle, emptying its 30-round translucent magazine in one long burst that raked across three windshields, one after the other. Already reloading with a fresh mag, Bolan called back to his unarmed sidekick, "Run like hell!"

They ran, and he supposed that it was hell all right, inside the battered captive's borrowed shoes. The good news: all three of the late-arriving cars were stalled and going nowhere, with their drivers dead, wounded or hunkered down to dodge incoming fire. They couldn't turn, and didn't want to risk reversing down the driveway yet, if they were even capable of doing so, which meant the other cars Bolan had seen on his approach were bottled up.

For now, but likely not for long.

They ran and made it to his rented ride, but as he dropped into the driver's seat, Bolan saw one car rolling backward from the driveway he had just escaped, its driver working on a three-point turn that would allow him to give chase.

They weren't clear yet, and Bolan knew that it could still go either way.

CHAPTER TWO

Skyline Drive, Shenandoah National Park, Virginia
Two days earlier

A mountain lion stepped into the middle of the road and paused there, straddling the white line, glaring at the man and his machine that were approaching from the north, all noise and stench of oil. The driver slowed, then stopped, his engine idling while the tawny cat decided what to do. At last, after a long two minutes, it proceeded, crossed the pavement, leaped into the shadowed woodland on the east side of the highway and was gone.

Mack Bolan wished it well. He'd read somewhere that cougars had been extirpated—fancy, neutral word for slaughtered, hounded to extinction—in Virginia by the tag end of the 1880s. Sightings still continued, more each year in fact, as Mother Nature mocked humanity. It was a privilege for him to see the cat.

When it was clear, he brought the Ford Mustang he'd rented out of Washington Dulles International Airport back up to cruising speed, watching for other wildlife as he motored south on Skyline Drive, along the backbone of Virginia's Blue Ridge Mountains. The scenic drive ran for 105 miles, from Front Royal to Waynesboro, but he wasn't seeing all of it today.

In fact, he never had.

His destination was around the midpoint of the north-south journey, at a farm named for a nearby rocky promontory often photographed by hikers, christened for its rugged profile: Stony Man.

HE WAS HEADED for the Farm. Capital *F* because he rarely used its full name, much less any of the more obscure code names it had been tagged with over time, since it was founded by a President now out of office and relieved of dealing with the nonstop crises that pertained to national security. The Farm survived because its usefulness—its sheer necessity—was demonstrated yearly in a host of ways that most Americans would never recognize.

The System worked, but only to a point. When danger was so clear and present that it couldn't wait for a wrangling vote in Congress, when some human predator appeared to be above the law, when a catastrophe could only be averted by immediate decisive action, then America had the Farm.

Mack Bolan was the operation's first recruit—its inspiration, if the truth be told. His long and lonely war against the Mafia, begun as retribution for the slaughter of his family, had echoed in the halls of power. Some who'd heard the rumblings were afraid, and rightly so, based on their personal corruption. Others saw a gleam of possibility for swift reactions in an age where terrorism was an end unto itself, and certain nations had linked hands with thugs to loot the world.

These days, a visit to the Farm felt like a homecoming of sorts to Bolan. Family, with any luck, was where a person found it, and adoptive links were often stronger, more substantial and supportive, than the accidental bonds of blood.

Another thirty miles to go. He'd given up on fiddling with the Mustang's radio. Religious shouters put him off, and while he liked the country stations well enough, they faded in and out with too much static for him to enjoy the music.

Silence was its own reward.

He didn't have an inkling of the reason why he'd been invited to the Farm this morning. It would be another mission, certainly—but what? And where?

He couldn't second-guess it from the tide of breaking news. No matter where he looked, there was a war in progress, starting up, or winding down. Police were being murdered or were killing protest marchers. Governments were reeling from rebellions, scandal and the threat of bankruptcy, while criminal cartels made billions feeding habits, peddling misery.

Enough work for a soldier's lifetime, anywhere he turned.

But Bolan wasn't called unless a job was something special. Something no one else could tackle with a reasonable expectation of success *and* secrecy. Or, rather, say *deniability*.

Whatever happened once he had been pointed at a target and agreed to take it on, the end result could not blow back on Washington, or on America at large. If victory was claimed in whispered tones, behind closed doors, there could be no proof that the White House or its several agencies had intervened.

He was expendable—but hey, what else was new?

During his one-man war, he'd been a hunted fugitive. Then he had "died," a staged event to wipe the slate, and been reborn. New face, an ever-changing list of names, no fingerprints on file.

Except, of course, at Stony Man. Along with DNA.

The Farm would know if he went down for real. Somehow, they'd verify it and his dossier would formally be closed. There'd likely be a brief and very private mourning party—and beyond that, nothing.

When he was two miles from the Farm and closing, Bolan knew the hidden cameras would be tracking him, an officer assigned to morning-shift security reporting his approach, guards drifting toward the gate, well armed, in case there was a problem. At the gate, before he was allowed to enter, Bolan's ID would be verified by facial recognition software, and a heartbeat sensor would determine whether anybody else was with him in the car, concealed.

They weren't, but if there had been, neutralizing measures would be taken. Any extra heartbeats would be stilled.

Technology. You had to love it—sometimes, anyway.

But in the crunch, a clear solution still required boots on the ground.

He cleared the rolling gate, no lookouts visible, and watched it close behind him as the Mustang powered toward the farmhouse and nerve center of the Stony Man facility. Off to his left, a guy dressed all in denim drove a John Deere 6D Series tractor with a disk harrow hitched up behind it, turning up the soil before another field was seeded. Stony Man had always been a working farm, unique in that its hands were all on active duty with the U.S. military—Army Special Forces, Navy SEALs, Marine Corps Force Reconnaissance, Air Force Combat Control Team—sworn to silence under pain of closed-door prosecution before the secret Foreign Intelligence Surveillance Court. They served a tour of duty at the Farm, moved on and were replaced.

Only the hard-core staff remained in place, year in, year out. And some of them were waiting for him on the long porch of the farmhouse now, as Bolan pulled into the yard.

Up front, and not a full-time resident, was Hal Brognola,

from the upper echelons of Justice back in Washington. He ranked as Bolan's oldest living friend, had hunted him across the country in another life when the big Fed was with the FBI and Bolan topped the agency's most-wanted list. They had begun collaborating then, outside the law, and knew each other well enough to recognize what was and wasn't possible.

Brognola knew, for instance, that he couldn't ask the Executioner to kill simply because some politician wished it or considered it desirable. He needed something more than "national security" mentioned in passing as a cover for some personal agenda. Bolan, for his part, knew that Brognola would quit the program in a heartbeat if it turned into a tool for greedy bastards feathering their own nests at society's expense. They trusted each other, held that trust inviolate.

Beside Brognola, on the porch, stood Barbara Price, the Farm's mission controller, heart and soul. And to her left, bolt-upright in his wheelchair, Aaron Kurtzman wore a smile for Bolan's benefit, his bulk reminding Bolan why the techno-wizard's friends called him "the Bear."

"Good trip?" the big Fed asked as they shook hands.

The cougar stalked through Bolan's mind as he responded, "Uneventful."

"Good. We're set up in the War Room."

They entered through a door of armored steel, disguised with wood veneer. Along their route to reach the elevator, here and there, familiar faces nodded to Bolan as he passed. Some stood in awe of him, while others simply knew him as a man who came and went irregularly, doing business for the Farm. None but the three accompanying him to the elevator knew about the other life he had discarded, who he'd been or what he'd done for family and honor. Grateful to have him on their side, in whatever capacity, they didn't press their luck.

The elevator took them down to basement level, and Brognola led them to the War Room tucked away there, leaving them to sort out seating at the table built for twenty. When they'd settled in, the big Fed seated at the table's head and a huge flat-screen TV wall-mounted at his back, he asked Bolan, "Have you been keeping up with news from India, by any chance?"

"Can't say I have," Bolan replied.

"You missed the stampede, then?"

An eyebrow arched, Bolan allowed, "I must have."

"It's a weird deal," Brognola pressed on. "I won't call it tradition or a ritual, because it isn't planned. But every year, they have mob scenes—stampedes, in fact—at various religious sites around the country. Thousands come to celebrate and worship, mass hysteria kicks in somehow, and when the dust clears, you've got dozens, even hundreds, dead and injured."

On the flat screen behind Brognola, projected still shots showed the aftermath of violence, replaced by video clips of stampedes in progress. Men, women and children were flattened, left bleeding and dazed, some unconscious or dying. All for what? To get inside a building or away from one, without apparent cause?

"I've got a list here, going back to 1954," Brognola said. "At least 350 dead at Kumbh Mela that year, with two hundred missing and over two thousand injured. Fifty dead and seventy-four injured in 1992, at Kumbakonam. Two years later, 114 dead and five hundred hurt at Nagpur. It goes on like that through 2011, with 106 dead and at least another hundred injured at Sabarimala."

"And then," Price said, "there was last week's stampede."

"Mumbai," Brognola said, more bloody footage coming up on the TV behind him. "The official tally says 267 dead and something like a thousand injured. Only this one wasn't just another mob kicked into high gear over nothing."

Bolan had it now. "The bombing."

"Bombing *and* shooting," Brognola amended. "A full-scale terrorist attack, involving three confirmed participants, and maybe more. The early count says eighty-six killed, around 450 wounded. Some of those will likely die."

Mumbai—formerly Bombay—had suffered brutal terrorist attacks over the past two decades, starting with coordinated bombings that had killed 257 and wounded more than seven hundred in March 1993. Ten years later to the day, a blast on a commuter train killed ten and injured seventy. In August 2003, two bombs killed forty-four and wounded 150. In July 2006, more railway bombs claimed 209 lives and injured seven hundred victims. In November 2008, eleven closely timed bombing and shooting attacks killed another 164 people and wounded at least 308. The bustling city had learned to live on edge, never knowing when another disaster might strike.

"So, where do we come in?" Bolan inquired.

"G-troop," Brognola answered. "That's a spin-off from the so-called Mumbai Mafia, run by a character named Riyaz Geelani and his number two, Sayeed Zargar."

At the far end of the table, Aaron Kurtzman pushed a button on the console that controlled the War Room's audiovisual system. Brognola didn't have to turn. He knew that candid shots of both Geelani and Zargar had come up on the flat screen at his back.

"If you've read much history—or saw the movie *Gandhi*—then you know there's been a major split forever on the Indian religious scene," Brognola continued. "Four of the world's major traditions were born in India—Hinduism, Buddhism, Jainism and Sikhism. Then comes Islam, in the seventh century, to make a five-card hand. Before the Brits could pack their bags in 1947, fighting between Hindus and Muslims got so bad that India celebrated its independence by splitting up, which gave us Pakistan. They've been fighting over border territory ever since, and the Sikhs aren't happy, either. They want Punjab to themselves, and they've been waging war against the federal government since the 1970s."

"G-troop," Bolan reminded him.

"Geelani and his clique are more than gangsters," the big Fed went on. "They're heavy into drugs, of course. Prostitution's legal, but brothels are banned, so they've cashed in there. Gun-running, human trafficking, pornography—it's banned outright by law in India—and trafficking in endangered species. Tiger skins are big, I hear, and snow leopards. You've got your ivory, your rhino horns, bear spleens, whatever else they claim to use for medicine in China. Anything your little heart desires, G-troop can fill your order for a price."

"What makes them special, then?" Bolan asked.

"Aside from playing godfather, Geelani and his crew are hard-core Muslim fundamentalists—or, anyway, that's what they claim while breaking damn near every law that's on the books. From what I hear, they've been involved in every major act of terrorism in Mumbai over the past ten years, at least. That marks the time when Geelani and Zargar split up with their old boss, Haji Khan. He was a Tamil, and the Muslim mafiosi didn't think he showed enough respect. One night, somebody slips a couple cobras in his bed, and when the fallout settled, you had G-troop holding most of Khan's old territory, picking off his loyalists when and where they could."

"And terrorism doesn't put a crimp in business?" Bolan asked.

"Ah, there's the rub," Brognola said. "Geelani seems to see himself as both Mumbai's Don Corleone *and* a crusader for Islam. Moneywise, word out of Langley and New Delhi is that when he puts on his terrorist hat, he's probably bankrolled and taking his cues from Pakistan's Directorate for Inter-Services Intelligence. They've been around since 1948, with active spy rings documented from Afghanistan, Bosnia, France, Russia, Israel, the States—and, of course, India. Pre-9/11, they collaborated with the CIA on several operations. Today, not so much. They've been linked directly to the Mumbai terrorism and to agitating Sikhs in Punjab."

"With a goal of…what?" Bolan inquired. "Destabilizing India?"

"Why not? The countries have been at each other's throats since Pakistan was born," Brognola said. "They fought wars in 1947 and 1965. In 1971, India supported East Pakistan's claim for independence as Bangladesh and fought Pakistan's army to a standstill. They started fighting over Siachen Glacier, in Kashmir, in April 1983. That's still ongoing, though they called a cease-fire after twenty years. Another two-month war in 1999, and when they aren't overtly killing one another, the DISI prints counterfeit Indian currency by the carload. Basically, they've been at war for sixty-plus years, with no end in sight."

"And you say G-troop's been around for at least ten years. Why are they our urgent business now?" Bolan asked.

"They've been branching out," Brognola said. "As of 2010, one percent of America's population has roots in India. That's about three million, all together. And we know the vast majority of them are law-abiding, smart, productive, yada-yada. But—and it's a *big* but, as my old man used to say—some of them bring their bad habits from home. We know that G-troop definitely has a cell in New York City, and another in Los Angeles, and one up in Ontario, Canada. Big picture, we believe that they're collaborating with al Qaeda and the Taliban—in Pakistan and in Afghanistan, for sure. Here on our doorstep…well, nobody wants to wait and see."

"The FBI can't handle them? NYPD? LAPD?" Bolan asked.

"They're all over it. We have a list of sealed indictments, good to go on racketeering. Raids are pending, but the latest blowup in Mumbai made someone think we need to yank the weed up by its roots."

"Someone," Bolan repeated.

Brognola could only shrug at that. One name was never mentioned in the War Room. Understood, perhaps, but not pronounced.

"Okay, then," the soldier said. "Let's hear the rest of it."

"I've got a contact over there," the big Fed said. "What they would've called my 'opposite number,' back in the Cold War. Well-placed with the Central Bureau of Investigation, which is something like a merger of our FBI and CIA, combining criminal investigation and intelligence."

"The best of both worlds," Price remarked.

"Depends on who's in charge, I guess," Brognola replied. "My pal's been in the driver's seat for six or seven years now. Long enough to prove himself and let me know he gets it right more often than he's wrong. He says Geelani's contact on the Pakistani side is probably one Ibrahim Leghari."

Cue another scowling photo on the flat screen.

"He thinks 'probably,'" Bolan said.

"Right. I know. But like I said, he's right more often

than he's wrong. Whether Leghari's personally working hand in hand with G-troop or not, we know he's tied in with the Taliban, al Qaeda and the Sword of Allah. Funding and intelligence, plus hardware made in Pakistan, shipped out by their Defense Export Promotion Organization. And we're not just talking AKs or grenades. They run a cash-and-carry business from Islamabad, with merchandise including JF-17 Thunder fighters, Al-Khalid tanks and the odd submarine."

"We're going after Pakistan?" Bolan asked.

"Negative. It's G-troop, front and center, top priority. But if you see an opportunity to shut the pipeline down…"

His old friend got the message, nodded, and the deal was done.

His flight from Dulles, west to LAX, was scheduled to depart at 8:15 a.m. Bolan decided he would leave at four o'clock, plenty of time, and he preferred to sit around an airport than beside a highway, with a flat tire, wishing he'd left time enough for an emergency. That still left time for him to watch the CD-ROM Brognola had provided. More details on the G-troop operation, mug shots of Geelani's known associates from their police and prison files, more photographs of properties the gang maintained in Mumbai and environs.

After dinner, Bolan went to his quarters on the second floor and started poring over the files, committing the information to memory, together with a street map of Mumbai.

Another battlefield. More enemies. The names and faces changed, but Bolan's goal remained essentially the same.

Light rapping on his door distracted him, just when he had begun to think that he could use a break. There was a peephole in the door, but Bolan couldn't picture anybody using it. The Farm was one place where you didn't have to worry about personal security once you were safely on the inside, looking out. As far as Bolan knew, there'd never been an incident of any kind, including petty theft, except for the occasion when a traitor in the world outside had nearly brought them down.

Old scars, still painful now and then, at unexpected times.

Barbara Price stood in the doorway. "I thought you might be tired of reading."

"You were right." He stepped aside to let her pass, then closed the door behind her.

"So, Mumbai," she said.

"Good thing I've got a taste for curry."

"You can take a tour of Bollywood."

"Get a map to the stars' homes."

"Learn that dance from *Slumdog Millionaire*."

"I'm more a cha-cha kind of guy," Bolan advised.

"We ought to go out dancing sometime."

"Given time and opportunity."

"Right. There's the rub. What's checkout time tomorrow?"

"Oh-four-hundred."

Price checked her watch. "That's more than eight hours," she said.

"Time for…?"

"Resting up. After."

"I could use a shower," Bolan cautioned her.

"I thought you'd never ask."

CHAPTER THREE

Mumbai

Bolan drove west on Kalyan Street, toward Nandalal Jali Road, with headlights of the chase car racing after his Suzuki Ritz. A second pair almost immediately joined the first, but neither car had flashing lights on top, and he heard no sirens yet, approaching from the police station.

"Two tails," Bolan told his passenger.

The stranger swiveled in his seat, checking the road behind them, grimacing as the exertion cost him pain. "They'll catch us," he declared, his voice sounding almost fatalistic.

"Not if I can help it," Bolan said. "And if they do, they may regret it."

"Were you sent to find me?"

"No. Hang on."

He made a screeching left-hand turn onto Nandalal Jali Road and powered south, traffic appearing now that they were on a larger street and headed toward a populated area. Three blocks, Bolan remembered from the road map in his head, and he would have a choice to make: turn right on Yusuf Mehar Ali Road and travel west, into the heart of town, or keep on driving southward, stay with Nandalal Jali when it changed names, becoming St. Tukaram Road, and ran on through a district of light industry to dead-end at the Carnac Bridge.

One choice would soon surround him with civilians, unaware of mortal danger in their midst. The crowds and traffic might aid Bolan's bid to shake off his pursuers—or the chase could turn into a running firefight and degenerate into a massacre of innocents. The other route had less potential for evasion, but it minimized threats of collateral damage and might give him somewhere to stand, face the hostiles and fight.

South it was.

"You feeling any better?" Bolan asked.

"Well…"

"What I need to know is whether you can fight—or run, at least."

"Are we about to fight?"

"I wouldn't be surprised."

"I'll do my best. But as you know, I am unarmed, wearing a dead man's clothes."

"It's not a fashion show," Bolan told him. "Can you use a gun at all?"

"I spent two years in military service, after graduating from the National Defense Academy in Pune."

"That should do it. On the floor behind you, there's a gym bag. Grab the Uzi out of it and load up."

He was gambling big-time now; there was no way of knowing what his passenger might do once he was armed. A simple accident in handling the Uzi could be catastrophic, spitting 9 mm Parabellum slugs inside their car at sixteen rounds per second, maybe taking Bolan out, maybe disabling the Suzuki. But he'd take the stranger at his word, for now, and trust he had no fuzzy feelings for the G-troop soldiers who were chasing them.

And if he froze in battle? Then what?

Bolan guessed he'd have to wait and deal with that if it occurred. His first priority was finding someplace relatively safe to fight, without attracting and endangering a crowd of rubberneckers on the sidelines.

Factories and shops closed for the night sped past them as he held his course, jumping the traffic light at Yusuf Mehar Ali Road, dodging the cross-traffic and hearing bleats of protest from a dozen horns.

Beside him, his companion had the gym bag open now, groaning with effort, rummaging around inside it for his weapon. Bolan heard the clank of magazines as they were pushed aside, and then a muttered, "There it is."

The Mini-Uzi was a compact weapon, 14.17 inches long with its stock folded, but it retained the awesome firepower of its parent weapon—and then some, since the shorter bolt allowed a cyclic rate of 950 rounds per minute, compared to a full-sized Uzi's six hundred. In trained hands, the piece was a man-shredder. Handled by an amateur, it was disaster looking for a place to happen.

Bolan saw a blink of gunfire in his rearview mirror, with the lead pursuit car gaining, someone in the backseat hoping for a lucky shot. He jigged the Ritz's steering wheel, but didn't have to worry as the shooter's aim was off. The guy wasn't used to firing on the go, he guessed, unless it was a drive-by with the target unaware of what was coming.

"Are you set?" he asked his passenger.

"I'm ready, sir," the man answered, cocking the Uzi as he spoke.

"I told you not to 'sir' me."

"Force of habit, I'm afraid."

The Tata Power company was coming up on Bolan's left, where St. Tukaram Road turned sharply to the east, then ended under Carnac Bridge, abutting railroad yards. The Tata plant was massive, part of India's oldest and largest private-sector electric utility company, manned overnight—Bolan hoped—by a skeleton maintenance crew. Somebody at the plant was bound to call police after the shooting started, but with any luck they'd have some time to wrap it up before the uniforms arrived.

Or, at the very least, die trying.

"FASTER, DAMN YOU!" Rajesh Singh snapped at his driver, then recoiled as Tabish Khan squeezed off a shot from the backseat, the muzzle of his AK-47 only inches from Singh's ear. Half-deafened, Singh turned in his seat and yelled at Khan, "Who gave you leave to fire? Did I?"

Khan blinked at him and answered, "No, Raj."

"Then why are you blowing out my eardrums?"

"I'm sorry."

"Shoot when *I* say shoot, and not before!"

"Yes, sir."

Singh's headache, throbbing by the time they left the factory in pursuit of their attacker and the prisoner he'd freed, was worse now, aggravated by the ringing in his left ear from the close-range rifle shot. He marveled at the idiocy of the men he had to work with, wondering how any of them had been cleared to join G-troop, much less to serve as fighting men. It was a commentary on the quality of men available that could depress Singh, if he let it occupy his mind for any length of time.

Worse yet, Singh knew beyond the shadow of a doubt that he would bear the brunt of punishment for this night's grim fiasco. Even if they managed to retrieve the prisoner and kill or capture the mysterious assailant who had rescued him, Singh would be held responsible for soldiers lost in the attack and loss of the facility when officers from Mandvi police station showed up to investigate the shooting. God only knew what they might find while searching through the one-time factory. Singh's mind was spinning, focused on the chase in progress, and prevented him from cataloging evidence that might be gleaned by raiders at the plant.

His fault, all of it, for the simple fact that he had been in charge.

"Faster!" he snapped, venting his rage and fear on Bidhan Dinker, at the wheel of their Mahindra Scorpio.

"We're near the limit, Raj," Dinker replied, grim-faced, his eyes locked on the Suzuki they were chasing.

"If you can't do any better—" Singh stopped short, wondering what he could demand. Order his driver to defy the laws of physics? Demand that he make the SUV's 2.1-liter inline-four engine perform like the 2.6-liter turbo-diesel Singh had declined when he'd purchased the car?

"What, Raj?" Dinker prodded him, wanting to hear the rest of it.

"Nothing! Just catch them, damn it!"

"Good news," Dinker announced. "They'll soon run out of road."

"What do you mean?" Singh asked, then understood before his driver had a chance to answer. "Ah, that's Tata Power."

"They can only turn below the bridge," Dinker confirmed, "or run off-road into the railway yard."

"Be ready for it, either way," Singh ordered, turning to his soldiers in the SUV's backseat. "When we get close enough, but only on my order, you will aim to stop the car. Tires first, if you can hit them. It's important that we take the prisoner alive, and hopefully the other, too."

"After the men he killed back there?" Phani Barua challenged.

"Information is the first priority. Revenge can wait," Singh said.

"I don't think—"

"No, you don't. *I* do. Remember that."

Barua gave him a sour look, but nodded his understanding of the order. He would obey, if grudgingly, because he knew the consequence of insubordination. In G-troop, the penalty for disobedience was death.

"You see?" Dinker called out. "They're turning!"

He was right. In front of them, the Ritz had slowed enough to make the left-hand turn where St. Tukaram Road turned eastward, running under Carnac Bridge. Singh glanced at his wing mirror, saw the Dacia Duster gaining behind them, four more of his soldiers inside and ready to fight. He could not speak with them, had no idea what any of their cell phone numbers were, but when they stopped, if it was possible, he'd pass his orders not to kill their quarry unless it was absolutely unavoidable.

If it appeared that two men—one of them unarmed—might manage to defeat his eight. If anything suggested that the two of them would get away. In that case, it was better to present Riyaz Geelani with two corpses than an empty bag and some excuse.

"Stay after them!" he snapped unnecessarily, and braced himself as Dinker powered through the turn.

THE FINAL EAST-WEST stretch of St. Tukaram Road ran for a quarter-mile or less before the railroad yards cut off escape. Bolan could see the dead end in his rental car's high-beam headlights, nothing on the street in terms of other traffic, no vehicles parked along the curbs on either side. There'd been no time or opportunity for him to check out the Suzuki Ritz for its performance in emergency maneuvers, so he'd have to wing it, hope he didn't roll the car pulling the stunt he had in mind.

Old-timers called it a bootlegger's turn. It required co-ordination of the accelerator and the emergency brake, plus a strong hand to crank the steering wheel, whipping the vehicle into a 180-degree turn, revving and ready to charge back in the opposite direction as soon as the driver had adequate control.

Easy, unless the driver got it wrong and flipped the vehicle. Or, less dramatically, stalled out the engine, maybe flooding it, so that the person's getaway turned into going nowhere, fast.

In fact, Bolan didn't intend to get away just yet. He'd started out his night looking for someone who could give him fresh intel on G-troop, and had come away with someone altogether unexpected. Now, rather than leading hostile troops all over town, he meant to finish with them as efficiently as possible, sending a message to Riyaz Geelani that his headache wasn't over yet.

The pain was only getting started.

"Hang on," he warned his passenger a second time, and made his move. Accelerated, yanked on the parking brake left-handed, cranking hard left on the Ritz's wheel with his right hand. The maneuver wasn't picture-perfect, but it got the job done, Bolan's twelve-foot vehicle squealing through a dizzy U-turn, in effect, on tortured rubber. By the time they came to rest, he figured they'd whipped through a fair 170 degrees, and that was close enough.

Downrange, the lead chase car made the sharp turn, barely braking, with a smaller SUV behind it, keeping pace. Opening his driver's door, one foot out on the pavement, Bolan asked his passenger, "Ready for this?"

"I hope so, sir!" the battered Indian replied.

It wasn't quite an ambush, since they weren't concealed in any way. Call it a rude surprise, then, getting in the first punch while he could before the other side got organized. A short burst from his autorifle stitched across the black Mahindra Scorpio's windshield, the 5.56 mm rounds spalling on impact, wreaking havoc on the inside of the speeding vehicle. Bolan had no idea if he had tagged the driver or the shotgun rider, but the Scorpio didn't recover from its hard-left turn, rolling to wind up on its roof and trailing sparks across the blacktop as it slid.

Next up in line, a smaller Dacia Duster. Bolan couldn't see its driver through the deeply tinted windshield, but the guy was fast and competent. He'd seen what happened to the lead car and was hell-bent on avoiding repetition with his own ride. Bolan could imagine panic in the second SUV, saw windows gliding down as shooters tried to get their licks in, and he sighted on the front tires, cutting loose with half a dozen rounds that shred the rubber from their decorative wheels.

A double *pop* rewarded him, the silver car swerving away to Bolan's right, its front end down and plowing pavement with its bumper. It was going fast enough to jump the curb, regardless, and to cross the sidewalk with an angry grating sound before it struck one of the massive concrete pillars that supported Carnac Bridge.

Bolan's sidekick hadn't fired a shot yet, staring almost awestruck at the tableau laid before him, but he had the Mini-Uzi raised, at least, and pointed in the right direction.

"Are you sure that you can use that?" Bolan asked him.

"Yes, sir."

At the far end of the short street, men were spilling out of damaged vehicles, all armed, all as mad as hell and spoiling for a fight.

"Okay," Bolan announced. "Here they come."

RAJESH SINGH WASN'T sure exactly what had happened. They'd been closing in on the Suzuki Ritz, reckoned its driver would be trapped at the dead end of St. Tukaram Road. He was looking forward to recovering his prisoner, adding another to the catch—or killing both of them, if they insisted. In the final seconds of his wild ride, either outcome had seemed satisfactory.

Now he was upside-down and sliding over pavement in the Scorpio, Bidhan Dinker still grappling with the steering wheel as if he had control of the inverted SUV. It might have been hilarious to watch him, under other circumstances, but Singh's driver was the only man who'd bothered fastening his seat belt when they rushed off from the factory. Now he was hanging like a fruit bat from a sissoo tree, while all the rest of them were wallowing around with twisted necks and flailing limbs.

Singh could remember glaring headlights at the far end of the street, then muzzle-flashes from an automatic weapon and their windscreen suddenly imploding. Something sharp and hot had scored his cheek, not safety glass, and then the Scorpio rolled over, dumping Singh and both his backseat soldiers on their heads before they had a chance to brace themselves.

As soon as Singh confirmed that he was still alive, he started cursing. It was all that he could think to do while testing out each arm and leg in turn to see if they still functioned, taking special care when it was time to move his aching head. When nothing cracked or shrieked with savage pain, Singh found the button for his window, pressed it and unleashed another round of curses when it failed to work.

He tried the door itself next, thankful that he hadn't pressed the power-locking button when they set off in pursuit of the escaping prisoner. The door still managed to resist him, likely jammed into a dented frame, but then he rolled around and kicked it with both feet in unison and popped it open with a sharp, metallic squeal of protest.

His AK-47 lay beneath him, pistol grip and magazine

both digging into Singh's rib cage. He wriggled through the open door on his backside, propelled by heels and elbows like a giant wounded spider, then rolled clear and flattened on the pavement. He reached back inside the Scorpio to fetch his weapon. Singh heard firing, but he wasn't sure where it was coming from. His other soldiers, in the Dacia? If they were still alive and fit for battle, Singh might have a chance to rally with his first team and support them. Maybe catch their targets in a cross fire, even though the person who had released his prisoner appeared to have the upper hand so far.

Behind Singh, Tabish Khan and Phani Barua were clear and squatting on the asphalt now, using the capsized SUV for cover. Singh looked back inside the Scorpio, saw Dinker still suspended from his safety harness and called out to him, "You plan to join us, Bidhan?"

"At once," their driver answered, and as if Singh's words had roused him from a trance, he started grappling with the catch that held his safety belt in place. It did not open on his first attempt, and he would never make another, since a burst of automatic fire whipped through the windscreen's open frame and sheared the upper half of Dinker's face completely off his skull. A stew of blood and brains slopped to the ceiling—presently the floorboard—and the faceless body spasmed for an instant, then hung flaccid in its sling.

Recoiling from the carnage, sickened—though he'd seen and done much worse in other situations—Singh turned on his two surviving men. "We have to clean this up before the police get here," he said, imagining police cars swarming toward the dead-end stretch of St. Tukaram Road, forcing Singh and his men to fight or flee on foot.

They would be walking out regardless, whether the police arrived or not, but if they killed their adversaries quickly, they could ditch their outlawed weapons, scatter in the darkness and regroup somewhere before he made the dreaded phone call to Riyaz Geelani. Otherwise, he'd have to make the call from jail, and if the law caught him red-handed with machine guns, close to bullet-riddled corpses, he could expect a term of life imprisonment.

Death might be preferable, Singh thought, but an enlightened state would not consider executing him—unless, of course, he forced the first responding officers to use their guns in self-defense. Something to think about, as he considered how Geelani might react to this night's series of humiliating failures.

His men were shaken, frightened, still intent on hiding in the shadow of the Scorpio. Singh saw that he would have to lead them by example, set a standard for Khan and Barua, which they would be forced to emulate.

Or what?

Singh might just shoot the pair of them himself.

BOLAN WAS RELIEVED when his companion fired the Mini-Uzi, not just making noise, but sending rounds downrange and dead on target. His first rounds took out the driver of the stalled, inverted Scorpio, and kept the others under cover, leaving Bolan free to deal with those erupting from the Dacia. Four men, all smart enough to bail out on the side away from Bolan and use the SUV for cover, like their pals across the street.

Starting a siege?

They had to know police were on the way, and wouldn't want to face six years in prison for possession of illicit weapons, much less stiffer charges that might follow from investigation of the one-time factory or running firefights on a public street. They'd want to hit and git, maybe snap photos of their trophies on a cell phone, for the boss, to verify the kills, then get the hell away from there by any means available.

Bolan had much the same idea, minus the photo album memories, but rushing either one of the disabled SUVs on open ground, to root out its defenders, could be tantamount to suicide.

Before the huddled hunters had a chance to pockmark the Suzuki Ritz with lead, he leaned into the car and found one of the satchels heavy with grenades. Extracting two, he set one on the pavement at his knee, then pulled the other's pin and lobbed the bomb toward the Duster, where the SUV sat nose-on to the massive concrete pillar it had rammed.

A sitting target, right.

It wouldn't do to bounce the grenade *under* the Dacia, since it might wobble to the left or right, before its impact fuse went off. Instead, he threw it high and long, dropping it behind the SUV and out of sight before it blew.

Cue screams and wailing from the patchy shadows over there, as shrapnel tore through flesh and shattered the remaining Duster windows. Bolan surmised that anybody still alive back there was wounded, out of action, maybe dying. If he had the time for mopping up, he'd deal with them at point-blank range—or leave them for the medics, if a mercy urge came over him.

His second grenade was for the Scorpio, its several surviving occupants starting to stir and poke their heads around the wreckage, looking for an angle of attack. Bolan's companion sent them scurrying back under cover with the Mini-Uzi, milking it for short bursts like a man who knew what he was doing. Military training, sure, but had he kept it up since then in some related occupation? That would answer Bolan's question as to why he'd found the man under interrogation, but the moment called for action, not a guessing game.

He lobbed the armed frag grenade toward the Mahindra Scorpio, not trying to get over it this time. Instead, he dropped it on the undercarriage, pointed skyward at the moment, and its detonation ripped the fuel tank open, spewing gasoline in fiery streamers that arched high, then splattered back to earth on all sides of the vehicle, igniting pools of flame on asphalt.

More screams, and the gunners who'd concealed themselves behind the Scorpio were running now. Two of the men trailed flames and batted at them with their empty hands, weapons forgotten as they burned. The third came out around the front end of the Scorpio, scuttling and firing from the hip.

Bolan's companion took the shooter, ripping him from groin to throat with half a magazine of Parabellum shockers, dropping him into a boneless heap. Bolan decided not to let the flaming shooters run their lives out screaming, squeezing off one mercy round for each that silenced them and left them smoldering on St. Tukaram Road.

He thought about the others, maybe still alive behind the Duster, but a distant wail of sirens reached his ears now, telling Bolan they were out of time. "Hop in," he said, and slid behind the Ritz's wheel. He shifted the manual transmission out of Neutral, into First.

"Ready," his companion replied as he dropped into the shotgun seat. No, *sir,* this time.

Better.

Racing away from smoky death and the police, Bolan half turned and said, "I think we ought to try those introductions, now."

"Sergeant Baji Sharma, at your service," his passenger stated.

"Sergeant?"

"In the Central Bureau of Investigation. And you are...?"

CHAPTER FOUR

Chinchpokli, South Mumbai

The neighborhood was named for trees, the tamarind (*chinch*) and betel nut (*pofali*), garbled on the tongue of some long-dead British colonial officer, gone and forgotten like the trees themselves, which had been sacrificed to urban sprawl. This day it was a melting pot of sorts, with Jain and Hindu temples, Muslim mosques, even a Jewish cemetery on the west side of the railroad terminal that shared the district's name. It was a fair place to get lost in—for a little while at least.

Sharma directed Bolan to a small house off Dr. E. Moses Road, with a garage-cum-shed in back that had room for the Ritz. They left it there, but Bolan took his mobile arsenal inside the house, hedging his bets.

"When you call this a safehouse, how safe *is* it?" Bolan asked his host.

"I rent the place myself," Sharma replied. "Under a pseudonym, of course. It is unknown even to my superiors." He hesitated, then asked, "You will excuse me for a shower before getting down to business? The accommodations at my last hotel were far from satisfactory."

"Sure thing," Bolan replied, gambling that Sharma wouldn't rat him out this quickly, after being rescued from the certainty of slow and agonizing death.

Bolan could hear the shower running while he looked

around the small and tidy house, thinking about what he had learned so far. The Central Bureau of Investigation, as he'd learned from Hal Brognola at Stony Man, was India's premier investigative agency, combining law enforcement functions with intelligence and national security. Most ordinary crimes, from petty theft to homicide, were handled by the State Police, leaving the CBI to deal with federal offenses, foreign spies and terrorists. Its motto—Industry, Impartiality, Integrity—stated the agency's ideals, but had not shielded it from charges of corruption and mishandling major cases, from the Bhopal gas-leak tragedy of 1984 to the unsolved murders of a dozen children at Nithari during 2005 and 2006.

Sharma had briefed him on the basics of the job that brought him to the factory where Bolan had discovered him, naked and duct-taped to a chair. He'd been assigned to infiltrate G-troop, sent undercover with a manufactured prison record that would stand up to computer searches through the Ministry of Law and Justice. Only his immediate superior had known where Sharma was at any given time, a risky deal designed for maximum security, which broke down on the night he'd been abducted and delivered to the plant for questioning—around the same time Bolan had flown out of LAX.

The shower stopped, and Bolan heard the normal sounds of someone dressing in a rear bedroom. He was studying a small bronze statue of a dancing four-armed figure, one foot planted on a smaller form, resembling a gargoyle.

"That is Shiva," Sharma said behind him. Bolan turned to find him dressed in clean clothes, looking slightly fresher, with his hair slicked back and glistening.

"A fearsome-looking guy," Bolan allowed.

"He dances to destroy a weary universe and pave the

way for Brahma to begin a new creation. Underneath his foot is Apasmara, a dwarf who symbolized ignorance."

"I've met a few of those," Bolan said.

"They are, sadly, all too plentiful."

"You have someone waiting to hear from you?"

"Indeed, but I'm uncertain what to tell him."

"Oh?"

"Officially, I have an obligation to report your presence in Mumbai, with an assessment of your plans."

"They'd be the same as yours," Bolan replied. "Get rid of G-troop."

"But without due process, I perceive."

"How's that been working for you?"

"Not well, as I'm sure you realize."

"Let's bottom-line it," Bolan said. "I stumbled onto you by accident. I'm glad I had a chance to help you out, but you're not obligated to me, and I'm not recruiting. If you want to share whatever information you can part with, comfortably, I'll be glad to get it. Otherwise, I'm on my way."

"You understand that I should be arresting you right now."

"I wouldn't recommend it," Bolan said.

"If I contact my superior, he may demand it."

"Then you'll both be disappointed."

Sharma smiled at that and said, "I would propose a different arrangement."

"Such as?"

"A collaboration, shall we say?" Sharma suggested.

"Define that for me."

"I am well acquainted with Riyaz Geelani's operations in Mumbai and elsewhere. I believe it may be time to try a new approach toward stopping him."

"I don't play by the book," Bolan reminded him. "I'm not collecting evidence for trial."

"The CBI has chased Geelani for the past ten years. He has a dozen different indictments pending, but he's still no closer to a courtroom. We have wasted time enough."

"All right, then," the Executioner said. "Let's talk."

Malabar Hill, Mumbai

EVERY CITY HAD a district where the rich and influential congregated. In Mumbai, that district was Malabar Hill, home to the governor of Maharashtra, various top-level CEOs, plus Bollywood stars and directors. One of the grand estates on Harkness Road, owned in the name of innocent third parties, was in fact home to Riyaz Geelani, one of India's most-wanted criminals, who managed to enjoy palatial splendor underneath the very noses of police, who, as they told it, labored day and night to bring him down.

On any other night, Sayeed Zargar might have amused himself, considering that strange charade. This night, however, he had bad news to deliver, and his master's unpredictable reaction had his nerves on edge. Killing the messenger was more than just a figure of speech with Geelani, as Zargar himself had witnessed firsthand.

He'd called ahead, reported trouble and explained that details should not be discussed by telephone. That was a gamble, since it gave Geelani time to fume and speculate, build up a head of steam before he heard the facts, but Zargar could not risk spilling the story where it might be plucked out of the air by eavesdroppers.

His driver turned in at the entry of Geelani's estate, and they sat waiting for the guards to recognize Zargar, open the gate and let them pass. Two minutes later, they were pulling up outside a grand two-story house with a colonnade in front. Behind it, sprawling over forty acres, was a private rain forest enclosed by ten-foot walls.

Geelani met Zargar on the front porch, an indication that the phone call from his second in command had agitated him. Without the normal salutations, he demanded, "So? Explain!"

Zargar detailed their losses while he trailed Geelani through palatial rooms to reach the master's office, its tall windows looking out on a veranda and large swimming pool. Geelani dropped into a thronelike chair behind a massive desk and scowled through the remainder of his lieutenant's report.

"How many dead, in all?" he asked when Zargar finished speaking.

"Fifteen, sir. Two more are not expected to survive."

"And now, police are in the factory."

"They have it, yes."

"And we have lost the spy."

"It's true, sir."

"Without learning his name or who employed him."

"Yes," Zargar replied.

"Someone came in and rescued him, you say."

"The five survivors all confirm it, sir. He was tall, a white man, maybe English or American."

"Maybe?"

"He did not speak. They're guessing, from his clothes."

"How does their guessing game help me?" Geelani demanded.

"It's all we have so far, sir. They were surprised and under fire."

"Enough excuses! Twenty-two of them were not enough to stop one man? What good are they?"

Zargar had no response to that. He sat and waited for the storm to break, perhaps to overwhelm him, or fade away.

"A white man, maybe English or American," Geelani said. "Tell me what that suggests to you, Sayeed."

"Not Interpol," Zargar replied, "since they have no enforcement arm. The CIA or MI6, perhaps, since our expansion to America and London."

"Not Afghanistan?"

"Another possibility, sir."

"Declaring war without the normal niceties," Geelani said.

"Washington thinks it owns the world," Zargar replied.

"Are we prepared to teach them otherwise?"

"At your command, sir."

"You still think that the spy was a policeman? CBI or State Police?"

"It's logical, but now that he's escaped…" Zargar could only finish with a shrug.

"Reach out to our connections in the agency," Geelani ordered. "Find out if they've called for any outside help. If so, I want the details—and I want to know why we were not forewarned."

"It shall be done, sir."

"We'll have no more surprises. Find these men, Sayeed. If you must turn the city upside-down, *find them!*"

Central Bureau of Investigation Headquarters, Mumbai

CAPTAIN VIVAK PATEL entered his office with a sense of foreboding, not quite of depression, but well on its way. He'd spent another night without word from the undercover agent who had broken contact three days earlier, and Patel had begun the mental process of accepting that his man—his friend—was dead.

CBI headquarters in Mumbai occupied the second floor of New Hind House, on Narottam Moraji Marg, in the South Mumbai district of Ballard Estate. The area was a European-style business district, for the most part, with a distinctly London feel about it, named for Colonel J. A. Ballard, founder of the Bombay (now Mumbai) Port Trust during the First World War. The Port Trust still maintained headquarters there, near gleaming offices of the Reliance Group investment company, surrounded by hotels and shops. Captain Patel sometimes imagined that the moneymen wanted police nearby to keep their funds secure.

Or had the CBI been planted in their midst as part of some grand scheme to keep them honest, knowing that roughly half its agents had been recruited from the Indian Revenue Service?

No matter. Money made the world go round, and always found its way back to the hands of those who had more than they needed, as it was. This day, Patel's concerns were more immediate.

He'd sent a plainclothes officer around to Baji Sharma's flat to look for any signs that Sharma had been home within the past few days. The officer had used his own initiative to pick a lock and search the place, but had found nothing to suggest foul play. No clues of any kind, in fact. He'd left the flat the way he found it and reported back, with an apology for failing to resolve the mystery.

Captain Patel was normally imbued with confidence, but he'd begun to second-guess his plan for G-troop from the moment Sharma had accepted the assignment. It was voluntary—no man should be sent into a cobra's lair against his will—and Sharma had seemed eager to proceed. Perhaps *too* eager, now that Patel thought about it. Had he underestimated their opponents? Had he made some small mistake that sealed his fate?

All things considered, preparation for the penetration had been relatively easy. Patel's rank and contacts in the Ministry of Law and Justice had facilitated fabrication of a prison record. They had called him "Ram Khatri," setting his crimes and prison time in Bihar, India's twelfth-largest state, along the border with Nepal. Patel had thought Riyaz Geelani would be less likely to see through Sharma's cover if they had no friends or enemies in common, but the convoluted underworld of crime could still surprise him.

If he'd been mistaken, if a former prisoner from Bihar asked Sharma who he'd known while doing time in Bimbisara Prison, for example, one wrong word could stamp his death certificate.

And how would Patel, then, explain to his superiors? What would they say on learning that he'd hatched the plan himself, alone, and forged ahead without permission or advice?

It shamed him, thinking of himself, when Sharma might be dead or worse, but Patel reckoned it was only natural. Self-preservation in the bowels of a bureaucracy was like a dance or mating ritual, each step and pirouette dictated by the complex rules of play. Throw in the shifting tides of politics, and it required a master's skill to stay afloat in the command ranks, much less to advance.

Captain Patel stared at the fat files stacked up on his desk, considering which one to open first. If nothing else, perhaps he could distract himself from worrying about—

His cell phone thrummed and vibrated against his hip. He checked the caller's number, did not recognize it, but decided he would answer anyway.

"Namaste."

"Captain."

Patel felt his throat clench tight. He cleared it, but could barely whisper in reply. "Baji?"

"I'm all right now," the weary but familiar voice informed him.

"'Now'? What happened? Where are you?"

"I cannot answer many questions," Sharma said. "You know about the killings overnight, in Dana Bandar?"

"What? Oh, yes, of course." A sudden chill lanced through Patel. "Were you involved somehow?"

"They would have killed me," Sharma told him, "but a friend arrived in time."

"A friend?" Patel's eyes flicked around the corners of his office, as if someone might be crouched in one of them and listening. "What are you saying?"

"Nothing more," Sharma replied. "I had to tell you that I'm well, or reasonably so, and am continuing with my assignment on a different path."

"I do not understand you. Baji, please explain yourself!"

"We never could have stopped Geelani using methods that have failed before. You see that, Captain?"

"Sergeant—"

"It is better if you do not try to find me. For your own sake."

"Baji—" But the link was lost.

Patel sat staring at the cell phone in his hand, trying to make sense of the weird, truncated conversation. Word of the Dana Bandar massacre had rousted Patel out of bed and brought him to the office hours early, for what promised—threatened—to become another grueling day. Now this, with Sharma calling up from who knew where, saying that he'd been in the midst of it—and what else?

Was the sergeant being forced to speak? Had someone scripted his peculiar comments? Patel didn't think so, but if Sharma had been speaking for himself, what was he saying? What did it suggest if he continued with his mission against G-troop "on a different path"? Who was the so-called friend who'd rescued him, presumably from Riyaz Geelani's enforcers?

And what did they plan to do next?

Directorate for Inter-Services Intelligence Headquarters, Islamabad, Pakistan

MAJOR IBRAHIM LEGHARI hunched over his laptop, watching grisly images streamed on the *Times Now* website, broadcast from Mumbai with English commentary. He had seen most of the footage several times already, but new clips were constantly uploading as the body count increased. Black rubber bags on stretchers disappeared into the yawning maws of hearses and were whisked away. Police tramped in and out of what appeared to be an aged factory, or circled around cars riddled with bullet holes. One of the vehicles—a black Mahindra Scorpio, he saw— lay upside down in early footage. Later, once the wreckers had arrived, it rested on its tires again, a dead man slouching in the driver's seat.

One of Riyaz Geelani's men.

"What is all this?" he muttered, taking in the carnage. Bloodshed had never troubled him. It was the damned adverse publicity, unplanned for, wholly uncontrolled, that made Leghari clench his fists in anger on his desktop.

Dealing with people like Geelani kept Leghari in a foul mood, feeling tainted by association with such hypocrites who claimed to serve God, but who corrupted everything they touched. Such men—and women, too—were necessary in the covert world of sabotage and terrorism, but Leghari went home every night feeling the need for long, hot showers with the harshest soap available.

Geelani and his creatures did the work that they were paid to do, creating havoc in the streets, but now it seemed someone had wreaked havoc on them. It was a price of doing business in the underworld, Leghari realized, but which of G-troop's several deadly rivals had the strength and will to cause such damage in a single skirmish?

There was Abdur Tarzi, the Pashtun mobster with a yen to dominate drug trafficking. And Dipesh Hossein, with his Bengali soldiers, breaking into prostitution and pornography. Nor could he overlook the Kumar brothers, Dharam and Azeez, who had been drawn from Bangalore to claim their slice of Bollywood. All were Geelani's enemies, but had they risen up last night—alone, or acting in collaboration—to attack him?

The beeping of his private sat-phone line cut through Leghari's rumination. Frowning at the instrument, he picked it up to silence the annoying sound.

"As-salaam-o-alaikum."

"Alaikum as-salaam."

He recognized the voice at once, and felt his frown turn to a scowl. Switching to English, he inquired, "Have you engaged the scrambler?"

"Naturally," Riyaz Geelani said.

"I see you've had some difficulty," Leghari stated, striving for a neutral tone.

"Some difficulty! It's a great deal more than that."

"Not one of your competitors this time?"

"My men unmasked a spy within our family," Geelani said. "I think he was police."

"You think?"

"They had no chance to finish his interrogation. Last night, he was stolen from their custody and my soldiers were massacred in the process."

"I've been watching it online," Leghari said. "What do your stooges in the State Police say?"

"Nothing, yet. It's not their style to hit and run without

arresting anyone. Survivors say the man who took him out looked English or American."

"One man did this?"

"One devil."

"THIS WILL BE difficult to understand, for my superiors. What should I tell them?"

Momentary silence on the line, before Geelani said, "Nothing is going to derail our plans. I'll find the bastard responsible and punish him accordingly."

"I hope so. Failing that…"

He did not have to say the rest. Geelani knew how much the DISI valued cunning and efficiency. An ally who could not control his own backyard was worse than useless. Under pressure, he might spill the secrets of his dealings with Islamabad and bring down scandal on the agency. Better to silence him for good before that happened, than to run unnecessary risks.

"Trust me," Geelani said.

"I do—until that trust is found to be misplaced."

"If we need help…"

"I'll see what can be done discreetly. All must be deniable."

"Of course. I understand."

"Khuda hafiz," Leghari said.

"Goodbye," Geelani answered back, and cut the link.

Another problem in Mumbai. Just what Leghari needed.

"Son of a bitch!" he muttered, as he put down the sat phone and reached out for the landline on his desk.

Chinchpokli, South Mumbai

"FEEL BETTER NOW?" Bolan inquired.

Sharma nodded. "I said nothing of our plan," he said.

"Okay."

The sergeant hadn't felt he could proceed without informing his superior that he was still alive. He'd used a prepaid cell phone, rather than the landline in the safehouse, to avoid a trace, and Bolan trusted him enough on instinct to believe he hadn't tipped their hand. Why would he?

As for blowing Bolan's cover, Sharma didn't know who he was dealing with. Bolan had introduced himself as Matt Cooper—not the name imprinted on the passport or the California driver's license he was carrying—and Sharma had not questioned it. An undercover cop himself, he would have recognized it as an alias and likely wouldn't care, as long as Bolan held up his end of their deal.

Which was to crack G-troop by any means available.

As Sharma told it, he had watched Geelani's goons run rampant through his two years with the Indian Police Service, and for the past eight, since he was recruited for the CBI. The small fry went to prison or were killed in shootouts, either with authorities or rival mobsters, but Geelani and the outfit's upper crust appeared to be untouchable. Sharma had offered the address where India's most-wanted fugitive was living at the moment, in a regal mansion, unmolested by authorities who suffered from a kind of self-inflicted blindness. Some of them, he ruefully admitted, had been paid to look the other way. Others were worried about jeopardizing their careers if anything went wrong in an attempt to capture him—as it was prone to do in India.

And finally, Sharma suggested—though he couldn't prove it—there were likely officers within the CBI who hoped Geelani could be turned against the men who pulled his strings from Pakistan, either exposing them to public scrutiny or undertaking covert operations that would blow up in their faces.

So far, those attempts had borne no fruit, and Sharma was convinced they never would.

"Geelani," he'd explained to Bolan, "*thinks* he is a mighty Muslim warrior. Truth be told, he is a heretic and hypocrite, who would be subject to a death sentence in Pakistan for dealing drugs if they enforced the law against their own agents. I'd be surprised if he has ever opened the Quran. Clearly he does not understand the teachings he espouses."

"What I have in mind," Bolan explained to him, "is hitting G-troop hard and fast, time and again, until it starts to fall apart. The fatter targets I can find, the better. Body count is part of it. The other part is emptying his wallet."

"So, a blitzkrieg, yes?"

"That's it," Bolan agreed.

"But why not simply kill Geelani?"

"Then his number two steps up, and it goes on like that forever, while they're busy hiring kids out of the slums to fill their ranks. I'll crush the snake's head when there's no hope that the body will revive and sprout a new one."

"Ah. The hydra!"

"Close enough."

Sharma's bruised lips produced a winning smile. "So, you—now *we*—shall be like Hercules!"

"Without the muscle-flexing," Bolan told him. "Or the immortality."

"Of course."

"So, are you ready for it?"

"I've been wishing for a chance like this," Sharma replied, "believing it was just a dream."

"The point," Bolan advised, "is not to let it turn into a nightmare. Not for *us,* at least."

"But for Geelani, eh? I understand."

"I don't suppose there's any way we could get access to your G-troop files?"

"No need. I've spent so much time following Geelani, studying his network, that I nearly have them memorized."

"Okay, then. First thing that we need's a list of targets. Bigger's better. Anything he values highly that's important to his operations. Anyplace his soldiers congregate, where we can find a good-size group of them together."

"And to kill them?" Sharma asked.

"I'm not taking anybody into custody," Bolan replied. "I may find someone who I need to question, while I'm at it, but they'll never see the inside of a courtroom, working either side."

Another nod, as Sharma said, "I understand."

"And you can handle that? It's no disgrace if you want to part company right now."

"No, no. After so many years," the sergeant answered, "I need to accomplish something. Let's begin."

CHAPTER FIVE

Kranti Nagar, Mumbai

The meth lab was concealed, after a fashion, in an old warehouse off Water Tank Road, with a view of Vihar Lake off to the west. The only light burning outside the place was mounted on a pole twenty feet tall, bathing the front parking lot in a halogen glow. Moths the size of sparrows dipped and dived around the pole light, worshipping its glare, while bats swept past at intervals to thin the crowd.

Three vehicles were parked under the light as Bolan and Sharma approached the plant on foot, through unkempt grass that grazed their calves and made the Executioner imagine snakes in waiting. He'd done some background reading on his flight from LAX, and one factoid that stuck had been a statement from a group of Indian physicians, claiming that the yearly toll of fatal snakebites had been underestimated by a whopping 98 percent—pegged at an average of 1,300 yearly, when the true total exceeded 46,000.

Thankful for his boots, he reached the chain-link fence with coils of razor wire on top and scanned the property that it protected. First, the vehicles. One was a San Storm two-seater, bright yellow, and likely the manager's ride. The second was a Tata Sumo SUV, showing some wear and tear, probably used to make deliveries. The third was a little Hyundai i10 subcompact model that reminded Bolan of a clown car in a circus.

There were no signs on the fence suggesting that it was electrified, but Bolan checked it anyway, tossing a soda can against the lower chain-link skirt so that it grounded, failing to produce a crackling rain of sparks. "Okay," he said, and Sharma plied the wire cutters he'd brought from the safehouse, cutting a flap for them to crawl through. Once inside, a simple twist tie held the flap secure enough to pass a casual inspection by a lazy guard.

They wouldn't need much time, in any case.

Bolan moved around the cars while Sharma covered him, using his Tanto blade to flatten two tires on each vehicle. No matter what happened from that point on, they wouldn't have another high-speed battle through the city's streets. When that was done, he sheathed the knife and got out of the light, ducking around behind the warehouse, following the stench of ether and ammonia that could pass for rotten eggs and cat urine blown into the night by multiple exhaust fans.

THEY FOUND A SENTRY sitting on a deck chair, out in back, smoking a cigarette that could have set the place off if he'd lit it up inside. The droning of exhaust fans deafened him to death approaching and it helped muffle the single shot from Bolan's INSAS rifle, pitching the negligent lookout into a heap on the ground.

That left the back door to the lab unguarded, but the raiders didn't plan to go inside. They didn't need to, when the atmosphere throughout the plant was, in and of itself, combustible. Bolan moved past the useless watchman's body, tried the door and felt it open at his touch. A nod sent Sharma back to a safe distance, while he primed a frag grenade and pitched it through the doorway. He was turning, leaping, as it wobbled through the air, across a spacious room, toward impact with a plasterboard wall.

The detonation didn't sound like much, muffled by outer walls, but it was followed by a cataclysmic bang that rocked the warehouse down to its foundation. Gouts of flame like dragon's breath shot through the meth lab's painted-over windows, melting screens. The big exhaust fans choked and died, their power suddenly cut off as circuits fused and fried inside the building.

Screams echoed from somewhere in the heart of that inferno, but they instantly evaporated in the flames. How many? Bolan didn't know and wouldn't let it worry him.

The blitz was on. G-troop had just begun to feel the heat.

"The next stop isn't far away," Sharma said. "Perhaps two miles."

"The brothel?" Bolan confirmed.

"Near Guru Nanak College," Sharma stated. "Follow Sanman Singh Road to the east, then Pratap Singh Road northward."

SHARMA HEARD THE SIRENS now, the Mumbai Fire Brigade responding to the last site they had visited. Too late for any of the G-troop members who had died inside the meth lab, all reduced to ash and blackened bones by now. Sharma considered the sensations he had felt during the raid, watching the flames, and how he felt right now, waiting for guilt to overwhelm him, but it did not come.

He'd done his best, as both a soldier and a policeman, in the interest of law and order, only to behold the goal of a sincerely civilized society slip further from his grasp with every passing day. A part of Sharma's mind told him that joining Matthew Cooper signaled his failure, but he pushed that notion down, suppressing it.

To every man, there came a time when he had to make a choice: to stand and fight, or turn his back and slink away, branded a coward. It was not enough to simply tread the same path of futility for years on end, marking the calendar until he could retire—as what? A soulless shadow?

"There," he said, as Cooper approached the target. "In the middle of the next block. On our right, the pink house."

"Got it."

It was getting late—or early, all depending on your point of view—which meant that Mumbai's nightspots would be packed with pleasure-seekers, each trying to rent a taste of pleasure that eluded him or her in normal daily life. Whether the thrill was sexual or chemical, provided by another human body or a game of chance, the profits went to feed a monster most of G-troop's customers still failed to recognize.

And Baji Sharma, with the tall American he barely knew, was taking on that monster in a struggle that meant death for one side or the other.

Maybe both.

The brothel wasn't much to look at, had no advertising signs outside, depending on its patrons to promote the place by word of mouth. Local police knew where to find it, but they left the operation unmolested, blinded by the graft that they received to supplement their salary of 5,600 rupees per month. Convert it to one hundred U.S. dollars, and you'd understand how constables could be corrupted without thinking twice about the source of extra income.

If the guardians were living hand to mouth, how zealous could they be?

Bolan parked the Ritz a half-block from the brothel, killed its engine and took time to check his rifle's curved, translucent magazine. Counting the rounds, he frowned, replaced it with a fresh one, then faced Sharma in the dark.

"All set?"

Holding the Mini-Uzi, Sharma nodded once and stepped out of the car. Bolan locked the Ritz's doors, using the button on his key fob, making sure the vehicle would still be there when they returned.

In keeping with the brothel's clientele and neighborhood, no guards were posted on the street outside. Sharma and Bolan moved rapidly along the sidewalk, mounting concrete steps to reach the brothel's narrow porch. Bolan pressed the doorbell and they heard it chime inside, something from a Bollywood soundtrack.

It took a moment for the door to open on a slender, androgenous figure dressed all in white, with straight hair hanging down to his/her shoulders. The greeter saw their guns and tried to slam the door, but Bolan was faster, pushing through with Sharma on his heels. He fired a short burst from his INSAS rifle toward the ceiling, shouting after it in tones that echoed through the house.

"Two-minute warning! Up and at 'em, people! Hit the bricks, or stay and burn!"

Their frightened greeter was the first one out the door.

Malabar Hill, Mumbai

RIYAZ GEELANI CLUTCHED the handset of his desk phone in a strangling grip, fighting an urge to hammer it against the desktop until its plastic and his knuckles shattered. Slowly, speaking through clenched teeth, he said, "The laboratory *and* the playhouse? There is no mistake?"

"Unfortunately no, sir." The nervous voice came back to him, reed-thin and tremulous.

"I want full information, as you get it."

"Certainly. Without delay."

Geelani cut the link without another word, leaving the

young police detective on the other end to go about his business. The alert would cost Geelani extra—bitter irony, considering the losses he'd already suffered in the past few hours—but it was a basic cost of doing his illicit business in Mumbai.

Geelani snapped open his cell phone, selected Sayeed Zargar's number from the speed-dial menu, thumbed it down and waited.

One ring. Two. Zargar picked up before the third ring was completed, and Geelani snapped, "Sayeed! To me!" then broke the link.

He stood beside his desk, fuming, counting the seconds in his head to keep from smashing something, anything within his reach. Stark rage consumed him, burning in his veins, raising the short hairs on his nape and forearms as if they were charged with electricity.

Riyaz Geelani was a man on fire.

A rapping on his office door distracted him. "Enter!"

Zargar came in and shut the door behind him, gently, careful not to let it slam in case it triggered an explosion from his master. He stood waiting for instructions, an expression on his face that fell somewhere between perplexity and fear.

Geelani faced his second in command. "You have not heard, I take it?" he inquired.

"Heard...what?"

"That we have lost the laboratory on the lake, and the campus playhouse."

"What?"

Geelani saw his chief lieutenant shiver for an instant, nearly staggered by the news—or was he simply acting? Was it possible that Sayeed had a hand in treachery? No, he decided. Sayeed was a gifted liar, of necessity, but if his current shock was feigned, he should receive a Bollywood award as the best actor of the year.

"Still no trace of the missing prisoner?" Geelani asked, before his friend was able to recover.

"No, sir. I have our men out searching everywhere."

"We need to call some of them back," Geelani said. "Assign them to security on the remaining labs and at the Bhandup West casino."

"Right away."

"It's most important that we find your prisoner, Sayeed, together with his white friend."

"You believe they are responsible for these attacks?"

"If nothing else, we need to rule it out. We need to find out who the spy is working for, and how he called on an outsider to come rescue him. Above all, we must punish them for soldiers lost and damage suffered during the escape."

"It will be done."

"And soon. I have no patience with excuses."

Zargar seemed to take that personally, as it was intended. He had been in charge of questioning the prisoner, had delegated that responsibility to others, and the men he picked had failed. Geelani could not punish them, since they were dead, but someone had to be held accountable.

That would be G-troop's second in command.

"I will report immediately when I have some news," Zargar assured him.

"I want *hourly* reports," Geelani said, "with full details of progress."

"As you say, sir. I'd best get started now."

"Indeed you should." Geelani turned his back without another word, waiting until he heard the office door open and close again.

Who would send a spy to infiltrate the city's largest syndicate?

The possibilities were limited, and it was time to squeeze some of the law enforcement officers who owed their style of living to the man whom they had pledged to lock away.

Central Bureau of Investigation Headquarters, Mumbai

CAPTAIN VIVAK PATEL examined his appearance in the men's room mirror, fudged his necktie's Windsor knot a fraction of a millimeter to the left, and frowned at the result. It was the best that he could do, and he was running out of time.

A summons from his colonel automatically put Patel's nerves on edge. As with so many supervisors in the average bureaucracy, Major Arutla Yugandhar never delivered praise, except to *his* superiors, for personal advancement. With subordinates, he could—and did—find fault in anything, from stacking chairs to executing mass arrests in riot zones. Major Yugandhar seemed to think no conversation was complete until he had dissected some event and found a way in which the person who'd performed the given task had fallen short of expectations.

A call from Major Yugandhar *this day,* after Patel's terse conversation on the telephone with Baji Sharma, raised Patel's blood pressure to the point where he could hear each heartbeat pulsing in his ears. The very last thing that he needed, in the present crisis, was a lecture on the proper way to fill out requisition forms or rotate ammunition crates in his division's storeroom. Patel feared that he might crack if Yugandhar droned on and on about some pointless trivia that made him want to scream.

The major's aide gave Patel a minimal salute and told him Yugandhar was running late. Important calls from the director's office, vital business, classified. Patel sat down in an uncomfortable plastic chair and tuned him out. He turned his thoughts to Sergeant Sharma once again, and nearly missed it when the aide said, "Captain? Major Yugandhar will see you now."

The major was a short, wide man, whose general appearance offered the impression that he'd been constructed out of building blocks: square head, square torso, chunky arms and legs like stout limbs from an oak tree. When his face was etched onto the block that was his skull, the artist had not bothered to include a smile.

Patel saluted and stated the obvious, "Captain Patel, reporting as ordered, sir."

"Shut the door, Captain, and sit."

This time the chair was wooden, even more uncomfortable than its plastic mate out in the waiting room.

"You wonder why I've called you here," Yugandhar said, not asking him.

"Yes, sir."

"It seems we have a problem."

"Sir?"

"A missing officer."

Patel exerted every ounce of willpower he had to keep his face deadpan. "Missing, sir? Who might that be?"

"That's half the problem, Captain. I don't know."

Patel allowed himself a frown at that. "I'm sorry, sir," he said, "but I'm afraid I don't—"

"We have intelligence," the major interrupted him, "that gangsters in Mumbai have captured someone from the bureau, possibly an officer assigned to undercover work. Details, alas, are vague. We're asking all unit commanders to contact whichever men they have involved in covert operations and confirm that they're secure. If anyone cannot be reached…well, then, we have the name and can take steps to help him."

"Sir, if I may ask, who are the specific gangsters you believe may be involved?"

Major Yugandhar considered that for several seconds longer than seemed necessary, then replied, "A group from Bangalore, trying to crack the Mandrax traffic. Strictly classified, of course."

"Of course, sir."

"So, you'll check your rolls immediately, and report back any officer who's fallen out of contact in the past few days."

"Yes, sir."

"Dismissed."

Patel retreated from Yugandhar's office, his thoughts in turmoil. He had not been criticized for anything—except, perhaps, by implication that he might lose track of officers he supervised—and it was clear the major had been lying about methaqualone smugglers out of Bangalore. Most of the Mandrax sold illegally in India or shipped on to South Africa came from the stockpiles of domestic pharmaceutical concerns, diverted for the extra profits it would earn as contraband.

No, it was G-troop, trying to identify and then recapture Baji Sharma. Patel had no doubts on that score. And the only question left: was Major Yugandhar himself on Riyaz Geelani's payroll, or was he acting under orders from a rotten apple higher up the ladder of command?

Bhandup West, Mumbai

THE CASINO OCCUPIED the top floor of an otherwise legitimate department store, located two blocks east of Madhu Hospital. Sharma described it as a full-scale operation, mingling East and West with a range of traditional Indian games, plus the clattering marvels of modern technology. A Public Gambling Act from 1867 made it illegal to operate or patronize a casino, but the penalties were relatively minor: fines did not exceed three hundred rupees—less than six U.S. dollars—and the stiffest jail term capped at ninety days. More recently, the Information Technology Act of 2000 had imposed a 100,000-rupee fine and five years in prison for electronic transmission of gaming information prone to "corrupt" public morals.

Which, of course, only encouraged gambling, pouring cash into the coffers of G-troop and its competitors.

Mack Bolan had a different approach to the problem.

He had never been a blue-nosed moralist and saw no reason why gambling couldn't be legally managed like any other industry. What motivated Bolan was the outlaw gambling profits funding other crimes, from the narcotics trade to terrorism in the present case. The games weren't evil, nor the players, but the end result, as witnessed in Mumbai, came down to death and suffering.

Players called G-troop's club the Mayfair, though it had no name in fact, after the posh department store that served it as a front. Geelani stood to profit twice, in some cases, as winners from the upstairs games were lured to purchase jewelry, stylish clothing and accessories before they left the premises for home. It was the closest thing to a Las Vegas operation found in India, and Sharma estimated that it paid Geelani something in the neighborhood of eighty million rupees yearly.

It was time to shut down that pipeline.

They parked the Ritz a block east of the Mayfair and walked back to reach their target. With the store closed for the night, Sharma led Bolan to a service entrance used by gamblers after hours, in an alley at the rear. A young guard

answered Bolan's knock, declared that entry was for members
only, then abruptly changed his mind with two guns leveled
at his face. Disarmed, he led them to an elevator, where they
took a second lookout by surprise, relieved him of his pistol, and stood waiting for the car he summoned to descend.

Access to the casino was restricted, but the elevator
operator had a special key to get them there. The car rose
smoothly, stopped on four, and sighed as its door opened
to the right. Another lookout greeted them, blinked once
before a slug from Bolan's sidearm drilled his forehead,
then another pair of shots put down the soldiers they had
bagged downstairs as the men went for their weapons.

Predictably, all hell broke loose.

Confronted by a pair of gunmen at the elevator, players,
dealers and assorted other personnel raced for the nearest
exit, stairs descending to street level as a backup system
if the power failed. A fourth and final guard was on that
door, drawing a pistol as the human tide washed over him.
Bolan saw him stumble backward, lost to sight inside the
stairwell. Shots exploded there, followed by screams and
sounds of bodies tumbling over one another in a wild, self-
mutilating rush downstairs.

"Grab as much loose cash as you can carry," Bolan
said. "I'll hit the bar and start the fire. Two minutes, and
we're out."

"Two minutes," Sharma echoed, whipping out a shopping bag he'd tucked beneath his jacket, double-timing toward the nearest card table and smiling all the way.

Juhu, Mumbai

"You're sure the only people here will be Geelani's men?"
Bolan asked.

"I am certain," Sharma answered. "Earlier tonight—

or, I should say, on any normal night—they would have brought their women. Not their *wives,* you understand, but *randee.* You would say—"

"I get it," Bolan said, as they walked through early morning darkness, headed south on Juhu Tara Road. "No danger to civilians, then."

"None whatsoever."

"Fair enough."

The Bombay Club was nothing much to look at from the outside, clearly no competition for the tourist traps that fronted nearby Juhu Beach, a onetime sandbar that developers had turned into a lavish popular resort. G-troop would tap the wallets of those visitors in other ways, leaving its shooters in the background, out of sight and out of mind.

Two guys were loitering outside the entrance to the Bombay Club, not standing watch per se, but checking out the cars that passed, alert to any look or gesture that suggested disrespect. They spotted Bolan and his partner from a long block out, exchanging comments, not advancing, but prepared for trouble if the new arrivals wanted some.

Or, anyway, the two guys *thought* they were prepared.

It was a different story when the INSAS rifle rose in Bolan's hands, cracked twice and slammed their lifeless bodies to the pavement, twitching in the crimson pond that spread from shattered skulls. Bolan and Sharma stepped around them, pushing through the entrance in a rush before the sounds of gunfire fully registered with anyone inside the bar.

It looked to be a slow night at the Bombay Club—or maybe the half-dozen shooters facing toward the door as Bolan entered were relaxing briefly, in between patrols. They all stood frozen for a heartbeat, looking at the strangers on their threshold, armed with automatic weapons, then they broke for cover, diving every which way, pistols coming out.

Bolan started on his left, tagging a long-haired shooter with a droopy Fu Manchu mustache. He slammed a 5.56 mm shocker through the target's chest and pitched him over backward, arms outflung and flapping like a pair of broken wings as he collided with a table, tipped it and went down with glasses shattering around him.

Next in line, a short, stout gunner with a shiny automatic pistol in his fist, firing his first round without aiming, in a bid to buy some time. It didn't work, as Bolan stood his ground and gave the little guy a double-tap from twenty feet, spinning him through a jerky little dance that took him halfway to the bar before he fell.

Behind that bar, another member of the crew had given up on pouring drinks and was prepared to spill some blood. He'd dragged a shotgun out from underneath the bar, but Bolan caught him with a hot round through the throat before he had a chance to level it. The barkeep got his shot off anyway, but sprayed the left side of the room with buckshot, raising howls from someone over there, then dropped from sight.

Baji Sharma did the rest of it, his Mini-Uzi chattering in short, well-measured bursts, spent brass cascading to the concrete floor beneath their feet. A moment later, deathly stillness fell over the Bombay Club. Bolan surveyed the scene, saw scattered plates of food and asked, "They have a kitchen in the back?"

"A gas stove," Sharma said.

"Cover the door," the Executioner replied. "I feel another fire sale coming on."

CHAPTER SIX

Central Bureau of Investigation Headquarters, Mumbai

"All clear?" Colonel Hamid Rahman inquired.

"Yes, sir," Captain Arjun Durani replied. "The scan shows no taps on your private line."

"All right. Dismissed."

It was impossible to be too cautious at the CBI. In Colonel Rahman's business, paranoia was not mental disorder; it was a survival tool.

There was no time to waste. His private line was clear right now, but might be tapped at any moment in the future. A delay in placing the unpleasant call only increased his risk. He tapped the number out from memory, not trusting any database or microchip to keep it safe from prying eyes. Across Mumbai, another phone rang twice before a flat voice answered.

"Namaste."

Colonel Rahman ignored the greeting, spoke the coded phrase that had been selected for this contact, and sat waiting while Riyaz Geelani's stooge ran off to fetch his master. It only took a moment in real time, but Rahman felt as if he had been hanging on the dead line for an hour when Geelani spoke.

"Colonel. You have news for me?"

"Nothing yet, unfortunately, but my captains have been

ordered to discover and report if any of their officers are missing in the field."

"And can you trust them?"

Rahman hesitated for a fraction of a second, then replied, "I think so, yes."

"I hope so, Colonel."

"We maintain strict discipline."

"In theory, certainly." A hint of mockery had crept into Geelani's tone. He did not need to state the obvious—that true strict discipline would have prevented Rahman from accepting G-troop's money and collaborating with a gang of criminals.

"If one of them conceals an undercover operation," Rahman said, "he violates the bureau's protocol."

"Or, as another possibility," Geelani said, "he may be acting under orders from an officer who outranks you."

Rahman had no ready response for that. It was, in essence, what he feared the most: entrapment from within the CBI itself. Eliminating him would not be easy for his adversaries, though. Rahman had seen to that by documenting guilty secrets of his own subordinates *and* his superiors, including sexual transgressions and pecuniary sins alike. Blackmail was not beneath him, and if that failed, anyone who took him down would find his reputation smeared and blackened in the process.

"This spy who got away from you," he said. "How certain are you that he is connected to the bureau?"

"We've considered all the possibilities," Geelani said. "Inquiries are proceeding with the State Police, the IPS and IRS, as well."

Referring to the Indian Police Service, or *Bhāratīya Pulis Sevā,* and Indian Revenue Service, the *Bhāratīya Rājaswa Sevā.* Both agencies investigated various aspects of organized crime nationwide, and the CBI recruited officers directly from their ranks.

"With what result?" the colonel asked.

"Still inconclusive," Geelani replied.

"You got nothing out of him, before you let him slip away?"

"*I* did not let him slip away."

"Your soldiers, then."

"He was…resistant to interrogation."

"Then you have no reason to suspect my bureau more than any other agency."

"Until the matter is resolved," Geelani said. "Those who cooperate in our attempt to find the spy will be rewarded. Those who fail us should expect no thanks."

And, Colonel Rahman thought, no payoff.

"As you can see," he said, "I *am* cooperating."

"I prefer cooperation with results," Geelani countered.

"If my men have anything to hide, I shall uncover it," Rahman assured him.

"From an officer of your accomplishment," Geelani said, "I would expect no less. Good day, Hamid. And good hunting."

The line went dead before Colonel Rahman could speak again. His cheeks warmed with a flush of anger at the mobster's rude behavior, but he cradled the receiver softly, swallowing the urge to hammer it against his desktop. Unchecked fury was a luxury that he could not afford. It clouded judgment and could blind him to potential threats.

Whether the spy Geelani was obsessed with had connections to the CBI or not, Rahman knew something strange and perilous was brewing in Mumbai. The recent bloody raids against G-troop were totally unprecedented in Mumbai, despite the city's history of simmering, sporadic gang warfare. It was unique and startling to see Geelani's syndicate on the receiving end of so much mayhem when he normally was dishing out the death and suffering.

Rahman supposed that many people in Mumbai would be delighted by Geelani's discomfiture, and the colonel himself derived a certain satisfaction from seeing Geelani on the defensive. His supplemental salary, however—twice what he received in monthly paychecks from New Delhi— still depended on Geelani, and for that reason alone he had to keep the smirking bastard satisfied.

Which meant more pressure on the officers beneath Rahman, until he satisfied Geelani—and himself—that the elusive spy was not one of his own.

And if he *was*…well, any soldier was expendable.

Naikwadi, West Mumbai

DAWN BROKE OVER Mumbai with the implicit promise of another muggy, steaming day. Commercial vehicles were first out on the streets, making deliveries to restaurants, hotels and grocery stores. The Bombay Stock Exchange, which stubbornly refused to change its name, would not start trading until 9:00 a.m. Most shops and offices would stall another hour before opening their doors for business, then proceed to serve their customers over the next twelve hours. Six-day weeks were standard, though some lenient managers allowed their workers to punch out at five o'clock on Saturdays.

Mack Bolan's destination was Wicker Lane, a shop that manufactured custom rattan furniture—and which concealed a G-troop arms depot. The hardware was employed as needed by Riyaz Geelani's soldiers, with the surplus sold to anyone with ready cash on hand: bank robbers, kidnappers, assassins, would-be "liberation warriors"—

take your pick. Eliminating it would be another step toward pulling G-troop's fangs.

Directed by his sidekick from the CBI, Bolan drove north on Lal Bahadur Shastri Road to Castle Mill Circle, then branched off on a street of stylish shops to reach his target. Parking in front was possible this early in the day, but too risky for Bolan's taste. An alley running past the rear of shops along the street's west side, wide enough for garbage trucks to pass, had ample space to leave the rented Ritz outside Wicker Lane's back door.

The door's two locks were both good quality. Instead of taking time to pick them, Bolan used the muffled Mini-Uzi, blowing them apart. Inside the silent building—no guards stationed there, for reasons that eluded him—he followed Sharma to another locked door and repeated the procedure, then descended metal steps into a basement armory.

The place was stocked for war, and then some. In addition to a large supply of standard-issue assault rifles and submachine guns, the cache included Indian-made MG 5A general purpose machine guns, Israeli Negev light machine guns, and a Russian NSV heavy machine gun. Other items on hand included a stockpile of Shiva-lik grenades, adaptable for throwing or use as rifle grenades with simple change in the outersleeve, and an 84 mm Carl Gustav recoilless rifle.

After setting some of the grenades aside, Bolan homed in on the arsenal's stash of Semtex plastic explosive. Whoever stocked the arsenal had wisely kept their case of detonators separated from the Semtex, but Bolan had no trouble finding them. With Sharma helping, he distributed a chain of half-pound charges evenly around the basement, extra helpings set with the grenades he'd left behind and the Carl Gustav's stock of high-explosive rounds. They planted detonators, linked them with a web of insulated wires, and linked those to a handy kitchen timer with a battery attached, the timer ticking down from ten minutes to doomsday as they scrambled back upstairs.

Back in the car, Bolan circled the block, passed Wicker Lane once more and satisfied himself that no one had reported in for work so far at the adjoining shops. There would be damage to surrounding property, of course, but Sharma had reported that Riyaz Geelani owned most of the buildings, holding their deeds through companies that fronted for his syndicate. The lion's share of damage would fall squarely onto G-troop, where the grief belonged.

With no civilians visible around ground zero, Bolan motored four blocks east, then pulled into the curb and left the Ritz's engine idling while he waited for the earth to move. Sharma was half-turned in his seat, expectant, watching through the car's rear window. Bolan kept an eye out for police cars while he waited, counting down the doomsday numbers in his head.

The blast was right on time, shattering windows in a two-block radius, raising a cloud of dust and smoke in Bolan's rearview mirror at the spot where Wicker Lane had stood. A crater had replaced it now, as if a bolt from heaven had descended to eradicate a plague spot from the street. And if the shop's innocent neighbors never recognized the danger that had lurked beneath their feet—so what?

A portion of his job was done.

The Executioner was moving on.

Ashok Nagar, Mumbai

EVERY PARAMILITARY OUTFIT needed at least one motor pool. G-troop's largest was located on Pipeline Road, a quarter-mile west of Chhatrapati Shivaji International Airport.

The layout included an acre or so of blacktop surrounded by chain-link fence and the expected razor wire, plus a metal building that appeared to serve as a garage of sorts, complete with gasoline pump standing twenty feet from its front door.

It was broad daylight now, and Bolan watched three men moving around the yard, wiping windshields, checking tire pressure, fetching drinks from a machine inside the building. All of them were wearing pistols underneath loose-fitting shirts. Bolan chalked them up as soldiers and fair game.

The rolling stock included twenty-seven vehicles, ranging in size from tiny Tata Nano subcompacts to Mahindra Scorpio SUVs, a black Humvee, and a MAN-Volkswagen Constellation semi rig minus its trailer. Overall, it was a sizable investment that would leave Riyaz Geelani hurting when it all went up in smoke.

Right now.

Mack Bolan peered through the 8-by-42 power scope atop his Vidhwansak sniper rifle, giving the G-troop motor pool a final sweep. The piece was normally a two-man weapon, since it tipped the scales at fifty-five pounds and measured five feet six inches long, but Bolan was going solo this morning, with Baji Sharma watching out for cops and any other interlopers near the sight he'd chosen for his roost, eight hundred yards southwest of his intended target.

The Vidhwansak was a rotary bolt-action weapon, feeding ten rounds from a curved detachable box magazine inserted on the left side of its receiver, in the style of British STEN and Sterling submachine guns. The hellish kick from its 14.5×114 mm rounds was absorbed—at least in part—through a damping system that permitted the barrel and receiver to recoil inside the chassis frame. There was no cushion for a target out on the receiving end, where bullets weighing up to sixty-six grams traveled 3,300 feet per second and struck with a shattering 24,000 foot-pounds of destructive energy.

Bolan's first magazine was loaded with armor-piercing incendiary rounds. He zeroed on the gas pump first, a target too inviting to resist, and stroked the rifle's trigger, sending hell downrange. The pump exploded, lofting skyward with a *whoomp!* and rising on a tongue of flame, a minimissile striving for escape velocity. Without a booster system, though, it quickly tumbled back to earth—or, rather, to the roof of the garage, where it disintegrated on impact.

By that time, Bolan had moved on. He caught one of the G-troop soldiers gaping at the fireball rising where the gas pump used to be, and slammed a round into the Tata Safari behind him, detonating its fuel tank. The SUV stood on its nose, buoyed on a cushion of fire that enveloped the man near its tailgate. Bolan couldn't hear the soldier screaming, and he didn't bother watching as the guy performed a jerky break-dance in a pool of flames.

Next up, the big rig parked beside the prefab building. Bolan pumped a round into its engine block, letting the bullet's tungsten carbide core deal with the penetration, while its incendiary tip lit fires along the way.

The soldier didn't have to take out every vehicle, only enough of them to spark adjacent cars and turn the lot into a smoky wrecking yard. The Vidhwansak's bolt-action wouldn't handle rapid-fire per se, but it was fast and smooth enough for Bolan's purpose as he worked his way around the yard, placing his next eight rounds in under fifteen seconds, concentrating on fuel tanks.

None of the vehicles downrange were armored, nor would standard armored bodies have saved them. The Vidhwansak's ammo was designed to penetrate 1.5 inches of steel at 325 feet, and 1.25 inches at 1,600 feet. The sheet metal bodies of passenger cars offered no more resistance than cardboard. After ten rounds, it was hell down there, with one survivor out the gate and running for his life down Pipeline Road.

Bolan let him go. It couldn't hurt to have a witness out there, spreading horror stories on the street and shaking up his pals. Whatever damaged G-troop, mentally or physically, was beneficial to the cause. He broke the rifle down in seconds flat and stashed it in the Ritz's trunk, while Sharma piled into the shotgun seat.

Pulling away from there, Bolan had an idea. Turning to Sharma, he inquired, "You wouldn't know the number to Geelani's private line, by any chance?"

Malabar Hill, Mumbai

"FOR YOU, SIR," Shyama Chauhan said, his hand extended with a cell phone nestled in its palm.

"Who is it now?" Riyaz Geelani asked.

"He would not say. Only that it is vitally important."

"Idiot! How hard is it to get a name?"

"I—"

"Never mind." Geelani snatched the phone and spit another curse at Chauhan. Turning cautiously, then, as if the cell phone he was holding might explode, he raised it to his ear and said, *"Namaste?"*

"I suppose you're wondering where you went wrong," the caller said in a voice Geelani did not recognize.

"I do not understand you," he replied.

"Well, think about it. This time yesterday, you were on top, no competition worth considering. Today, you're in the crapper, circling the drain. It has to make you wonder.

Why is all this happening? Who dropped the ball? What happened to your so-called friends?"

"You speak in riddles, Mr....?"

"Hey, what's in a name? My point is that the names you know, the ones you trust, have obviously let you down."

"Again..."

"I get it," the stranger said. "Since we're talking on an open line, you have to play it dumb. No problem. What you *really* need to do right now is *think*. Imagine how this show is playing in Islamabad. You think they're pleased with your performance so far? Or are they the ones behind it all?"

A nervous tic sprang into life below Geelani's left eye, causing him to wink involuntarily. He swiped at it, swallowed the angry and impulsive answer that was on his tongue.

"I SUSPECT YOU have confused me with some other party," he replied at last.

"Okay. So, in the past few hours you haven't lost a meth lab, a casino or a whorehouse? You don't have a private army running short of soldiers who keep dropping dead? You didn't just lose twenty-seven vehicles and a garage? My mistake."

"Garage?" Geelani blurted out. "Vehicles?"

"No one tipped you yet?" the caller asked him. "Jeez, I guess the one guy who got out's still running. He was headed north on Pipeline Road, last time I saw him."

"Who *are* you?"

"Just a contractor," the caller said. "This time around, the contract's got your name on it."

"Why call me, then?"

"Maybe I like to keep it sporting."

"I don't think so."

"You're right. Let's say that I like working for the highest bidder, and I've only had one bid so far. You've got a lot to lose. Maybe you want to ante up and turn the game around."

Geelani smelled the trap. Only an idiot would fall for such a ploy, negotiating murder on the telephone, where every word can be snatched from the air, recorded without warrants and played back to hang him at his trial.

"You spin an interesting fable," he replied. "It has been most amusing, but I have no further time to waste."

"Your call. Don't say I didn't warn you."

There was more Geelani might have said, but dead air whispered in his ear. He snapped the cell phone shut and shouted for Shyama Chauhan. When the house man stood before him once again, Geelani said, "I need to speak with someone at the Pipeline Road garage. Immediately!"

Chauhan now wore a sick expression on his face. "That is not possible, sir."

"Not possible? Explain yourself!"

"While you were on the other line, Baba Gurera called. He says that the garage and all the cars are gone."

"All gone? What does that mean, 'gone'?"

"Exploded, sir. He believes it was a rifle firing from a distance, possibly explosive rounds. Jitendra and Mukut are dead."

Geelani stared at Chauhan, realized that he was gaping, and immediately shut his mouth, striving for an expression that suggested thoughtfulness instead of panic. Finally, the only thing that he could say was, "Go! Get out!"

He thought of calling back the stranger, but he did not know the caller's number, and could not permit himself to beg for help in any case. Whatever the assassin offered to him, it was bound to hide a snare. Better to trust the devils that he knew firsthand—assuming he could trust them now.

Geelani started tapping out a number on his private cell. The country code for Pakistan was 92; the area code for Islamabad was 51. Geelani knew the number by heart, and while he regretted calling it a second time within a few short hours, he could think of no alternative.

He needed reassurance, answers to a hundred questions that were roiling in his mind.

And, more important, a place to hide.

His call was answered on the second ring.

"As-salaam-o-alaikum."

"Alaikum as-salaam," Geelani echoed.

"Again, so soon?" Major Ibrahim Leghari said, sounding out of sorts.

"I realize the imposition," Geelani stated, "but we need to talk."

"So, talk."

"Not on the telephone," Geelani said. "In person. Face-to-face."

Grant Road, Mumbai

"He put you off, then?" Sharma asked.

"About what I expected," Bolan answered. "He's not dumb enough to spit out any secrets on an open line. He's thinking, though. Wondering how far he can trust his buddies out of Pakistan."

"And calling them, perhaps?"

"I wouldn't be surprised. Another little push could do the trick."

"What trick?" Sharma inquired.

"I don't know, yet. Maybe divide and conquer. Maybe

spook Geelani into making a mistake he can't recover from."

"So now we visit him at home, but not to kill him?"

"Just to shake him up a little more," Bolan agreed.

The Ritz was rolling west along Grant Road, toward Malabar Hill. Bolan was hoping that he'd have another opportunity to use the Vidhwansak again. Reach out and touch somebody from a distance, without getting in too close and personal this time, giving Geelani room to duck and cover while his world kept on unraveling around him.

Rolling up the G-troop network still meant more than taking out the man on top. Eliminate Geelani, and his number two, Sayeed Zargar, would simply step into his vacant slot. Would it be Z-troop, then? A label made no difference to Bolan if the juggernaut kept rolling on, disrupting lives and killing innocents. He wanted to dismantle the machine from top to bottom, and it helped if he could get the man at the controls to make a critical mistake.

Another angle that he hoped to work was G-troop's link to Pakistan. Spies were not protected under Bolan's private ban on hitting law enforcement officers, and he had tangled with the DISI's thugs before. Their record of supporting terrorism hung a bull's-eye on their backs whenever Bolan saw the opportunity to take a shot.

Grant Road took Bolan to Gamdevi Lane, a looping run to the southwest, connecting to Marine Drive, then Walkeshwar Road, rolling along with ocean on his left, and houses turning into grand estates off to his right. He picked up Harkness Road, turned inland, following his guide's directions toward Riyaz Geelani's not-so-little piece of paradise.

About to be a slice of Hell on Earth.

They were a quarter-mile from target acquisition, give or take, when Sharma's cell phone rang. The sergeant snagged it on the second ring, glanced at the LED display and frowned as he announced, "Captain Patel."

"He keeping track of you?" Bolan asked.

"I advised him not to contact me," Sharma replied.

"He take you seriously?"

"I believe so."

Three rings. Four.

"You want to get that?" Bolan prodded.

"NAMASTE!" HE SAID into the phone.

Sharma listened for a moment, frowning at whatever he was hearing. Finally, he answered back, *"Dhanyavad. Namaskar."*

Bolan waited while he put the cell away, but when the moment started dragging out, he interrupted Sharma's reverie. "What is it?"

"It appears we are too late," Sharma replied.

"For what?"

"To catch Geelani at his house."

"How's that?"

"He's left, with half a dozen men. Leaving the city, it appears."

"Right now?"

Sharma was nodding. "My superior maintains surveillance on Geelani, even though the officers above him do not care to take advantage of it. He is halfway to the airport, where a private jet stands waiting."

"Going where?" Bolan asked, though he thought he had a fair idea.

"To Pakistan."

It was a change of plans, but Bolan had survived his lonely war this long by learning to adapt and improvise. He might be taken by surprise, but never let it stagger him or throw him off his game.

"Okay," he said, watching the traffic for a break, some-place to turn the Ritz around. "I need to make some calls myself, and see if we can bag ourselves a set of wings."

CHAPTER SEVEN

Sion, Mumbai

Captain Vivak Patel had not risked calling Baji Sharma from his office at CBI headquarters. Already in the field when he received the news of Geelani's abrupt departure from home, with a jet standing by to extract him, Patel had placed the call from the lobby of the Hotel Ashray International in Sion, a suburb separating Mumbai proper from the bulk of Salsette Island. Sharma had absorbed the information and had thanked him for it. What might happen next was out of Patel's hands.

He felt a pang of guilt—or was it guilty pleasure—from his act of subterfuge. Breaking the rules was not a tactic he preferred, or that he normally would countenance among his officers, but something strange and great and terrible was happening around him, and he'd found himself sucked into it against his better judgment.

If he had not been interrogated, if the bureau's upper echelons were not apparently collaborating with Riyaz Geelani's thugs to find his sergeant, then Patel likely would not have felt compelled to step outside the law. During his years of service, he'd grown accustomed to biting his tongue and averting his eyes while justice was bartered or sold to the highest bidder. That was the way of the world, in Mumbai and everywhere else. But the plague of terrorism changed all that, and if his own superiors turned out

to be accomplices, Patel had no choice but to act without
their knowledge or approval.

No choice, in this case, except to break the law.

Leaving the hotel lobby, he walked westward, against
one-way traffic, on the north side of Swamy Vallabhdas
Road. A young man passed him, going in the opposite direction, and while he was one of many on the sidewalk,
there was something in his hasty sidelong glance that rang
a faint alarm bell for Patel. The captain dawdled at a shop
window, ostensibly admiring a display of jewelry, and
sneaked a look off to his right while he was at it.

Half a block behind him, the young man had met two
others walking in Patel's direction, and the three of them
were idling, forcing other foot traffic to flow around them
while they put their heads together in an earnest conversation. On his second peek, Patel caught one of them staring
at him, then awkwardly averting startled eyes.

A tail, then. And they weren't police, that much was
clear. Two of the three were too young for plainclothes assignment, while the third had prison tattoos rising from the
open collar of his shirt on both sides of his neck.

G-troop.

Patel moved on toward Station Road, not hurrying or
looking back to see if his three followers were still in
place. They wouldn't lose him here, despite the crowds
surrounding them. The vital question, for Patel, was how
could *he* lose *them*.

Not on the train downtown to headquarters; that much
was obvious. They'd have him cornered once he went
aboard, and if they chose to force a confrontation in a
crowded car it could degenerate into a massacre. Patel was
carrying his standard-issue semiauto pistol with a pair of
backup magazines, and while he would not hesitate to fire

in self-defense, he didn't relish touching off a shoot-out in the midst of innocent civilians.

Not that he would necessarily be given any choice.

So it came down to him. Patel could seek some method of evading his three stalkers, or select the safest place available in which to challenge them, demand that they surrender any weapons they were carrying and come with him to jail.

Not likely. All the less because he only had a single pair of handcuffs with him, and the nearest help available was nearly two miles distant, to the north, at the Mahim Police Colony.

In short, no help at all.

Patel resigned himself to shooting as he spotted Sion Railway Station West ahead of him and knew he absolutely couldn't take the train. He passed the station, and someone's fate was sealed. His own? That of his followers? Maybe all of them together?

Where should he go to make his stand?

He knew the answer instantly, instinctively. Where better to attempt losing a tail than in Dharavi, the pathetic slum due west of Sion, where a million souls were crammed into two-thirds of a square mile? Perhaps the world's most famous Asian slum—featured in *Slumdog Millionaire* some years ago—Dharavi boasted five thousand shops and fifteen thousand single-room "factories" turning out pottery, textile and ready-made garments.

Patel followed his nose toward Dharavi, no great challenge for a district with one toilet for every 1,400 inhabitants, and felt his stalkers following. His choice was made, and so was theirs.

Now it only remained to be seen who would survive.

Juhu Aerodrome, Mumbai

To BOOK A CHARTER flight, Bolan and Sharma bypassed
Chhatrapati Shivaji International in favor of the city's
smaller airport, located adjacent to Juhu Beach on the
Arabian Sea. Juhu Aerodrome handled all helicopter operations out of Mumbai, while hosting the Bombay Flying Club, plus various executive and charter services. The
city's plan, at least in theory, was to move all small private
aircraft operations from CSI to Juhu, thereby decongest-
ing the international airport, but as usual, bureaucracy and
simple inefficiency had left that program hanging.

Bolan had selected Kismatwala Airlines after Sharma
told him that the name meant *Lucky,* and a phone call fixed
a price for carrying two passengers from Mumbai to Karachi, some 550 miles one way. That city would not be their
final destination, but the pilot only had to set them down
at Jinnah International Airport and await their return for
a reasonable length of time. If they did not return to meet
him, for whatever reason, he could take off on the deadline with full payment for the round-trip flight.

Their aircraft was a Gippsland GA8 Airvan, manufactured in Australia, with seating for eight that included its
pilot. Its power plant was a six-cylinder, 300-horsepower
Lycoming O-540 engine, with a cruising speed of 138
miles per hour at ten thousand feet and a range of 840
miles. Call it four hours to Karachi, once they lifted off,
and while Geelani had escaped them for the moment,
Bolan wasn't worried about losing him.

Sharma knew where the G-troop chief was going, if he
didn't alter the normal pattern of his other trips to Pakistan. Geelani had a place midway between Karachi and
Hyderabad, about fifty miles inland, and a map showed
them the layout in fairly close detail. There would still be

things to learn once they were on the ground, but for the moment, Bolan figured they were points ahead.

Their main advantage, if they pulled it off, would be surprise.

Getting through Customs at Jinnah International would be the first stumbling block, and their pilot had some thoughts on that score. His name was Bharat Deshpande, and he smiled too much for Bolan's taste but seemed to know what he was doing with his preflight checklist on the Airvan. Bolan left him to it, while Sharma made small talk with the younger man in Hindi, saying things that made the pilot laugh either from glee or force of habit when it came to stroking customers.

Ten minutes later they were airborne, climbing steeply to the Gippsland's cruising altitude, then circling out to sea before Deshpande aimed the aircraft northwest, toward Karachi. As he'd explained it, they'd be flying over water all the way, with coastline on their right, until they reached their destination and turned inland. Through his little window, Bolan watched Mumbai retreat and dwindle, other coastal towns passing to starboard, and they made their way toward Pakistan.

Oddly—at least, to Bolan's mind—air traffic between India and Pakistan continued quasi-normally, despite the generations of hostility and armed conflict between the two belligerent neighbors. "Quasi," because Pakistan International Airlines operated daily commercial flights across the border, while Air India refused to enter Pakistani airspace. Transit overland depended chiefly on crowded buses and trains, both prone to breakdowns and sporadic terrorist attacks.

Bharat Deshpande "knew a man" in Customs at Karachi, he'd explained, and could ensure that any baggage passed inspection without being opened for a "handling fee" of ten thousand Pakistani rupees—roughly a C-note and change. It was another gamble, but their only other option had been driving from Mumbai, eight hours on the road if they were lucky, interrupted by a border checkpoint where the trip could end abruptly, even fatally.

He hoped the pilot's system worked. Beyond that, he was counting on Riyaz Geelani running to the hideout Bolan had surveyed by satellite, instead of running off to meet his DISI contacts in Islamabad or somewhere else beyond their reach. A car was waiting for them, theoretically, when they touched down at Jinnah International, but Bolan didn't plan on chasing his elusive prey all over Pakistan.

A tidy hit-and-git was what he had in mind, preferably driving the boss of G-troop back to India and rattling his connections to the Pakistani government while they were at it. Anything they did to stem the tide of terrorist attacks in India would be a bonus.

And Geelani, once he started running, would be on the fast track to his grave.

Sindh Province, Pakistan

RIYAZ GEELANI WAS relieved to put Karachi in his rearview mirror. Its population—roughly twice that of Mumbai—was spread over a larger area, but driving through its streets still made Geelani feel a kind of claustrophobia that put him in an angry funk for no apparent reason. He felt better in the open countryside, riding in air-conditioned comfort, with a carload of his soldiers out in front of him, another carload bringing up the rear.

Trouble had come too close for comfort in Mumbai. The stranger's phone call to his home had been the final straw, convincing him to take a holiday from all the chaos. Hiding out in Pakistan also had other benefits, including an

appointment to meet Major Ibrahim Leghari face-to-face.
The Pakistani would be flying in by helicopter to Geelani's
rural compound, paid for in large part by his own agency.
Geelani hoped their talk would be productive—in particular, contributing to resolution of present difficulty.

It was in Leghari's interest to support him. Who else
had done more wet work around Mumbai, in service to
the DISI, than Riyaz Geelani? Surely, no one. It was true
enough that he had been rewarded for his service, but in
order for that service to continue, he required assistance in
eliminating the infernal vermin who were plaguing him,
inflicting major damage on the empire he'd established for
himself. He was a loyal Muslim, naturally, but he also had
to make a living if he was to carry on helping the cause.

Allah would understand that. So should Major Ibrahim Leghari.

"Five more miles, sir," his driver said.

Geelani grunted in response, still focused on his problem. So far, he'd lost soldiers, money, property and critical
prestige. The latter was most painful, and potentially most
dangerous, since it encouraged rivals in Mumbai and elsewhere to believe that he was vulnerable, weak and failing.
Once that perception took root, it could become reality.

Geelani's compound was situated outside Thano Bula
Khan, a town built at the meeting point of five converging roads that qualified as *highways* only in the broadest
definition of that term. The four-lane M-9 Motorway, on
which he traveled now, was rated as a "superhighway" by
Pakistan's National Highway Authority, linking Karachi
to Hyderabad, but plans for a Malaysian company to build
two additional lanes had been stalled for years. The other
roads to Thano Bula Khan were two-lane tracks at best,
rumbling with truck traffic day and night.

Geelani's retreat covered forty-five acres of hilly terrain

on the southern fringe of the Kirthar Mountains, nothing to compare with the towering Karakoram, Himalayan or Hindu Kush ranges for climbing appeal, but the territory bred rugged tribesmen who looked askance at strangers and were willing to alert Geelani to intruders, once his generosity toward those who served him well was recognized.

He kept a dozen men in residence at the retreat year-round, well stocked with weapons, ammunition and emergency supplies. Not quite a home away from home, it still provided relatively plush accommodations for the boss of G-troop, with an eight-room house that most Americans would designate as ranch-style. Other buildings on the property included barracks for his soldiers, with a mess hall and latrines, a bungalow stocked with communications gear and a Quonset hut containing an all-purpose maintenance facility for vehicles and buildings.

Geelani spent a portion of each year in Pakistan, evading periodic outbursts of "reform" by Indian authorities who took his bribes with gratitude but still had to impress the citizens they claimed to serve by raiding vice dens or pursuing those responsible for acts of terrorism. Some of it was just for show, but certain officers still took their oath of service seriously, and it helped to have a hiding place beyond their jurisdiction when the heat was on.

Like now.

Geelani still did not believe officials were behind the recent raids against G-troop. Not *Indian* officials, anyway, though he was undecided on the CIA and MI6. London, he was convinced, could not forget that it once owned the whole of India and Pakistan together, ruling it with bayonets and bullets, forcing peasants to grow indigo and sell it below market value to British planters who leased them the land, taxing the very salt required to season humble food. He felt that the queen and parliament would grasp at any opportunity to punish former colonies for claiming independence from the British Raj.

As for America, who could predict what tactics the Great Satan might adopt in its new crusade against Islam? Geelani lived in secret dread of killer drone aircraft, but never let the fear show to his followers, the soldiers who depended on him for direction and support.

A little rest and consultation with Major Leghari would be helpful. If the trouble was not settled soon, he would return and teach the fleas that pestered him the perils of provoking a bull elephant.

Dharavi, Mumbai

MOST OF THE SHOPS and houses in Dharavi were illegal, built from any stray materials at hand, without regard for public health and safety codes. The fetid streets and alleyways branched off in all directions, odd lopsided buildings leaning this way and that. Every open doorway, every window without glass or screen, showed furtive movement in their shadowed spaces. Over all hung a miasma, cooking odors mixed abominably with the stench of rotting trash and sewage.

It was an infernal maze—and still, Captain Patel could not lose the three hunters who were stalking him. He was not sure of their intent, whether to capture and interrogate him or to kill him outright, but Patel was running out of prospects for evasion.

It was nearly time to stand and fight.

Passing the headquarters of Eman Enterprise, a manpower recruitment firm for clients in the Persian Gulf, Patel drew his 9 mm Smith & Wesson M&P pistol, holding it against his thigh as he turned right into another narrow street of sorts, where beggars vied for space with men and women selling pottery and bolts of brightly colored fabric. Some saw the pistol, careful averting eyes that seemed to have seen everything, no longer much impressed by any fresh surprise.

Another moment, and he'd make his move. He would identify himself, of course, as if the hunters didn't know already who and what he was. A mere formality, and he did not expect them to retreat, much less surrender into custody. Patel would have preferred an empty street, but there was no such thing in the Dharavi slum.

Reaching an intersection, he stopped short, spun on his heel and raised the pistol in a firm two-handed grip while shouting at the stalkers, "CBI! Put up your hands!"

Instead, of course, they tried to scatter, each man groping for a hidden weapon of his own. Patel fired two shots at the older, tattooed gunman, striking him at least once in the upper chest. The target dropped, and then two pistols hammered back at him, putting Patel to flight.

He ran through filthy winding streets with no direction clear in mind. He knew Dharavi mainly as the site of many crimes he had been called on to investigate, without a great deal of success. The slums inhabitants saw nothing, knew nothing, when the authorities asked questions. It would be the same after this incident, Patel thought, whether he survived or died facedown in stinking muck.

The two remaining hunters kept pace with him, firing shots when either of them saw an opening, not caring if their misses wound up hitting men, women or children. They'd been hired to do a job and were committed to fulfilling the assignment. If Patel meant to survive, he knew that he would have to match their ruthlessness, perhaps even surpass it.

Five long minutes into aimless flight, he ducked into an

open doorway, startling the inhabitants of a pathetic hovel shared with chickens and a cringing, skeletal dog. Patel stood with a finger pressed against his lips, warning the family to silence, emphasizing it by angling his pistol in their general direction. From the street, he heard advancing footsteps, anxious questions flying back and forth.

He let the hunters pass him, then stepped out behind them. No further warning as he shot the taller of them in the back and dropped him, twitching, onto the perpetually damp and reeking earth. The other spun, trying to save himself, but Patel hit him with a double-tap before the young assassin had a chance to raise his pistol.

He was off by inches, trying for a heart shot, but his bullets drilled the gunman's throat and chin, snapping his head back sharply. He went down without a murmur, Patel closing in to check the pair of them for any signs of life, detecting none.

He could report the shooting now, forced to explain what he was doing in Dharavi, why he might be hunted there—or he could simply walk away. Another glance around the street, at dead eyes watching him, made up his mind.

Patel holstered his gun and walked.

Over the Arabian Sea

BLUE WATER GLISTENED from ten thousand feet, giving a false impression of passivity. Observing it, with ships reduced to tiny flecks of color on the azure field, no one would guess that pirates from Somalia trolled those waters more or less at will, seizing commercial ships for ransom of their crews and cargo, adding smaller pleasure craft to their expanding fleet after the rightful owners had been killed and dumped at sea.

From two miles up, you couldn't see the blood at all.

Looking inland, from the Executioner's perspective, there was no dividing line between the territory claimed by Pakistan and India. The nearest region, Gujarat, was the cradle of the ancient Indus Valley Civilization, this day an industrial center with sixty million inhabitants. Beyond it, Rajasthan—the largest state in India—had witnessed more bloodshed than most embattled nations twice its size. Throughout recorded history, its native tribes had struggled to exterminate each other, while successive waves of plundering invaders claimed the territory for themselves. No trace of mortal combat or demented ethnic cleansing lay upon the land this day.

From two miles up, it all looked fresh and clean.

The same was true of Pakistan, as they approached it from the sea. A country born in blood, spawned by religious hatred, showed no blemish from the horrors it had witnessed or the mayhem that continued on a daily basis. Constantly at odds with India, walking a razor's edge while dealing with the Taliban and U.S. occupation forces in Afghanistan, the land whose motto—Faith, Unity, Discipline—failed to allow for its complexity had found its territory breached by killer drone aircraft and raiding parties like the one that had finally eliminated Osama bin Laden. Was another war impending? Or a breakthrough in diplomacy?

The landscape didn't say.

Bolan glanced at his watch and saw they had another hour of flight time yet. Across the aircraft's narrow center aisle, Baji Sharma was dozing in his seat, or possibly pretending to. Bolan did not disturb him, had no pressing questions left to ask at this point, though he'd doubtless think of some when they were on the ground.

First hurdle: Customs. If their pilot wasn't snowing

them about his greedy friend—and if said friend wasn't off-duty for the day, leaving them to deal with someone else—they should be reasonably safe on touchdown. Or, at least, as safe as any other foreigners arriving with a small but potent mobile arsenal and traveling with clear-cut criminal intent.

Sharma had briefed him on the laws of Pakistan, including the state's list of capital crimes. There were twenty-seven in all, ranging from blasphemy, adultery and ripping off a woman's clothes, to treason. Murder could be flexible, downplayed in some cases as "mischief on earth," whatever that meant. Conviction required an eyewitness or a confession. Most condemned inmates were hanged, though stoning was reserved for the adulterers.

The story's moral: leave no witnesses and don't get caught.

As Sharma broke it down, there were at least a dozen federal law enforcement agencies in Pakistan, plus a local force in each of the nation's ten provinces. Most wore uniforms, but he would have to watch his step regardless, most particularly if Geelani called up reinforcements for his compound in the hinterlands. He didn't plan to violate his ban on killing cops, even by accident, even when they were clearly acting on behalf of terrorists like G-troop.

And if something happened in the heat of battle, if he somehow didn't recognize a target as a law enforcement officer—what then? Would he stand down? Give up his long and lonely war? Surrender?

Bolan wasn't sure, himself. He'd never thought it through that far, and saw no point in dwelling on it now.

He thought of the last movie he had watched from start to finish, in a New York hotel room. A killer comedy, *In Bruges*. The plot hinged on a rookie hitman who had killed a child by accident, and wound up marked for execution by his boss, a stickler for decorum when it came to kids. During their final showdown, said boss accidentally gunned down a dwarf dressed in children's clothing for a film shoot, then "stood by his principles" by blowing out his own brains on the spot, while his intended hitman-victim tried to set him straight on the mistake.

The message Bolan took from that: identify your target to the best of your ability, and if something went wrong, think first, before reacting.

Basic rules of combat, sure.

That settled in his mind, at least, he leaned back and closed his eyes.

CHAPTER EIGHT

Jinnah International Airport, Karachi, Pakistan

Bharat Deshpande's contact was on duty when they landed and, as advertised, he happily accepted payment on the spot. An extra thousand rupees got their passports stamped without the bother of explaining any travel plans to nosy immigration officers, and Sharma went to fetch their rental car.

He returned with a silver Suzuki Liana, right-hand drive, with five-speed manual transmission. Bolan stowed their gear and got behind the wheel, found Airport Road, and merged with traffic flowing westward, toward Karachi proper.

When they'd departed Mumbai, the plan had been to find Geelani at his rural compound, shake him up and send him running home again, follow, and finish mopping up G-troop. In flight, however, Bolan had decided that they shouldn't waste an opportunity to crush the Pakistani end of G-troop's operation while they had the chance. Sharma had briefed him on Geelani's operations in the ostensibly straitlaced Islamic republic, including opium poppy plantations, a heroin lab in Karachi, meth kitchens, another casino.

Everything, in short, that should have made imams see red.

The fact that he'd been operating virtually without opposition for a period of years told Bolan that the fix was in, most likely from the powerful Directorate for Inter-Services Intelligence that used Geelani to carry out terrorist raids in Mumbai. It would be easy for the DISI to divert local police, and if payoffs found their way to certain people in the upper ranks of government...well, they were only human, after all.

Plan B—the new Plan A—was a Karachi blitz, before they hit Geelani's hideaway. Give it the afternoon, maybe the evening, and have their target reeling from his losses by the time they dropped in, unannounced, to prove his Pakistani safehouse wasn't safe at all.

Karachi was Pakistan's largest and most populous city, its primary seaport, and its financial center, also the capital of Sindh province. In global terms, it constituted the world's ninth-largest urban agglomeration, with some 15,500 residents packed into each of its 1,362 square miles. Pakistan's largest corporations were headquartered there: textile and shipping firms, automotive factories, fashion and entertainment, advertising, publishing and medical research.

Not one of which held any interest for the Executioner.

Bolan was looking for the dark underside of Karachi: human trafficking, money laundering, counterfeiting of Indian currency—anything at all, in short, that profited G-troop. Drugs were the key, of course, with poppy cultivation yielding four tons of heroin yearly, while Pakistan served as a major transhipment point for Afghan drugs as well, including opiates and hashish bound for Western markets.

The problem wasn't finding targets, but selecting which to tackle first.

"Something in town, perhaps," Sharma proposed, "before we move into the countryside."

"Heroin lab?" Bolan suggested.

"Perfect."

Pakistan had been a minor player in the smack trade prior to autumn 1996, when the ultrafundamentalist Taliban had seized control of neighboring Afghanistan. The Taliban had waffled on drugs, first raiding opium plantations and executing smugglers, later adjusting their attitude and imposing a 20 percent tax on all shipments of heroin leaving the country. Angry growers had shifted next door to escape the taxation, planting the literal seeds of a new opium empire in Pakistan before 2001, when American troops invaded Afghanistan, seeking Osama bin Laden. The new "democratic" Afghani government, while formally condemning the heroin trade, made millions from trafficking that flourished under U.S. occupation, but production had continued on the Pakistani side, as well.

Targets enough to go around, and then some.

How much of the money that Riyaz Geelani earned from drugs was channeled into terrorism on behalf of Pakistan, against the Hindus both regarded as their mortal enemies? Enough, at any rate, to keep the wheels of mayhem turning, grinding up the innocent and spitting out atrocities. Stopping the flow of drugs entirely was not possible, but Bolan knew that he could slow it enough—right here, right now—to make Geelani feel the pinch.

And that could be enough.

Sharma had their target spotted on a large-scale city map, aerial photographs providing extra detail for their approach and withdrawal. Neither could give them any kind of head count for the guards on hand, or prep them for security precautions that Geelani might have set in place, but target acquisition was the first critical step in any strike. The rest of it was eyeball work once they were

on the scene, and some would still come down to luck, no
matter how well Bolan had prepared.

A new front opening in Bolan's war against G-troop.

The opposition didn't know it yet, but Hell had come
to town.

Central Bureau of Investigation Headquarters, Mumbai

CAPTAIN PATEL MOVED through the drab, familiar hallways,
feeling strange and out of place. Since his near-miss with
death in the Dharavi slum, nothing he saw or heard seemed
quite the same to him. Headquarters, in particular, seemed
alien and hostile.

It was knowing that he'd been betrayed, set up to die—
or worse, be tortured to extract the name of Baji Sharma—
that had jaundiced Patel's view of everything around him.
When familiar faces passed him in the corridors, smiling,
he looked for guilt behind the eyes, waiting for someone
to appear surprised that he was still alive.

Could it be mere coincidence that he'd been sent out to
investigate a theft, then found himself pursued by G-troop
thugs? Impossible. Geelani's soldiers had no reason to be
interested in Patel, unless someone at headquarters suspected him of knowing more than he'd admitted when he
was interrogated by Major Arutla Yugandhar.

Was *he* Geelani's source? Or was it someone higher up
in the chain of command?

Patel knew that he had to be extra cautious now, after
the bold attempt on his life. Whoever had betrayed him had
to have weighed the consequences and decided that protection of Geelani warranted a human sacrifice—or two,
since Baji Sharma would be killed as well, if G-troop managed to locate him. Killing fellow officers went far beyond
the pale of typical corruption, which diverted evidence,

offered advance warning of raids and saw files disappear. From simple graft, the man or men who had conspired to kill Patel were rogues in every sense.

And they were doubly dangerous.

Patel could not confront Yugandhar with an accusation, clearly. Even following the major's movements would be difficult, when anyone—including members of Patel's own squad—might be in league with G-troop. He could tip his hand with one careless remark, and that would be the end of it. Of him.

Riyaz Geelani, for his part, had fled to Pakistan, leaving his problems in Mumbai, no doubt conferring with the Pakistani agents who bankrolled his terroristic crimes. He would return eventually, and Patel could try some moves against him then…but in the meantime, what to do?

His mind rebelled against the path Sharma had chosen, casting aside every law that he'd sworn to uphold and defend. But, then again, Patel had done the same thing in Dharavi, leaving three men dead without a call to headquarters, much less completing all the forms required whenever deadly force was used against civilians. He had crossed a line himself, and something told Patel that there could be no going back.

What, then? Should he become a vigilante outlaw?

Rising crime rates throughout India had sparked reactions from the populace. Of late, there had been lynchings in Bihar, some carried out—or so newspapers said—while the police looked on. Within Mumbai itself, and very recently, a young man had been clubbed to death by vigilantes who accused him of abusing his mother and sister. Organized hoodlums had been spared, so far, but should they be exempt from retribution just because their money bought them friends in government?

Patel sat at his desk, cleaning his pistol, a routine activity that would arouse no questions if one of his officers stopped by to ask a question or report on an investigation's progress. When he'd finished and replaced the spent rounds from the weapon's magazine, he shuffled files, pretending interest in the paperwork laid out before him. All the while, his mind was racing, searching for an angle of attack—and self-defense—against his enemies.

He would not leave Mumbai, his lifelong home. Nor could he simply wait for those arrayed against him to decide on their next move, if he intended to survive. The trick was to decide upon a starting point, begin with nerve and see the action through with grim resolve.

But where to start?

The only lead that he could think of, risky as it was, involved Major Arutla Yugandhar. With rank against him, he'd get nothing out of his superior by simply asking questions. Not unless he turned the circumstances to his own advantage. If Yugandhar found himself in a position where refusal to cooperate had painful, even lethal, consequences—and if he could not identify the junior officer asking the questions—then Patel might have a chance.

But would he even dare to try it?

If the major or someone above him had decided to eliminate Patel, it meant that Patel had nothing to lose. Why *not* take more aggressive measures, if it meant the difference between survival and his death?

Why not, indeed?

Sindh Province, Pakistan

AT LAST, RIYAZ Geelani had received a welcome phone call, one that did not bring him news of some fresh problem threatening his life or reputation. This call, from Karachi, was about his second most favorite thing in the world: piles of money, with his name all over them.

Not that the cash would be traceable when his investors finished washing it. But it would still be *his*.

"The shipment's ready, then?" he asked.

"Ready to go, sir," Farouk Aziz said. "Four trucks, as we agreed."

One packed with heroin, three with hashish. There was no need to name the cargo, even though the telephones they used were scrambled, with their signals bouncing off a satellite in outer space.

"Three men per truck, at least," Geelani said.

"I thought you might prefer a complement of four, sir."

His deferential tone was always pleasing to Geelani's ear. "I would, indeed. And you—"

"Will lead the convoy personally, as agreed."

"I leave it in your hands, then. You'll be met as usual, with escorts and your final payment."

"As always, it's a pleasure doing business with you."

"Salaam alaykum."

"Alaykum salaam."

The link was broken, and Geelani found that he was smiling. He did the simple mathematics in his head: one ton of processed heroin cut down for street sale made five tons, and sold on the streets of Mumbai for 606 rupees—about eleven U.S. dollars—per gram, for a gross take of nearly ten million dollars. Cannabis was cheaper, selling to users for five rupees—eight cents, American—per gram, but Geelani's take from six tons would still exceed $435,000.

Why shouldn't he be smiling?

Still, money remained Geelani's *second*-most favorite thing in the world. The top spot on his list was claimed by revenge—slow and painful and bloody—against those

who wronged him. That pleasure was denied him at the
moment by the failure of the people he had searching for
his nameless enemies around Mumbai. So far, Geelani's
men—both G-troop and the various officials they controlled—had failed to give him simple names, much less
locations for the men he planned to keep alive in howling agony for weeks, lamenting the discomfort they had
caused him.

Razor blades and fish hooks. Electricity and flame. Perhaps a dose of nitric acid for variety, but nothing to excess.
Geelani had a doctor, long since stripped of his official
license, who repaired the wounded members of his family when they could not seek service at a public hospital.
The same man also served, in certain special instances,
to keep Geelani's enemies alive and more or less alert as
they were slowly, oh so lovingly dissected on a morgue
table he'd purchased for that very purpose. By the time
Geelani finished with them and released their worthless
souls, they would be unrecognizable to people who had
known them all their lives.

Unrecognizable, in fact, as human beings.

Sweet revenge.

But he could not indulge himself unless he had a subject on his table, and that pleasure was denied him by the
fumbling failures of his people in Mumbai.

Perhaps, if one of *them* became a lesson and example
to their friends, the rest would be encouraged to succeed?

Something to think about, as soon as he returned—but
not just yet.

He hoped the mayhem in Mumbai would be suppressed
by the authorities, if not by his own men. Geelani could
forego protracted vengeance if he had to, in the certain
knowledge that his enemies were dead and gone, but he
still needed to discover who had sent them. No one in his

right mind undertook a hopeless struggle against fatal odds unless directed by some high authority.

Or, possibly, if driven by a personal vendetta?

No. The spy his men had caught but couldn't hold had been a native Indian; that much was clear. The man who'd rescued him was white, either American or European. Nothing in Geelani's life experience allowed him to conceive a situation in which two such mismatched individuals could have a killing grudge against him, or against G-troop.

Impossible.

They had been sent, then. And Geelani had to learn which agency employed them. Once he held that information in his hand, he could obtain a name or names. And once he had the names of those who wished him dead…

Revenge.

It would not matter if he had to track them down in London, Washington or New York City. They could try to hide with MI-6, the Secret Service or the FBI—whichever.

They would die like pigs at slaughter, squealing for their lives.

Jamshed Quarters, Karachi

THE HEROIN LAB occupied a modest house near Karachi's Islamic Law College. The neighborhood was 99 percent Muslim, nearly one million residents in all, split into ethnic quarters that included Balochis and Bohras, Ismailis and Kashmiris, Memons and Muhajirs, Pakhtuns and Punjabis, Seraikis and Sindhis.

The men Bolan wanted to visit were scumbags. If they'd had a Latin scientific name, it might have been *Humana vastum*—human waste—or *Spumae universalis*—universal scum. Wherever Bolan found them, they behaved exactly like the last ones he had stepped on, be it in a nearby town or halfway round the world.

What other species murdered, raped, looted and terrorized its own kind for amusement or for profit? Only the one that should have been extinct by now, in anything resembling truly civilized society.

Bolan was on his way to blitz another infestation now, inside a neighborhood where he stood out like the proverbial sore thumb.

"Maybe they'll think that we're Jehovah's Witnesses," he said, while fastening the short suppressor to his semi-auto pistol's snout.

"I hope not," Sharma said. "Mobs beat them everywhere they go in India, then the police arrest them for inciting riots."

"It's a good thing we're in Pakistan," Bolan replied, and stepped out of the car, with Sharma close behind him.

It was drizzling rain, a bonus, since they both wore lightweight raincoats to conceal the weapons they were carrying. They'd parked a half block from their target, to the north, and locked it. That wouldn't protect it if a thief came by while they were gone, but in another moment, Bolan thought, the hell they'd raise inside the drug lab should distract attention from a new car at the curb.

A sentry occupied a folding chair out front, holding a black umbrella overhead since there was no porch roof to cover him. He saw them coming, frowned and started reaching for a bulky shopping bag that leaned against the left side of his chair, but Bolan got there first and plugged him with a Parabellum round between the eyes. The guy went limp and slid out of his chair, the contents of his bag clattering on the deck as it went down.

Bolan replaced the pistol in its holster and unveiled his INSAS autorifle, Sharma doing likewise with the Mini-

Uzi. Bolan fired a 3-round burst into the doorknob, just
in case it had been locked behind the lookout from inside,
and followed with a snap-kick at the threshold, charging
through with Sharma on his heels.

They caught the lab crew by surprise, one shooter to
their left, four baggers working at a table in what once had
been a living room. The five gaped at them in surprise,
and then the baggers bolted for the nearest exit, while the
shooter stood his ground and made his play.

It was a plain case of too little and too late, as Bolan
shot him in the chest and dropped him thrashing onto
cheap linoleum, his pistol still inside its holster, and an
AK-47 propped against a nearby wall forever out of reach.
Sharma took down a couple of the runners, short bursts
from behind that left them facedown on the floor, and
Bolan dropped the other two as they got hung up in the
doorway to another room, jammed in the space like players in a slapstick comedy.

They cleared the other rooms, found more smack waiting to be bagged and shipped, along with all the other
chemicals required for a refinery: acetic anhydride, chlo-
roform, ethyl alcohol, ether, acetone, slaked lime, sodium
carbonate, ammonium chloride, and activated charcoal.
The acetone, ether and alcohol were highly flammable,
which made the last part of their job much easier.

When they had doused the processed heroin and stocks
of morphine base, along with walls and window drapes,
both men retreated to the open door through which they'd
entered. Bolan held a sofa cushion drenched in ether, lit it
with a match and skimmed it back into the one-time din-
ing room. It landed on the table heaped with plastic bags
and poison, caught the fumes there, and the workstation
erupted into brilliant, roaring flames.

Bolan waited a moment longer on the threshold, watched

as trails of fire raced across the floor to other destinations, spurting up the walls and finding more fuel in adjacent rooms. The house was old and soon would be consumed, together with the corpses and the misery it held.

One target down.

They jogged back to the car, climbed in and rolled toward number two.

Chaklala Air Force Base, Rawalpindi, Pakistan

MAJOR IBRAHIM LEGHARI scowled at the Dassault Falcon 20 sitting on the runway before him, its twin General Electric CF-700 turbofan engines already whining, devouring fuel. He did not feel like flying anywhere this morning, much less to Karachi for a meeting with Riyaz Geelani, but as usual, it seemed he had no choice.

Once they had lifted off, the flight to Karachi's Faisal Air Force Base should take about an hour and a half. They would not stop en route, since the Dassault could fly more than two thousand miles without refueling. Leghari would be comfortable, as far as that went, the only passenger aboard a jet with seating for eight, but this was not a pleasure trip, and flying in the lap of luxury—at least, by Pakistani air force standards—did not compensate for what awaited him upon arrival in Karachi.

First, the drive out to Geelani's compound, then the meeting with his thug—a useful one, no doubt, but still a lowly felon in Leghari's eyes—which would inevitably lead to more demands for help with the ongoing troubles in Mumbai. Troubles, Leghari thought, which had nothing to do with him, but which could easily ensnare him if he was not cautious in his answers to Geelani. He had to empathize, perhaps suggest solutions if they came to him, but promise nothing that committed him, much less his agency, to join the fight.

Leghari boarded on the left side of the aircraft, forward of the wind and just behind the cockpit. Neither member of the two-man crew appeared to notice him, likely because they'd been informed that every detail of the flight was classified. A third crew member, not required by any means to operate the jet, greeted him formally with a salute and offered him his choice of seats. Leghari picked one on the right and halfway back, agreed that he would like a cup of black coffee when they were airborne, then turned toward his small round window as he put the flight attendant out of mind.

There was no need for courtesy when dealing with subordinates.

Leghari wore civilian clothes for this unpleasant, unofficial errand, and he had no luggage with him, as he did not plan to spend the night camped out with G-troop criminals. He *was* armed, as a matter of routine, with a Steyr M9-A1 semiautomatic pistol that was standard-issue for his service, chambered in 9 mm Parabellum with 17-round magazine, and a built-in trigger safety modeled on the mechanism pioneered by Glock.

His backup weapon, for an ultimate emergency, was a straight razor with an ebony handle and a blade forged from Damascus steel, which could serve double duty for shaving at need. He had used the razor twice, in situations likely never contemplated by its manufacturer, and it had served him well both times. One adversary was deceased, the other blind and permanently scarred as a reminder of his folly in attempting to surprise Leghari.

Precautions.

They should not be necessary with Riyaz Geelani, but the man did have a wild streak. Some might even say—*had* said—that he was certifiably insane. The perfect terrorist and gang leader, perhaps, but no one that Leghari would permit to jeopardize his life or rank in the Directorate for Inter-Services Intelligence.

His bottom line, as the Americans would say: all contract agents working for the agency had to be regarded as deniable and, finally, expendable. They danced upon command, but did not call the tune. Leghari would be pleased to help Geelani, within reason, and with no thought that he was empowered to commit his own troops or resources to an internecine war.

The aircraft lifted off, and he had steaming coffee on the fold-down tray in front of him five minutes later, nodding his thanks to the attendant and dismissing him at the same time. As he settled back to sip the rich, dark brew and pass the time, Major Leghari hoped that he had not embarked upon a fool's errand. If he decided it was time to let Geelani go his own way, sever his connections to the agency, it had to be handled deftly.

A sane man would accept dismissal. But a lunatic with homicidal tendencies?

In that case, Leghari thought, he should have a standby candidate in line to fill Geelani's empty post, when the Mumbai godfather was removed.

With extreme prejudice.

CHAPTER NINE

Baldia Town, Karachi

A major aspect of the covert Pakistani war on India involved counterfeit currency. At any given moment, India's National Investigation Agency calculated that some 160 billion in counterfeit rupees—nearly three billion U.S. dollars—were in circulation throughout India, Nepal, Bangladesh and Afghanistan. The majority of those bogus bills were printed in Pakistan, either by the DISI directly, or by criminal syndicates working in alliance with the Pakistani government. Counterfeit bills were so common that they had been tagged with the shorthand designation FICN—for fake Indian currency note. Despite an increasing trend toward prosecuting counterfeiters as terrorists under India's Unlawful Activities Prevention Act, the volume of FICN in circulation increased with each passing year.

Bolan intended to put a small dent in that traffic this day.

G-troop's largest printing plant filled a house in the Ghous Nagar district of Baldia Town, a suburb on the west side of Karachi with one million residents. To reach it, Bolan drove four blocks west of the Mohajir Camp Muslim graveyard, spied the blue door Sharma had predicted and made a half circuit of the block to check the rear approach.

There was a guard out front and another at the back, lounging with minimal attempts to hide the fact that they were armed. Pistols or compact submachine guns, Bolan thought, judging from the bulges visible beneath their baggy shirts. Whether they were skilled at using them was anybody's guess. He had to figure G-troop wasn't hiring any virgins, but a lookout's job might well be handed to a rookie while the veterans took care of other, more demanding jobs.

"I don't believe they've heard about the drug plant yet," Sharma said.

"If they have," Bolan replied, "it didn't spook them. Ready?"

"Ready."

They were parked in seconds flat, then went EVA, with no efforts whatsoever to conceal the weapons *they* were carrying. The back-door guard leaped to his feet and drew some kind of chunky little automatic weapon clearly modeled on—if not, in fact—a MAC-10 SMG. He hadn't cocked it in advance, though, and his grappling with the bolt delayed the shooter long enough for Bolan's single silenced round to punch his left eye through his brain and out the back of his skull.

Dead before his dropping weight collapsed the chair he'd occupied a moment earlier, the guard still managed to obstruct them as he fell across the doorstep. Bolan had a choice of dragging him aside or just pretending that he wasn't there. He picked the latter, blew the back door's lock apart at point-blank range and stepped across his fallen adversary as the door swung open to admit him.

Computers and photocopy technology had revolutionized counterfeiting in recent decades. It wasn't done on rolling presses any longer, with the rumbling noises guaranteed to wake your neighbors from the soundest sleep. Hundreds of bills per hour could be spit out in the proper size and colors—all, in this case, with a smiling portrait of Mahatma Gandhi on their face—without resorting to the hand-tooled printing plates of yesteryear.

A whole new world of fraud.

Bolan and Sharma caught a second lazy lookout rising as they entered, and another silenced round from Bolan's pistol dropped him in his tracks. The useless watchman managed to cry out, though, and a voice responded from a back room, with a question Bolan couldn't translate.

Sharma answered back, incomprehensibly, then whispered at Bolan, "Hurry!"

Bolan led the charge along a narrow hallway toward the rear, where walls between a pair of smallish bedrooms had been cleared for space to organize the printing plant. Three startled men with matching oily hair and thick mustaches, nearly triplets, stood around a copier that stood chest-high to Bolan and was roughly five feet long, disgorging sheets of uncut hundred-rupee notes into a stack of five trays on its left side, all five nearly full.

Seeing the guns, their targets bolted, but they didn't have a prayer. Bolan took one down with his pistol, while short bursts from Sharma's Mini-Uzi dropped the other two. The copier kept working through it all, spitting its funny money into tidy stacks, until a double-tap from Bolan's semiautomatic silenced it for good.

They took time, then, to look around the printing room. Against each wall, the product of the counterfeiters' labors sat in cardboard cartons, trimmed and banded, delicately oiled to give the notes that proper "greasy" feel, shrink-wrapped for transport to whichever destination was expected to inflict the most damage on India's economy. In monetary terms, they were inside a lab where lethal toxins were produced, then set adrift to poison each transaction that they touched, from global trade to shopping at a local marketplace.

The place was old and rickety. It only took brief application of a flame to set the curtains burning, which in turn lit up the walls. They waited until the flames were rolling, spreading on their own, then backtracked to the door where they had entered, passing through and out to reach their car.

"You've cost Geelani millions here today," Sharma said as they pulled away.

"Consider it a small down payment on his tab," the Executioner replied.

Faisal Air Force Base, Karachi

MAJOR IBRAHIM LEGHARI'S flight landed on time and taxied down the main runway of Faisal Air Force Base, stopping near the point where two Land Rover Defenders stood waiting, surrounded by armed men in camouflage fatigues. Leghari stepped from air-conditioned comfort into glaring sun that made him wince despite the dark glasses he wore, heat baking through his clothing to his skin.

Faisal AFB housed the Pakistani air force's Southern Air Command and its Air War College, where midcareer officers received their tactical training.

One member of the welcome party stepped forward to greet Leghari with a crisp salute. Captain Ghulam Malik was in his early forties, getting soft around the middle, with the first suggestion of a double chin. His bristling eyebrows matched his mustache and might have given his face a humorous, almost cartoonish cast, if he were not entirely devoid of humor himself.

"Do you have luggage, sir?" Malik asked.

"I won't be staying overnight," Leghari said. "Let's go."

The aircraft would be waiting for him, prepared for the return flight to Islamabad. Leghari did not want his visit with Riyaz Geelani dragged out any longer than was absolutely necessary for conclusion of their business. As he climbed into the backseat of the nearest Land Rover, the major's mind returned to plotting out a script for his discussions with Geelani, hoping he could keep the talk on track.

Geelani would, of course, rant on about his troubles in Mumbai, but Leghari was more concerned about keeping up business as usual. He knew the monthly drug shipment to India was almost ready to depart, tons of hashish and heroin to keep the Narcotics Control Bureau hopping, while India's heroin addicts—conservatively estimated at seven hundred thousand, with an estimated seventy-five million Indians addicted to drugs of all kinds—continued their annual drain on the nation's economy, fomented crime and generally undermined the culture Leghari despised.

His agency protected those shipments as far as the border, and would continue doing so if Geelani could get a grip on his personal problems, bringing his home base back under control. If not…

The other item on Leghari's personal agenda was acceleration of the DISI's covert terrorist campaign against India. The agency preferred to work through local elements and thus preserve deniability. Geelani was his front man in Mumbai, as others served in Jammu and Kashmir, in Bihar, Punjab, New Delhi and Uttar Pradesh. Leghari kept his hands clean, more or less, providing money and matériel, without involving his own agents in the bombings and other attacks. So far the system had worked well, despite broad accusations from the enemy, unsupported by proof.

But if Geelani was cracking…

Counting Malik and two drivers, Leghari's party included ten armed men. He guessed Geelani would have more than that on hand, but fighting was not on Leghari's

primary agenda. He preferred negotiation and agreement—
meaning that he got his way—but Malik had been advised
to prep the team for action, just in case. Eight carried
AK-103 assault rifles chambered in 7.62 mm, the folding-
stock model with 30-round magazines made of phenolic
resin. Some also carried Russian-made F1 fragmentation
grenades. Captain Malik wore a Steyr M9-A1 pistol matching Leghari's, and in the Land Rover carried a futuristic-
looking FN P90 submachine gun feeding fifty rounds of
5.7 mm ammunition from a detachable box magazine.

It should be adequate for self-defense during their drive
out from the city to Geelani's compound, but if they were
forced to move against their host, Leghari knew they had
to strike quickly and decisively upon the signal he had
arranged.

A last resort, of course, but no soldier had ever died
from planning too far in advance.

Saddar Town, Karachi

SADDAR TOWN WAS the heart of old Karachi, originally com-
prising the neighborhoods of Kharadar ("Salty Gate") and
Mithadar ("Sweet Gate"), facing the Arabian Sea and the
Lyari River, respectively. Most of the district's inhabitants
were members of the Gujarati ethnic group, which included
Mahatma Gandhi, but the Great Soul would have scowled
on Bolan's second target in the city.

Pakistan was rated as a source, transit and destination
country for human trafficking, with thousands of men,
women and children dragooned into forced labor and prostitution. While no firm figures were available, authorities
estimated more than one million victims were bought, sold,
rented or kidnapped each year into service as slaves. Illegal
labor agents pocketed large fees from parents, promising

lucrative work for their children, then sold their young victims into sexual slavery or leased them out as domestic servants, farm workers, brick-makers—even camel jockeys in Middle Eastern countries.

One such operation, run by G-troop, was Lakshmi Limited—a name that Bolan found ironic, since Lakshmi was the Hindu goddess of good luck, wealth and prosperity. Good luck was nonexistent for the outfit's human chattel, while the wealth was funneled to Riyaz Geelani and his staff of overseers, who kept bodies moving through the cruel machine. Located near the wedge of territory designated railroad ground on Bolan's map and aerial photos, west of Karachi's General Post Office, Lakshmi Limited operated from a refurbished warehouse on a railroad spur line that facilitated delivery and removal of living cargo.

Bolan parked the Suzuki Liana west of their target, behind another warehouse that appeared to be abandoned. Hitting Lakshmi Limited was different from taking down a drug lab or the counterfeiting plant, since most of those inside the building would be innocents, perhaps children. Some might be drugged or injured. Bolan's goal was to eliminate the G-troop goons assigned to watch the captives, then alert local authorities before he cleared the scene.

And what if said authorities were allies of Riyaz Geelani?

He would think about that problem if it came to pass.

"Precision work on this one," he reminded Sharma, as they hiked from the car to reach the firm that dealt in human misery.

"No automatic fire," Sharma confirmed, switching the fire-selector on his Mini-Uzi into semiautomatic mode. With its folding stock extended and suppressor mounted on the muzzle, the Israeli stutter-gun made an impressive little carbine, accurate—at least in theory—well beyond one hundred yards.

No guards or CCTV cameras were visible as they approached the warehouse, leaving Bolan to decide between attacking from the front or rear. He chose the back door, with its loading dock adjacent to the spur line, in a bid to minimize exposure from the street. Sharma stood watch while Bolan checked the door, confirmed that it was locked, then punched the dead bolt with a point-blank 5.56 mm NATO round. A solid kick and they were in, rushing along a narrow concrete corridor into warehouse proper.

First up on their right, a glassed-in office cubicle where one man sat behind a cluttered army-surplus desk and two more stood before it, startled out of contemplating ledgers lying open on the desktop. Bolan met them with his rifle shouldered, shot the nearest of them in the face and dropped him in a cloud of scarlet mist before the others could react. The seated man, a chubby specimen, was yanking at a desk drawer on his right when Bolan's second round exploded through his throat and sent him spinning from his chair, doing a one-man wave before he hit the floor facedown.

The third guy made it to his gun but never got a chance to use it. Sharma slammed a Parabellum double-tap into his chest and knocked the life out of him where he stood, legs buckling under him, collapsing in a heap that twitched the final throbbing pulses of his life away.

By that time, Bolan had moved on in search of other targets, and was suddenly among long rows of cages that resembled kennels: bars on four sides, concrete underfoot, a plastic pail in each cage for the huddled inmates' hygenic use. The eyes tracking Bolan ranged from panicky to dull and nearly lifeless, some bloodshot, others with their pupils dilated by drugs. None of the captives made a sound as Bolan passed their cages, all of them apparently conditioned by harsh treatment to maintain a regimen of silence.

Bolan moved with silent strides, his ears straining for the sounds of bustling movement that would mark his adversaries, presently invisible. The *click-clack* of a weapon cocking warned him just before a shadow loomed up in a narrow passage to his left and automatic fire ripped overhead.

Kranti Nagar, Mumbai

MAJOR ARUTLA YUGANDHAR had lost whatever minimal surveillance skills he'd learned in training as an agent of the CBI. Not that he was assigned to a surveillance job that afternoon, but he took no precautions to avoid a tail when he left headquarters, oblivious to the idea that anyone might wish to follow him.

This day, that was a critical mistake.

Captain Vivak Patel, by contrast, took pride in his skill at trailing suspects and observing actions that were never meant to be recorded for posterity. Before promotion to his present rank, he'd been renowned for undercover work that got convictions—when corruption in the courts allowed it—and that earned him deadly enemies. So far, he had survived seven attempts to kill him, while the would-be assassins had not.

This day, he planned to turn the tables.

Major Yugandhar had not requested that a driver take him home from headquarters that afternoon, Patel's first clue that he planned something worth investigating. Patel had given Yugandhar a lead, then followed in his own civilian vehicle through winding, crowded streets until they reached Kanti Nagar, in Mumbai's northern quadrant. The major's destination was a building that appeared to be a rooming house, between a restaurant and a dental clinic.

Boardinghouse?

Not quite.

Patel sat watching from his car as Yugandhar approached the door and pressed a buzzer, waited, then was greeted by a lovely woman in her twenties, hair upswept, wearing a jet-black sari with a purple snake embroidered on it wound around her body. He saw the woman kiss Yugandhar on both cheeks and welcome him inside. Before the door closed, Patel glimpsed two other women in the background, standing side by side and dressed in little more than scraps of lace.

A brothel then.

The major risked his job—and theoretically, his freedom—for commercial sex in a prohibited establishment. The brothel, standing as it did within two hundred yards of several public places, made its clients up to three-month prison terms based on geography alone. If any of the females working in the place were seventeen or younger, Yugandhar could be jailed for seven to ten years.

Patel considered that a decent bit of leverage.

His cell phone had a camera, and he'd already snapped the major entering the brothel, being greeted by its hostess. Although not prepared to go inside and see what Yugandhar was doing, he would wait and take more time-stamped photos when his quarry next emerged. The evidence might be dismissed as circumstantial, but unless Yugandhar called in officers to raid the place, a reasonable inference would peg him as a customer.

It was enough to spark a scandal, even if Yugandhar managed to survive it with his rank intact. Patel could not be certain it would crack the major, but he also had a pistol and the will to use it, after what had nearly happened to him in Dharavi.

He would have the truth today, no matter what it took.

An hour and a quarter passed before the major showed his face again. Patel snapped off his shots, emailed them to himself in nothing flat, and had his engine running by the time Yugandhar climbed into his car. He trailed the major's car westward, along Andheri Kurla Road and into Mota Nagar, yet another suburb. There, Yugandhar pulled into the parking lot of an apartment building, heedless to the final moment that he had been followed home.

Patel already knew Yugandhar's address, down to the apartment number on the fifth floor of the building. He had "cased" it, in the language of American police, and knew there was no doorman to prevent his entry from the street. He sat and waited, letting Yugandhar arrive upstairs, relax a little, possibly begin undressing. After ten minutes had passed, Patel went in and rode the elevator up to the fifth floor, easing his pistol from its holster as the car reached its destination.

It was a short walk down the hall to reach apartment 513. A cheap, square doorbell had been mounted in the middle of the door, below a peephole with a fish-eye lens. He pressed the button, heard the *ding-dong* of its chimes inside and put his best face on for scrutiny. A shadow blocked the peephole seconds later, followed by another hesitation as the major recognized his unexpected visitor.

At last, the door eased open, Major Yugandhar in shirtsleeves, glowering unhappily. "What are you doing here, Patel?" he asked.

The captain showed him the pistol as he pushed his way inside and said, "We need to talk."

Saddar Town, Karachi

SHARMA FLINCHED AT the staccato sound of automatic fire and moved in that direction, trailing Cooper and hoping

he would find the tall American alive. He could not bring
himself to meet the eyes of people caged on either side of
him as he proceeded, nearly hopping sideways as a small
girl reached out to him through the bars that held her captive, whimpering an incoherent plea for help.

He could do nothing for them yet, until he'd helped
Cooper to eradicate the other warehouse guards. And if
he found his comrade dead or dying, he would have to
carry on alone.

Sharma had come too far to turn back now.

Ahead of him, more gunfire, and he saw the muzzle-
flashes now, a submachine gun firing full-auto, while Cooper replied with single shots. The second of them found
its mark, and the machine-gunner collapsed, still firing
as he fell, his bullets ripping into long fluorescent fix-
tures overhead, sprinkling the floor and cages with a rain
of shattered glass.

Sharma called out to Cooper as he advanced, not wishing to be taken for a G-troop sniper creeping into range.
The big American answered with a nod and moved on,
hunting through the human zoo for other keepers who
might spring from hiding to attack. When no more sur-
faced after two long minutes, he returned, stone-faced,
moving past prisoners who plainly didn't know if they were
being liberated or if they were on the verge of being shot.

For some, Sharma supposed, death might have come
as a relief.

"How many do you figure?" Bolan inquired, clearly
referring to the prisoners.

Sharma had not been counting, but he made a hasty
estimate. Eight rows of cages, back to back, ran down the
full length of the warehouse. Counting off one row, he
multiplied, then said, "Five hundred cages."

Some of them unoccupied, perhaps; he couldn't say. In

several, he had glimpsed multiple children, three or four together behind bars.

"Even if we had the keys," Bolan said, "we can't take time to let them out. You'd better make the calls."

Four calls, as they'd agreed: one to the Federal Investigation Agency, one to the Sindh Provincial Police, and one to the nearest Karachi police station. All would send investigators, and amid the squabbling over jurisdiction, having all three agencies involved would guarantee that none of them deliberately dropped the ball. Sharma's fourth call, to Karachi's AAJ News television channel, would focus public scrutiny on everything that happened to the prisoners henceforth—and hopefully stir up enough heat to get prosecutors moving on the case.

If there was anyone to prosecute....

With each call, Sharma rattled off the warehouse's address, announced that human traffickers had been discovered and eliminated, while their prisoners required immediate assistance. He allowed no questions, gave no further explanation, and was finished by the time he reached the exit, trailing Cooper. It went against the grain for him to leave so many humans trapped and at the mercy of whoever entered next, but Cooper was right. The two of them could do no more unless they meant to stay and face arrest.

Unthinkable.

He had considered what might happen if the Pakistanis captured them. Cooper, an American, would certainly be treated as a spy and/or a terrorist. Whether the state placed him on trial or tried to ransom him, demanding favors from his homeland, there was some chance that he might survive.

Sharma, an Indian and Hindu, cherished no such hope. He would be executed as a lesson to his countrymen, most likely after torture that would leave him praying for a bullet to release him from his torment. Certainly, his agency would not negotiate or even publicly acknowledge his affiliation with the CBI. In custody, he was as good as dead.

Better to go down fighting, Sharma thought, and he was not concerned about Cooper's private rule concerning the police. Whatever guidelines the American imposed upon himself, Sharma would not surrender meekly to arrest.

And when he fell, he would not go alone.

"I hate to leave them," he told Cooper.

"We'll wait and watch as planned until we see them coming out."

Risky enough, at that. "And then?"

"I feel," Bolan said, "like visiting a poppy farm."

CHAPTER TEN

Mota Nagar, Mumbai

"Captain, you are making a disastrous mistake."

"Perhaps," Patel replied. "But I cannot undo it now. We shall proceed."

Major Arutla Yugandhar sat duct-taped to a kitchen chair, eyeing Patel with a mixture of fear and contempt. Clearly, he wasn't sure which attitude he should project in an attempt to end their confrontation peacefully.

Patel, for his part, thought it was too late.

"We can forget about this, if you let me go immediately," Yugandhar suggested. "Call it stress, related to your heavy caseload, eh?"

"Why call it anything, if we are going to forget it happened?" Patel challenged him.

"I meant to say—"

"Enough!" Patel lifted the pistol from his lap and aimed it at Yugandhar's face. "Three pigs from G-troop tried to kill me, earlier today."

"They obviously failed," Yugandhar said. "What happened to them?"

"Did you hear about the shooting in Dharavi, Major?"

"*You* did that? Why didn't you report it?"

"I have reason to believe someone within the agency arranged it," Patel stated.

"Within *our* agency?"

"What else are we discussing?"

"But—"

"You call me in for questioning about a missing officer, whose name and rank you do not know. Then, out of nowhere, I find G-troop killers stalking me when I've been sent into the field. By you."

Yugandhar blinked at that. Patel could almost see the wheels turning inside his head, straining for a coherent explanation. What he came up with was bluster.

"Think of what you're saying, Captain. Why would I have someone try to kill you?"

"Out of fear, perhaps. The fear that my investigator might discover your connection to Riyaz Geelani and his crimes."

"Ridiculous! There is no—"

"Stop!" Patel commanded. "I have no more time for lies. Before you speak, remember that my officer has been *inside* G-troop for thirteen months. His life means more to me than yours."

Patel was bluffing—with regard to Sharma, anyway. As to Yugandhar's fate, he realized that life had changed irrevocably for him when he'd barged into the major's flat with gun in hand. No matter what he said or did now, his career—his life itself—was finished if Yugandhar lived.

But could he pull the trigger in cold blood?

Yugandhar heaved a deep, dramatic sigh. "Vivak, you can't believe that I—"

The pistol rose again, rock-steady at eye level. "Would you die with a lie on your tongue?" Patel asked.

The major hesitated, then said, "If I speak, you'll let me go, unharmed?"

"You have my word." Patel surprised himself. The lie felt effortless.

"All right. What is it that you wish to know?"

"How long have you been working with Geelani?"

"Him, particularly? Five or six years."

"And before him?"

"Others. They're all gone," Yugandhar replied.

"With your assistance?"

"In some cases." Smiling now, Yugandhar added, "I always recognize a winner."

"How much does he pay you?"

"It depends. Each month, for the base rate, five thousand U.S. dollars. Special services have special prices."

"And finding my officer? Sending the thugs after me?"

Yugandhar shrugged, the move made awkward by his duct-tape cocoon. "A matter of self-preservation," he said.

"So, for free?"

The major nodded, worried-looking. He seemed to realize that he had made a critical mistake. "But you must understand—"

"Are any special operations presently in progress?"

"Only one."

"Which is…?" Patel prodded.

"A drug shipment. Well, *convoy* is more accurate. From Pakistan."

"Arriving how and when?"

Yugandhar told him, spelling out the details. Patel wasn't sure what he could do about it on his own, unless…

"One last thing," he said. "Who else at headquarters is working for Geelani?"

"What? You think I know them all?"

"The ones you *do* know then. Quickly!"

Yugandhar spoke two names. One was a captain whom Patel had thought to be his friend. The other was a special deputy director supervising operations in Mumbai. The weight that settled on Patel's shoulders made him feel small and helpless.

Yugandhar seemed startled when he rose and went into the living room. "Where are you going?"

"Just a moment." Patel came back with a decorative pillow from the sofa in his left hand, pistol in his right.

"What's that for?" Yugandhar demanded.

"Silence," Patel said, pressing the pillow against the major's chest, pinned with the muzzle of his gun.

"You promised me!"

"I lied."

The shots were muffled adequately, and Yugandhar had no time to scream. Patel carried the smoking pillow to the kitchen sink, and soaked it until he could squeeze it with his hands and feel no trace of heat. He left Yugandhar in his chair, chin on his bloody chest, without a thought for how long he might sit there, undiscovered.

Patel had touched nothing with his bare hands in the major's flat, except the sodden pillow that would hold no fingerprints. He'd kicked the door closed when they entered, and he used a handkerchief to turn the knob as he was leaving, unobserved. Before he reached the street, his car, he was already wondering how he could use the information that he'd got from Yugandhar.

And instantly, he knew.

Sharma.

Orangi Town, Karachi

THE ARMS DEALER'S shop was a small, shabby place with tarnished jewelry in the window. Baji Sharma knew the address from his research into G-troop's dealings with the Pakistani government, a target he could never reach because it lay outside his lawful jurisdiction while providing weapons and explosives used on raids around Mumbai. This day, the dwarfish owner greeted them with a suspicious mien, then welcomed them like long-lost friends when Bolan flashed his wad of rupees and explained, through Sharma, that cost was no object.

He had what they needed, the little man said. For a price.

Bolan had known they couldn't raid a poppy farm with nothing but the small arms he had acquired in Mumbai. There would be buildings and stockpiles of opium paste to destroy, with an uncertain acreage of plants in the field. He couldn't hope to blitz the place entirely—that would have required an air strike with defoliants or napalm—but they *could* inflict sufficient damage to retard the operation and to make Riyaz Geelani feel the heat.

First on his shopping list, an M9A1-7 flamethrower. American made, the weapon had evolved from models used by Marines in the Pacific Theater of World War II: the M1, M1A1, and M2. Each in turn had been lighter in weight, with increased striking range. Safety features had improved on the M2A1-2 and M2A1-7, used in the Korean War, before the M9A1-7 made its fiery debut in Vietnam. Although considered obsolete, like any other weapon that was well maintained, the M9A1-7 still did its job.

It weighed sixty-eight pounds, with two full tanks of jellied gasoline and one of nitrogen, employed as the propellant. With a maximum range of 132 feet, the M9A1-7 released a half-gallon of fuel per second, emptying its tanks in eight seconds of sustained fire, unless the operator milked it for short bursts. Changing tanks under fire was too cumbersome for Bolan, but he reckoned he could make his point with the initial load—and with the backup weapon he'd selected.

The Milkor MGL—for multiple grenade launcher—was a South African weapon, chambered in 40 mm and built on the revolver principle. It resembled an old-fashioned

Tommy gun on steroids, but its revolving aluminum cylinder held only six rounds, permitting the shooter to mix and match high-explosive, incendiary, smoke, gas or canister rounds. Bolan chose an assortment, omitting the gas shells used for crowd control in riots, and the smoke rounds utilized for marking troop positions on a battlefield. The rest, he thought, would come in handy for their next raid and whatever lay beyond it.

The vendor's asking price was steep—330,000 rupees, or about six grand U.S.—but Bolan didn't mind. In fact, he didn't plan on paying anything. The little gnome had been supplying terrorists for years on end, and he was out of time. The shocked expression on his face, as Sharma pressed a pistol to his head, revealed belated understanding that he'd picked the wrong side, after all.

The basement arsenal was something else. Its concrete ceiling, walls and floor were thick enough that bullets shouldn't penetrate. The Semtex stored in one corner would burn without exploding, since its blasting caps were kept entirely separate and well away from the plastique. Even a fire should be contained, once Bolan closed the metal door between the basement and the shop upstairs.

Convinced that taking out the arsenal would not incinerate a city block, Bolan let Sharma go ahead of him, lugging the flamethrower and a Kalashnikov assault rifle he'd picked up for himself. Once those were stashed in the Liana's trunk, Bolan followed Sharma with the Milkor and its ammunition, then went back inside. From hand grenades in stock, he chose two thermite cannisters, removed their pins and tossed the bombs toward the middle of the room. The door was shut and latched behind him by the time they detonated, spewing white heat that would leave no weapon functional, no round of ammo unexpended.

Call the stop a win-win situation.

And the Executioner was on his way.

Sindh Province, Pakistan

"APPROACHING NOW, SIR," Ibrahim Leghari's driver called out to his backseat passenger.

The major offered no acknowledgment, but shifted in his seat between the riflemen who flanked him. Things were always tense when he was forced to meet Riyaz Geelani, even though the pair of them wore smiles and feigned something that might resemble friendship to a stranger's eyes. In fact, both understood that their relationship was based on mutual convenience and nothing more, linked through the nexus of their mutual hatred for Hindus.

Leghari's prejudice ran in his blood. His parents were among those who had been uprooted from their homes and driven out of India in 1947, when the newly independent nation was divided on religious grounds, birthing the Muslim state of Pakistan. He had been raised on secondhand accounts of massacres and mayhem in the streets, women and children slaughtered, shops and homes destroyed in pograms spawned by sectarian spite. The venom he'd ingested from his parents and grandparents had propelled Leghari into military service, hoping for the opportunity to liberate disputed border areas or, at the very least, to kill some of the Hindus he despised. From there, the move into political subversion was a natural progression that he'd never questioned, never second-guessed.

Leghari did not know Riyaz Geelani's story, nor could he pretend that it held any interest for him. Geelani was a criminal who served a sacred cause by chance, either from greed alone, or based on motives best known to himself. He was an instrument Leghari and the DISI used to do their dirty work, while publicly denying any link to terrorism inside India. They were required to meet from time to time, of course—and Pakistani agents, by extension, had become accomplices in G-troop's crimes—but that would never make them friends.

Leghari saw armed guards manning the compound's gate, tracking the two Land Rovers as they slowed on their approach. It was the same thing every time, moments of silent scrutiny before the gate was rolled aside and they passed through to meet the Mumbai mobster at his home away from home. More riflemen kept pace with the two vehicles, jogging, once they had passed the gate, trailing them all the way to the squat, cream-colored bungalow.

Riyaz Geelani waited for them there, outside the modest house, flanked by a pair of bodyguards. Major Leghari noted that he was not smiling, and in fact, seemed to have trouble standing still. Geelani wasn't pacing the threshold, exactly, but he shifted nervously from one foot to the other, clearly restless and on edge.

Leghari's car stopped, and he waited for the agent on his left to step out first, then hold the door for him. He exited, subtly brushed wrinkles from his suit and walked around the vehicle to shake Geelani's hand. The handshake was perfunctory, Geelani's palm clammy with sweat. Leghari fought an urge to pat his own hand on his trouser leg.

"You had a good trip from Islamabad?" Geelani asked.

"No difficulties."

"You are fortunate. I find myself harassed by adversaries, even here."

Leghari looked around the sprawling compound and saw nothing out of place. "Here?"

"Here, in Pakistan," Geelani clarified. "It seems my men are being murdered in Karachi, even as we speak."

"Karachi?" Now Leghari had begun to feel like someone's parrot, simply echoing what he was told. To break the trend, he turned to a lieutenant at his side and ordered, "Call Karachi. See what's happening."

"Yes, sir!"

While the young man scurried off to make his call via the Rover's two-way radio, Leghari faced his host once more. "Explain," he said.

Geelani rattled off the bare details of two attacks, against a counterfeiting plant supported by the Pakistani government and something that he called "the slave market." Leghari did not ask for details on the latter target, thought it better not to know too much. His agents in Karachi could supply whatever details he required, if they were necessary. What mattered, at the moment, was delivering his consolations to Geelani—and discovering who dared to bring a private battle from Mumbai to Pakistani soil.

"It seems your enemies have followed you," Leghari said when Geelani ran out of breath.

"Perhaps." The gangster sounded skeptical.

"Perhaps? They raid you in Mumbai. You cross the border, and the raids start here. How can you doubt it?"

"What I know," Geelani said, "is that I seek protection from a trusted ally, and you can't provide it. How do you propose to make this right?"

Leghari forced a smile. He saw a long and bitter night ahead of him, beginning now.

N-5 National Highway, Pakistan

THE SIX-LANE BLACKTOP highway, laid in 1952, linked Karachi to Hyderabad, Multan, Lahore and points eastward. Bolan wasn't traveling that far that afternoon, only a few klicks from Karachi's eastern suburbs in fact. He was headed for a poppy farm that operated without interference from the government, despite a ban on smoking opium that dated back to 1953, and strict bans on drug trafficking that included capital punishment for smugglers caught with ten kilos or more. Protection by corrupt authorities explained the contradiction, but G-troop could not negotiate a payoff with the Executioner.

Satellite photographs had shown him where to find the nearest access road that would accommodate his rental car. Bolan turned off the pavement when he reached it, drove a quarter of a mile due north until he couldn't see the highway anymore, then parked and started suiting up for battle.

Bolan took the heavy weapons, first draping a bandolier of 40 mm rounds across his chest, then slipping into the flamethrower's harness, clipping its wand to his belt with a plastic twist tie for the moment. With that set, he picked up the Milkor MGL—another twelve pounds, his load approaching ninety overall—while Sharma took his new Kalashnikov, pockets loaded with extra magazines.

They hiked in from the west, proceeding through a field of poppies on their grayish, bristly stalks with bulbous heads and purple blooms, the pods already slit and leaking pearly beads of latex that would dry into crusty brown opium paste. The photographs they'd studied showed the farm extending over fifty acres, more or less, beyond what Bolan could eradicate with his selected weapons, so they planned to focus on the operation's heart: the drying shed and other buildings where the work of packaging was done before the paste went off to processing. When they had taken out those targets, if they still had time and ammunition left, Bolan would see what he could do about the fields.

There were no sentries in those fields, as far as he could tell. The first lookouts they saw were clustered at the target zone, guarding the inventory, buildings and equipment. Bolan knew that the initial harvesting was done by hand, grunt labor, but the plants were later mowed and harvested for "poppy straw," another source of opium that let each field produce a secondary crop after the seeds had been removed.

More fuel for Bolan's cleansing fire.

At fifty yards, they reached the end of any decent cover, sheltered by the final ranks of poppy plants before they had to cross a stretch of open ground. They were beyond the flamethrower's optimum range, but the Milkor had a more extensive reach—eight times their present distance from the mark, in fact. For Bolan, it was nearly point-blank range.

"Be ready when it starts to pop," he cautioned Sharma. "They won't spot me right away, but two or three rounds ought to do it."

"I'll take care of it," Sharma replied, bringing the AK-47 autorifle to his shoulder.

Bolan sighted on the drying shed, squeezed the Milkor's double-action trigger and lobbed an incendiary round into the open drying shed. Its detonation filled the shed with roiling flames and knocked two of the nearest sentries off their feet, one leaping up with pants on fire, the other scuttling lizardlike on knees and elbows to escape the broiling heat.

Before his adversaries could recover, Bolan fired another of his six rounds—high-explosive, this time—toward a kind of pole barn where the harvesting equipment stood in meager shade. The grenade struck a Chinese combine and detonated on impact, peppering an adjacent tractor and rotary cultivator with shrapnel. Another guard went down, this one for good, blood spouting from his throat in a bright arterial spray.

Sharma was firing them, to keep the other sentries off their mark and send them running for cover. Bolan left

him to it, worked the Milkor, pumping round after searing round into the buildings ranged before him. They'd
been cheaply built and wouldn't cost much to replace, but
with the product and equipment they contained, the price
tag took a flying leap into the stratosphere. Each blast increased Riyaz Geelani's losses, eating up his profit margin.

Smoking out the rats.

Six rounds, and he was empty. Rather than reloading
on the spot, he slung the launcher over his left shoulder,
adding to the weight already on his back, and freed the
flamethrower's wand from his belt. Its trigger and igniter
were located on the foreward pistol grip, while the rear
grip controlled the flow of fuel and had a safety catch
built in. His greatest danger, once he rose, would be a
bullet ripping through the tanks he wore and turning him
into a human torch.

No time to think about that now.

He bolted from the poppy field, advancing toward his
enemies.

BAJI SHARMA FOLLOWED Matthew Cooper out of the poppy
field, remaining to his left and half a dozen paces back as
the big American unleashed a searing gout of napalm from
his flamethrower. Two sentries tried to dodge the swoop-
ing arc of fire, but neither one succeeded. Within seconds,
they were transformed into lurching, screaming scare-
crows limned with flames that ate into their dying flesh.

Sharma was frozen for an instant, rifle at his shoulder,
then a sudden movement on his left brought him around.
Another guard was scuttling in to flank Cooper with a
submachine gun. Sharma drilled the shooter with a 5.56
mm bullet through the chest and dropped him as the dead
man's trigger finger twitched, firing off half a magazine
of wasted bullets toward the sky.

A pall of greasy smoke obscured the battleground, rising from structures Cooper had battered with his six incendiary rounds and now from swaths of fire laid by his flamethrower. The center of the poppy farm was an inferno, terrified survivors sprinting off into the fields, hoping to hide themselves and thus survive the holocaust.

Anticipating them, Cooper turned his hellish weapon on the fields and fired a blazing arc of flame over the purple blooms, reaching more than a hundred feet from where he stood. Five seconds later, and the tanks strapped to his back were empty, but they'd done their work. A wedge-shaped section of the nearest field was burning, and the flames were spreading rapidly, driven by a prevailing breeze, devouring dry stalks and bulbs.

Cooper dropped the M9A1-7's wand and shed its bulky harness, hastily reloading his grenade launcher while Sharma covered him. No vehicles or buildings stood undamaged in their strike zone; no surviving sentries challenged them. When Cooper said, "Time to go," Sharma responded with a nod and followed along the path back toward their waiting car.

Sharma realized, when they had traveled something like a hundred yards, that crackling flames were racing up behind them. The fields were dry, the crop approaching readiness for its conversion into poppy straw, but most of this yield would be going up in smoke.

The breeze was at their backs now, hastening the flames. Sharma smelled smoke and wondered if he was imagining a giddy sense of light euphoria. Could opium be smoked *before* it was processed? He didn't know, and didn't plan to find out if it meant having the flesh seared off his bones.

They ran, and in the distance, over the insistent rustling of the fire, Sharma heard someone screaming in the field behind him. One more of Riyaz Geelani's shooters treated to a taste of Hell on Earth, dying in agony. Unmoved by anything except his own fear of incineration, Sharma pressed himself to match Cooper's pace while poppy stalks whipped at his pumping legs.

The run back to their car seemed longer than the hike in from the access road, no doubt a product of the fear and the fatigue that Sharma felt. Since meeting Cooper, he had not slept—except for briefly, fitfully, during their flight from Mumbai with Bharat Deshpande. And, it struck him now, he had been kept awake for well over a day, before that, during his interrogation by the gunmen who had captured him.

How long could he keep going without sleep?

Until he cleared the field of flames, at least.

Cooper reached the access road, and Sharma stumbled clear a moment later, almost on his heels. They had outrun the fire, but still could feel its heat and smell the smoke it generated as they piled into their car.

Cooper cranked through a U-turn heading back toward the N-5 National Highway. Sharma fought to keep his eyes open, while his companion urged him to rest, conserve his strength for what still lay ahead of them.

Half dozing, Sharma watched smoke rising from the poppy fields and idly thought that it was his career in flames, as well.

Sharma had made a choice, to leave his mark regardless of the cost. But now, with smoke staining the sky and blood soaking the earth, he wondered what the final cost would be.

CHAPTER ELEVEN

Bandhup West, Mumbai

Captain Vivak Patel examined his own features in the rearview mirror of his Tata Nano city car and muttered, "Now I am a murderer."

There'd been no choice, of course. He'd known that Major Yugandhar, if freed, would either give his name to G-troop or report him to superiors within the CBI. In one case, Patel would be murdered; in the other, he'd be placed on trial, convicted and imprisoned—*then* he would be murdered. Silencing the major was his only option, but he wasn't finished, even then.

Patel possessed the details of a convoy moving huge amounts of heroin and cannabis from Pakistan, across the border into India. If Major Yugandhar had known about it, he assumed that others, higher up the ladder of command, had to also know. They had agreed, for pay, to turn a blind eye when the shipment was transported.

What could Patel do to stop it?

Nothing, on his own—but there was someone else who might be able to prevent the shipment coming through.

He'd parked near Guru Nanak College, watching students hurry past on foot, on bicycles. They made Patel wish he was young again, that he had chosen any other course in life besides the one that held him captive now. Too late, but he could dream, for all the good it did him.

He took the cell phone from his pocket, opened it and dialed the number he had programmed into it—and which he would delete for good, after this call.

Two rings. A third. He was about to cut the link, when someone picked up midway through the fourth. *"Namaste."*

"Sergeant?" He was not about to speak the name.

"Captain!"

"Forgive the interruption. I have information that you may find useful."

"Oh?"

Patel explained, omitting Major Yugandhar entirely, spelling out the convoy's route and schedule. Sergeant Sharma, wherever he was, listened with rapt attention, raised no questions until Patel had finished.

"Do you believe the information is reliable?" he asked.

"I'm sure of it," Patel replied. "I have it from a source inside the agency."

"Thank you. If there is nothing else…?"

"Nothing. Be careful, Sergeant."

"And the same to you, Captain."

Patel severed the link, then spent a moment purging Sharma's number from his cell phone's memory, together with the record of their conversations. He had no doubt that technicians could recover the incriminating information through some cybermagic that he did not fully understand, but at that moment, Patel didn't care.

He had decided that the best thing he could do, for now, was go back to his cubicle at CBI headquarters, behave as if nothing untoward had happened and wait to see what followed. Major Yugandhar had given him two names of officers allied with G-troop, though Patel had no idea if either one might be inclined to move against him now. They wouldn't know that *he* knew *them* as enemies, and with Yugandhar taken out of the equation—soon to be reported missing—they might hesitate to make a new aggressive move.

Patel, meanwhile, could make his own defensive preparations, relatively safe as long as he remained at headquarters. And on the street? If someone else came after him from G-troop or the CBI itself, he would defend himself by any means available.

With that in mind, he locked his office door and knelt before one of his two black filing cabinets. Opening its bottom drawer, he bent to work the combination lock securing a fire safe he'd installed for special items that required extra security. Inside, he kept a passport and assorted other documents in an alternative identity, and a Steyr TMP.

The little gun measured 11.1 inches long and weighed 2.9 pounds unloaded. Chambered in 9 mm Parabellum, it fed through detachable box magazines holding fifteen, twenty or thirty rounds, inserted Uzi-style through the main pistol grip. With a cyclic rate of nine hundred rounds per minute, it was deadly at close range and theoretically effective to one hundred meters. Best of all, it fit inside Patel's briefcase with room to spare.

As ready now as he would ever be, Patel logged on to his computer and began to search out information on his enemies within the CBI.

Sindh Province, Pakistan

RIYAZ GEELANI SWITCHED off his satellite phone, resisting an urge to fling it against the nearest wall. Instead, he clutched the instrument so tightly that his fingers ached, closing his eyes and taking a deep breath to calm the loud, insistent throbbing in his ears.

"More bad news?" Ibrahim Leghari asked.

Geelani turned, opened his eyes and faced the major. "It's the only kind I get, these days," he said.

"What now?"

"A poppy farm, not far from here," Geelani replied. "You know the place."

Leghari shrugged, withholding the admission of his own complicity. "What's happened?"

"Two men have destroyed the better part of it, with all the processed opium on hand. They used incendiary weapons on the buildings and the fields."

Leghari frowned. "Just now?"

"It's burning as we speak," Geelani said.

"Now there is no doubt that they are the same ones from Mumbai. They followed you."

Geelani shook his head. "Impossible. Someone has told them where to find me. After all, it's not much of a secret."

Leghari sat back and considered that, no doubt concerned about his own potential for exposure and embarrassment. "There was supposed to be security," he said, after another moment.

"So there was," Geelani agreed, "but ineffective. All but one or two of them are dead. Incinerated."

They were seated in Geelani's bungalow with mugs of coffee. Nothing stronger was permitted to a faithful Muslim under the Koran's explicit terms, although Geelani craved the sweet relief of alcohol. Perhaps hashish would do as well, but he required all of his wits about him while his empire was under attack.

"You said one of the men from Mumbai was American?"

"Or European," Geelani said. "On that point, the men who've seen him and survived to tell the story are confused."

"In any case, his presence here in Pakistan would constitute an act of war," Leghari said.

"Only if sanctioned by some government," Geelani stated. "And you would have to catch him first."

"I'll speak to the Karachi office," Leghari replied, "and coordinate with Sindh Police commanders. If your enemies are in the city, they'll be found."

"You think so?"

"This is not Mumbai," Leghari said.

"Indeed, not."

With a pinched expression on his face, Leghari said, "You might consider going back. Leave the elimination of your enemies to me, since they've unwisely placed themselves within my reach."

"*If* you can reach them. First, however, I have business with a shipment crossing into Gujarat."

"More drugs?" Leghari asked, pretending ignorance.

"What does it matter, if it serves the cause?"

Leghari did not take the bait. Instead, he simply asked, "Have you arranged security?"

"And will be doubling it, in light of recent incidents," Geelani said.

"All right. If there is nothing else…" Leghari did not check his watch, but he was clearly anxious to be gone.

"You're needed in Islamabad, no doubt."

"But in Karachi, first," Leghari said. "I will make sure our office understands the prime importance of locating those responsible for recent crimes against the public peace. They will be found, taken alive if possible and questioned. Otherwise…"

"As long as they're eliminated, I don't care," Geelani said. "I have friends in the CBI trying to learn if one of their detectives is involved."

"I smell a scandal," Leghari stated. "It could be in our best interest if police are implicated."

"And prevented from disrupting any further operations."

"That is why you pay them, eh?"

"Until a rogue appears and tries to ruin everything."

"Rogues," Leghari said, "are best exterminated for the good of all."

"And no time like the present to begin. I'll see you off."

Five minutes later, Geelani stood watching as the two Land Rovers cleared the compound's gate and rumbled back along the roadway toward Karachi. If Leghari found a way to end the raids that had bedeviled him, Geelani would be deeper in the major's debt than ever. It was not a situation that he relished, but he literally could not live with the alternative.

His top priority this day, above all else, had to be the shipment of narcotics bound for India. Geelani had a fortune riding on the convoy—and his reputation, too. Double security should do the trick, and he had warned his soldiers in advance.

In case of failure, no one should return alive.

Allahwalla Town, Karachi

"So, I HAVE to ask you once more, do you trust him?"

Baji Sharma spent about fifteen seconds pondering the question, then replied, "I think so. Yes, I do."

"He's under pressure," Bolan said. "No chance, in your mind, that somebody could be using him to bait a trap?"

"I cannot absolutely rule it out, of course," Sharma agreed. "But I do not believe that is the case."

"Okay, let's check the layout."

They were parked outside a shopping mall of sorts, their

heavy hardware in the rental's trunk, and Bolan's laptop open on the seat between them. On its screen, beamed via satellite, the landscape of their next prospective target lay revealed in detail.

"If your captain's right," Bolan said, "they'll be coming down the Coast Road toward Rehn Goth and crossing here, this bridge over Korangi Creek, and they're in India. Sounds simple, but there must be border guards, some kind of checkpoint."

"At the bridge, of course. I would assume the guards on both sides have been bribed."

"Our best bet," Bolan said, "would be to let them cross, then take them on the road that passes through these mangroves, here. They're clear of the police by then, we'd have good cover, and if someone's counting on us to attack the bridge, they'll think we got cold feet."

Sharma nodded. "The mangroves, then. The Vidhwansak won't be of any use to you at such close range."

"I'll use the Milkor," Bolan told him. "Backed up with the INSAS and your AK. Do it right, and that ought to be enough."

"Four trucks," Sharma said. "Geelani won't send that much heroin and hashish over without guards."

"I'm counting on it," Bolan told him. "It means fewer soldiers when it's time to take him out."

"Within the mangroves," Sharma told him, "we must be aware of dangers other than the convoy's guards. There may be tigers with a taste for human flesh. Not many, but the fishermen still live in fear of them. Also, the kraits and cobras. Crocodiles, of course."

"Sounds like a real safari," Bolan answered. "But I'm only hunting G-troop. If they want to send somebody from the DISI over with the drugs, that's fine."

"Discovery of Pakistani infiltrators could mean war," Sharma advised.

"If anyone acknowledged it. With both sides paid to look the other way, I don't expect a diplomatic incident."

"Too bad," Sharma said. "That might finally provoke some action against G-troop."

"No offense," Bolan told him, "but it sounds like you could use some housecleaning around the CBI before that happens."

"Certainly. And is it not the same in your United States?"

"In spades," Bolan agreed. "I've never seen a city or a country where police weren't linked to underworld activity."

"And yet, you have this rule about attacking them," Sharma observed.

"Sounds odd, I know," Bolan agreed. "But everybody draws a line somewhere. My thinking is that cops—*most* cops—start off wanting to do some good, help people, see that everyone's protected. Over time some of them get worn down. They weaken and begin to wonder what they're fighting for, if nobody around them gives a damn."

"But what of those who are no more than criminals themselves?"

"I've drawn my line. No killing cops."

"And what of soldiers? Spies?"

"Fair game, if they're in service to a criminal regime or syndicate."

Sharma was smiling now. "You are a very strange American."

"I've been called worse," said Bolan, glancing at his watch. "Don't want to keep Deshpande waiting for that border hop."

Directorate for Inter-Services Intelligence Headquarters, Karachi

"I UNDERSTAND," SAID Captain Ghulam Malik. "A strong guard on the convoy, sir. It shall be done."

"But only to the border, eh? Beyond that…" With a shrug, Major Leghari indicated that the G-troop smugglers would be on their own.

"Yes, sir."

"Now, about this other business," Leghari said. "The farm, the laboratory and so on. What have you learned?"

"Two men appear to be responsible, according to the few survivors we have found," Malik said. "One Indian or Pakistani in appearance, and the other white. They only spoke to the unfortunates collected from the warehouse, what Geelani's people call—"

"The slave market," Leghari said. "I know. Go on."

"Yes, sir. The white man spoke in English. No one questioned by police so far was able to describe an accent, whether British or American. The other spoke Hindi-Urdu."

No help with nationality from that, Leghari thought. It was the lingua franca of both northern India and Pakistan, facilitating communication between those who spoke standard Hindi and standard Urdu.

"They gave no indication of their reason for attacking these facilities?" Leghari asked.

"No, sir. Nothing beyond the obvious."

"Which is?"

Malik shrugged. "They hate Riyaz Geelani."

As do I, the major thought, but kept it to himself. For now, at least, Geelani was a necessary evil. But if things got worse, if he could not protect himself and function to

Leghari's satisfaction, then some drastic changes would be necessary.

First, however, he was obligated to protect the operations that they had already underway. Leghari's various superiors had deemed that anything was fair in efforts to destabilize the government and the economy of India. Hatred ran deep on both sides, rooted in religious conflict, fanned into flame by independence from the British yoke in 1947. Since the stroke of midnight on that day, the Indians who'd worked together under Gandhi's leadership to liberate their homeland had been bitterly divided, literally at each other's throats. Major Leghari reckoned that would never change until strict Muslims ruled the whole subcontinent, and he was confident that Hindus felt the same, whatever they might say in public.

So, the covert—sometimes *not* so covert—war went on. Leghari was a cog in the machine, but he would play his part, no matter how distasteful it became.

Once the drug convoy had made its crossing and no longer needed his protection, Leghari could turn his thoughts to a possible replacement for Geelani. G-troop's second in command, Sayeed Zargar, was an ambitious man. He'd met Leghari twice and showed the proper deference, although that could have been for show. Approaching him directly while Riyaz Geelani lived could be a dicey proposition, with Leghari never knowing if his overture might be accepted or reported back to Zargar's boss as an attempt to undermine him.

Which, of course, it *would* be.

On the other hand, if something happened to Geelani— more specifically, if it could be attributed to enemies still unidentified, who had been raising hell with G-troop's operations in Mumbai—then it was likely that Zargar would welcome help and sage advise from Pakistan. He was ostensibly a Muslim, after all, and had participated in their various campaigns against the common enemy.

That sounded like a plan, Leghari thought. Its details could be worked out on his flight back to Islamabad, and he was reasonably certain he could sell it to the DISI's brass. Their patience with Geelani had been wearing thin as well, particularly in regard to his extravagance and failure to conceal his links with Pakistan. Although the damage had been done, it might still be repaired to some extent, under a cooler head. And if Sayeed Zargar was not that man… well, there was never any shortage of young, avaricious gangsters in Mumbai. The city bred their kind like rats, and they were equally expendable.

Jinnah International Airport, Karachi

BHARAT DESHPANDE HAD the Gippsland GA8 Airvan fueled and ready when they reached the airport. His associate from Customs made another pass, doubling his daily bribe quota, and left them with delighted handshakes all around. Once they were airborne, Bolan's pilot spilled the details he'd arranged since answering the Executioner's last phone call.

They were headed for Shyamji Krishna Verma Airport at Bhuj, in the Kutch District of Gujarat, the farthest-western state adjoining Pakistan. The town, more than seven hundred years old, was famous for its native handicrafts, its several wildlife sanctuaries and as a filming location for Bollywood movies. With 290,000 year-round residents, two more just passing through should not excite much comment—even less, once they had greased more customs agents at the airport.

For their travel overland, Deshpande had called ahead and arranged for a ride. Upon arrival, they should find a "slightly used" Mahindra Scorpio waiting to take them north for their rendezvous with Geelani's drug convoy. Bolan, personally, didn't care how old the SUV was, as long as it got them to their contact point and back again. Bharat Deshpande, once again, would wait a reasonable time to take them back to Mumbai's Juhu Aerodrome.

Back to the main front in their war against G-troop.

Bolan could tell that Sharma was uneasy, following his final conversation with his captain in Mumbai. There seemed to be a level of respect between them, possibly a friendship spanning ranks, and Sharma doubtless wondered if the other man had laid a trap for them—or if, in fact, he still remained alive. The price tag of their war was rising hourly, and it was Bolan's job to make sure that the enemy finally came out in the red.

Red ink. Red blood.

Red faces when Geelani had to tell his troops—and those who bankrolled him from Pakistan—why he couldn't eliminate two men inside his territory. Bolan knew his adversary had to be feeling heat from every side by now, with no relief in sight. Losing the convoy just might tip him over—or, at least, prepare his dwindling private army for a knockout blow.

But first, they had to find the convoy, knock *it* out, and make their way back to Mumbai. If Sharma's captain was a ringer, they might find themselves out in the mangroves, facing enemies more dangerous than cobras and man-eating tigers. Soldiers, maybe—or the CBI itself, a law enforcement agency that put its members on the no-hit list, as far as Bolan was concerned.

Would cops roll out to guard a drug shipment? Sadly, it wouldn't be the first time.

On the other hand, had Sharma's captain dreamed up

the whole thing as bait to nail his renegade sergeant and spare himself from heat at headquarters?

Another possibility.

Bolan was ready for whatever happened next, whether it led to victory or prison—and, thereby, inevitably to his death. His war had started with the long view fixed in mind, a realization that no one got out of life alive. Escape from his selected destiny had never been an option. Whether it came in Gujarat, Guangzhou or Green Bay, Bolan was riding that train to the end of the line. The only thing he could be sure of: when it reached the final terminus, he damn sure wouldn't be alone.

That said, he never entered any contest with an expectation of defeat. The odds he'd faced and beaten in the past were proof enough that one man—or a pair of them, in this case—could come out on top when logic made it seem that he, or they, were bound to lose. Common sense—like "common knowledge"—didn't necessarily reflect reality, much less the fullest range of human possibilities.

Riyaz Geelani had already learned that lesson.

And his education wasn't finished yet.

CHAPTER TWELVE

Landhi Town, Sindh Province, Pakistan

Farouk Aziz completed his inspection of the trucks. All four were "army surplus," meaning they'd been sold to G-troop at a discount by the Pakistani government for use in operations meant to undermine the Indian economy or otherwise disrupt society in the continuation of their endless feud. Aziz had no idea why the two nations were at odds, beyond the basics of religion, and he didn't care. Although ostensibly a Muslim, like the rest of those who served Riyaz Geelani, he concerned himself primarily with worldly things and only prayed when there appeared to be a risk that he might die.

Was Allah listening? Who knew?

The trucks were standard 2.5-ton flatbed models, waterproof tarpaulins covering their cargo, which itself was wrapped in plastic inside sturdy wooden crates. The load of heroin, worth more than all three trucks of cannabis combined, would lead the convoy, with Aziz himself riding the shotgun seat. Or in this case, more properly, the AK-47 seat. Geelani had insisted that the guard be doubled, meaning that besides a driver and a shotgun driver, each truck would have two more gunmen riding in the cargo bay. Twelve automatic weapons and assorted sidearms would secure the drugs in transit.

Nor would that be all. Farouk Aziz had been surprised

to learn that they would have an escort to the border: two Land Rovers filled with riflemen provided by the Directorate for Inter-Services Intelligence. That nearly doubled the guard on their convoy until it crossed Korangi Creek and entered India, beginning their long journey through the mangrove country.

At the border, they'd be met by other vehicles, all strictly private, since the government of India—at least officially—was bent on driving G-troop to extinction. Unofficially, Riyaz Geelani paid good money to an ever-growing number of policemen, politicians and the like to keep his crime family in business, but it would not do for anyone to see soldiers escorting a narcotics caravan between Karachi and Mumbai.

In spite of all the trouble they had suffered recently, Aziz did not expect an ambush on the road. The other raids, as far as he could tell, had all been aimed at stationary targets and had caught defenders with their guard down, unprepared. He frankly did not understand how two men—*two,* and one of them a foreigner at that—could wreak such havoc without being killed or captured. If anything, he hoped they *would* attack the convoy, giving him a chance to punish them and prove himself worthy of a promotion into G-troop's upper ranks.

Why not take full advantage of adversity?

With that in mind, he had handpicked his convoy guards, selecting only those he personally knew as seasoned killers, fearless men who kept their wits about them under fire, all former soldiers or ex-tactical officers from various divisions of India's Central Armed Police Forces—Border Security, the Rapid Action Force, or COBRA, the Commando Battalion for Resolute Action. Aziz had staked his life on their ability to keep the shipment safe.

They were leaving from Landhi Town, east of Karachi, because of its proximity to the border. Some 667,000 people occupied the town, which included Karachi's largest industrial estate sprawling over eleven thousand acres. Four trucks would not be noticed there—or, if they were, no one would question why they rated paramilitary guards to keep their cargo safe from hijackers and thieves.

At last, they were ready to roll. One Land Rover would lead the convoy, with the other coming up behind to watch their backs, the four trucks sandwiched in between. The total distance of their journey was 550 miles one-way— ten hours on the road, at top speed for the trucks—which would require them to refuel en route, but each truck carried a reserve supply of gasoline on board. One stop along the way, to refill tanks, and they were good to go.

Aziz boarded his truck and settled in beside the driver, raised the walkie-talkie to his lips and gave the order to proceed. Six engines growled to life, the first Land Rover pulling out ahead and nosing southward, toward the border. With his AK-47 wedged against the door, immediately to his left, Aziz sat back and made a conscious effort to relax.

Whatever happened in the next ten hours, he would deal with it. If they could make delivery without a hitch, so be it. But if someone tried to intercept them on their way, Aziz would turn the challenge to his own advantage, making an impression on Riyaz Geelani that the man would long remember. Either way, it was a winning proposition.

All he had to do was reach Mumbai alive.

Bhuj Airport, Kutch District, Gujarat, India

THE GIPPSLAND GA8 AIRVAN touched down ten minutes ahead of schedule, as predicted by their pilot, making Bolan wonder why commercial airlines always managed to run late. Bharat Deshpande smiled his way through help-

ing them unload and pocketed a bonus, happily agreeing
to stand by and fly them back to Chhatrapati Shivaji International when they were finished with their business
in the mangrove country.

If they made it back in time.

Bolan had run the calculations while in flight. From
Bhuj up to the Pakistani border and back was 214 miles.
Two hours and change if they could hold a fairly steady
sixty miles per hour in the gray-and-rust-colored Mahindra Scorpio that waited for them near the terminal. Allowing time to pick an ambush site, wait for the convoy
to arrive, then deal with four trucks and whatever escort
vehicles they might have brought along, Bolan set a firm
eight-hour deadline for their rendezvous. Beyond that time,
Deshpande would be free to go, and they would have to
make their own way south, 360 miles to reach Mumbai
from Bhuj.

Assuming they had not been killed meanwhile, or taken
into custody.

Preparing to depart, after another friendly customs officer stopped by to claim his bonus for the day, Bolan considered all the things that could go wrong. Their vehicle
seemed fit enough, on first inspection, but nobody could
predict a breakdown on the tracks that passed for highways
through Gujarat's mangrove country. Anything beyond
a flat tire could derail their mission—and a second flat,
after they'd used their only spare, could do it just as well.

Meanwhile, there were roving gangs of bandits in the
district who survived by robbing travelers and raiding vil-
lages, kidnapping local merchants or selected members
of their families for ransom, or peddling contraband that
ranged from sandalwood and tiger skins to deadly snakes
shipped out as pets for eccentric collectors.

Bandits and smugglers also meant police patrols, conducted by India's paramilitary Border Security Force. Sixty-odd years of conflict with Pakistan had created one of the world's largest border patrols, with some 260,000 personnel divided among 186 battalions. The good news: they were spread along some 9,300 miles of borderline separating India from Pakistan, China, Nepal, Bhutan, Bangladesh and Myanmar, with a strong concentration on the Line of Control drawn between portions of disputed turf in Jammu and Kashmir. With luck—something he absolutely couldn't bank on in advance—Bolan surmised their risk of meeting a patrol in mangrove country, well back from the Pakistani border, should be relatively small.

Neither of the district's two state highways—GJ SH 6 or GJ SH 7—served the territory Bolan was traversing, leaving him to navigate a roadway that was barely two lanes wide, pockmarked by divots in the pavement that could snap an axle if they caught you by surprise, with no time left to swerve or hit the brakes. It would be worse in darkness, worst of all in rainy weather, but he'd take whatever Mother Nature had in store for him and do his best.

The trick was to find a spot where they could hide the Scorpio, conceal themselves and have a field of fire that let him use the 40 mm Milkor launcher. If he got a chance to use the Vidhwansak sniper rifle, so much the better, but he wasn't counting on that kind of long-range visibility within a mangrove forest. He'd never seen a perfect set on any battlefield, but time and grim experience had taught Bolan to work with the terrain available.

His targets, being motor vehicles, would be restricted to the road they traveled, walled by trees on either side. Their passengers could bail out once the shooting started, but the trucks themselves could only travel forward, or attempt to flee the ambush in reverse. With proper planning, timely execution, Bolan reckoned he could turn the two-lane road into a death trap for Geelani's men and send their cargo up in smoke.

If he was wrong…

They didn't talk about the downside, driving north. Sharma was quiet, staring off into the woods that flanked the roadway, occupied with private thoughts, while Bolan turned his mind to strategy. He knew only one way to play the killing game: full-throttle, leaving only scorched earth for his enemies.

A one-way race, perhaps, to victory or death.

Central Bureau of Investigation Headquarters, Mumbai

AFTER PONDERING HIS problem for the best part of the afternoon, Captain Vivak Patel decided there was no way to protect himself without eliminating his potential enemies inside the CBI. The death of Major Yugandhar had freed him in some way—or possibly, he thought, had driven him insane. In either case, it stood to reason that the other officers who had betrayed their oath of office for Riyaz Geelani knew about the bungled contract on Patel, and would do everything within their power to help G-troop carry out his execution.

That was, if he did not get them first.

He had two targets left, both named by Yugandhar. The first, Captain Kapil Ram, was assigned to the CBI's Special Crime Branch where, Patel now realized, he was ideally placed to warn Riyaz Geelani of investigations that affected G-troop's operations. The other, Special Deputy Director Jai Bhagwan Sherawat, was in overall charge of Mumbai, answering only to the CBI's director in New Delhi. Sherawat could cancel an investigation without explanation, and a detective's only recourse would be a complaint to the top man himself—in CBI terms, equivalent to invoking Lord Shiva, and about as likely to produce results.

For, after all, who knew if the director was corrupt, himself?

Patel was not about to take that chance. He had disposed of Major Yugandhar without assistance, and he reckoned he could do the same again. His targets, Ram and Sherawat, were only human, after all. A kind of numbness gripped Patel as he sat planning double murder, something that, just yesterday, he would have deemed impossible. But that was yesterday, before he had been hunted through the streets and nearly killed. His life might seem a worthless thing to his superiors and to Riyaz Geelani, but Patel would not surrender it without a fight.

Which traitor should he tackle first? Or was there some way he could catch them both together at a place where he could strike and have a reasonable expectation of escape? Perhaps, if he applied some ingenuity, but he would also need special equipment. Patel could not trust a sofa cushion for the bold, audacious scheme he had in mind.

Patel left his tiny office and rode the elevator down to basement level, where evidence from past and pending cases was archived. He signed in with a clerk who barely glanced at him, using Kapil Ram's name, and made his way through aisles of plastic tubs labeled with case numbers and names until he found the one he sought. The captain removed the tub to an examination table situated where the clerk could not observe him, if he'd cared to try, and opened it.

Inside, with other evidence from an old murder case, Patel found a Walther P-22 semiautomatic pistol. As indicated by its model number, the weapon was chambered for .22-caliber long rifle cartridges. Like all Walther P-22s, it came with an internally threaded barrel that allowed attachment of a sound suppressor, with the coupling of a separate thread adapter from the manufacturer—an assassin's weapon, in short.

Both the adapter and suppressor were inside the tub, each in its own plastic evidence bag. Patel removed them, put them in his trouser pockets, then tucked the Walther under his jacket and replaced the tub on its proper shelf. He did not worry about fingerprints, since he had worked the case originally and had handled every piece of evidence on multiple occasions.

And besides, after he used the gun, if it was traced to him somehow, it wouldn't matter.

He would already be dead.

The next step: how to bring his targets together without making either one of them suspicious. Patel believed that he could manage it, although the risk was great. If he could contact Sherawat by telephone and bait him with an offer to disclose Major Yugandhar's whereabouts, Patel believed he could arrange a private meeting. Then, the challenge would be duping Kapil Ram into arriving at the same time, unexpected by the special deputy director. Once he had the two of them together in the same room…

Could he do it? Two more killings in cold blood?

Why not, when one or both of them was bent on killing him?

They should expect no mercy from a man they had condemned. He was prepared to play by their rules, and if that prevented his soul's access to *moksha*—liberation from the endless cycle of death and reincarnation, into a state of completeness—so be it. Patel would take that chance to save the life he had this day, and strike a telling blow against his enemies.

Borivali West, Mumbai

SAYEED ZARGAR STOOD at his window, staring toward the greenery of Sanjay Gandhi National Park, sixty-five square miles of wilderness contained within this northern suburb of Mumbai. From where he stood, it seemed impossible that tigers, leopards, crocodiles and cobras roamed at liberty within the peaceful-looking forest, but he knew that during one month of a recent year, leopard attacks had claimed the lives of fourteen visitors. They hardly counted, though, among two million paying customers per year, and Zargar was convinced the tang of danger was a major lure for tourists.

Danger of another sort preoccupied the mind of G-troop's second-highest ranking officer as he observed the park's green treetops rippling underneath a squall of rain. He'd been expecting some word from Riyaz Geelani for the past half hour to confirm departure of their convoy from Karachi, but there'd been no call so far.

More trouble? One of his informants in Karachi had already briefed Zargar on the attacks within that city, starting soon after Geelani fled across the border into Pakistan. In truth, Zargar had been relieved, hoping the enemies he'd been unable to identify thus far would be content to stalk Geelani, leaving Zargar and Mumbai in peace. It was a selfish wish, perhaps, but perfectly in character for a ruthless purveyor of drugs, death and misery.

What would happen if the unknown enemies killed Geelani? Would they then come back for *him,* or view their mission as successful and withdraw? Zargar was not a seer, but just in case, he had begun preparing for succession to the throne, in case something should happen to his boss. All for the good of G-troop, naturally. And himself, of course.

The phone rang, finally, and Zargar snatched it up. *"Namaste."*

"How are you faring in our friend's absence, Sayeed?" the caller asked.

Zargar immediately recognized the voice but did not speak his name. If would be rankest folly to identify Major Leghari, when he had no idea as to who might be eavesdropping on the line.

"Doing my best, sir, as always," he replied.

"I would expect no less. It's why I've called, in fact."

"Oh, yes?" he asked, not quite confused, but definitely curious.

"Indeed. It seems his troubles are persisting," Leghari said. "Some who have supported him begin to wonder if he has the wherewithal to save himself, much less to be of further use."

How should Zargar reply to that? Was it a test of loyalty Geelani had concocted for his second in command? Or was Leghari offering the world up to him on a silver platter?

"I believe he will endure," Zargar responded, finally.

"You would know best, of course," Leghari granted. "It's something of a shame, though, don't you think?"

"What is, sir?"

"To see a thriving operation and successful partnership dragged down to ruin by a single man."

"If that were true, of course, I would agree."

"And if I told you sponsorship would be available for a successor to the fallen king?"

"I would be curious about the timing of the overture, sir."

"You see? I knew you were a wise man," Leghari said. "Waiting for the snare to close around you if you draw too near."

"With all respect, sir, it is a possibility."

"Consider this—I offer you the full endorsement of my agency, in the event our friend should not survive his present difficulty. You would take his place, no questions asked, with all of the cooperation he enjoys today—and possibly a good deal more."

Zargar's heart lurched against his sternum. He felt almost giddy for an instant, then recovered, coming back to earth with both feet planted firmly on the floor beneath him. In the park below him, he imagined that a tiger raised its head from sipping at a stream and snarled.

"If you are serious, sir, I would be honored to participate."

"Then say no more, for now," Leghari said. "But turn your mind to a solution of our mutual dilemma. No one wants it needlessly protracted, eh?"

"I'll definitely think of something," Zargar promised.

"Excellent. We'll speak again."

"Goodbye, sir."

Breaking the link, Sayeed Zargar could scarcely credit what had just occurred. Without quite saying so, a ranking officer of the DISI had given him the go-ahead to plot Riyaz Geelani's death and seize control of G-troop with cooperation from the agency. If he could pull it off, Zargar might well be set for life.

And if he failed, that life would be a short one, swept away in blood and agony.

Kutch District, Gujarat, India

THEY WERE IN mangrove country, north of Nirona, traveling along the only narrow road remaining to them. All around stood massive trees with arching roots exposed, resembling houses built on stilts, with rustling gray leaves emulating thatched roofs overhead. The mangroves thrived in coastal areas, planting their strange roots in the muck that lay below salt water, rife with barnacles, fish and crustaceans. Here, so close to the Arabian Sea and the Great Rann of Kutch—a seasonal salt marsh and sometime desert—they dominated the landscape, providing concealment for prey and predator alike.

Perfect for Bolan's needs.

He hadn't found the site he wanted yet, somewhere to hide the Land Rover without submerging it or bogging down, but they still had another forty-odd miles left before they reached his favored target zone, selected from satellite photos online. He didn't want a border crossing where police would be on hand, nor any village en route between Bhuj and Karachi. Someplace well away from human habitation, with no civilians in the line of fire.

A killing ground, in short.

They'd seen no wildlife yet except for birds, which didn't mean that other eyes weren't watching as they passed. There might be mugger crocodiles—named from the Urdu *magar,* meaning "water monster"—but they normally preferred fresh water. Whale sharks visited the coast of Gujarat sporadically, but they were harmless, once the shock of meeting one wore off. Not so the tigers, cobras, banded sea snakes whose bright colors were a warning sign for fishermen. Once they went EVA, Bolan and Sharma would be forced to watch their step.

The rented Land Rover had given them no trouble so far, and he hoped to keep it that way. Stash it somewhere cozy, where it wouldn't catch stray rounds or sink up to its axles in the muck. A smaller access road branched off occasionally from their route, but Bolan wasn't sure where any one of them might lead him, whether to a village, to a private residence or to a dead end in the marsh.

Bolan picked out an opening in the treeline, approach-

ing on his right, with what appeared to be a patch of solid
ground beyond it. Tall reeds screened it from the road,
so Bolan stopped, leaving the Rover's engine rumbling,
to explore on foot. He found that there was hiding space
and room to spare behind the trees and undergrowth,
better concealment from the eyes of southbound drivers
than from those northbound, which was another plus. The
ground was solid underfoot, with no indication that their
ride should sink.

The only problem: if he nosed into the hiding place,
he'd have to back out when he'd finished with the G-troop
convoy, which would leave him facing a narrow road littered with death and wreckage. To avoid that trap and to
facilitate their getaway, he'd have to turn and back into
the space he'd found, with the Land Rover pointing back
toward Bhuj.

It took a bit of time and effort, but he made it, Sharma
on the road, directing him with hand signals in Bolan's
rearview mirror. Once the vehicle was hidden—Sharma
jogging north along the road, then walking back to check
it from a hundred yards—they looked for places to conceal themselves.

That took a while as well, checking the trees, looking
for cover where they wouldn't be immersed in salt water
for hours on end, or have their boots sucked off by mud,
their weapons fouled. At length, each man found a place,
Bolan on the left side of the road, and Sharma to the right.
As Bolan had expected, there'd be no use for the Vidhwansak bolt-action rifle, so he took the Milkor launcher,
backed up with his INSAS rifle, Sharma ready with his
AK-47.

Bolan checked his watch. They had an hour and ten
minutes left to wait, if G-troop's convoy had started on
time and had not been delayed on the road. They spent

twenty minutes of that working out fields of fire, gauging distance, outlining the trap they would close on the trucks if it all ran according to plan.

Which it might, Bolan thought. But if not, he would play it the same way he had countless times in the past. He would adjust, adapt and do the best he could with what he had. Hit first, hit hard, hit often, until there was no fight left in his opponents. Nothing on the field in front of him but wreckage, be it human or mechanical.

Scorched earth, to send a message home that there was no escaping from the Executioner.

CHAPTER THIRTEEN

Sindh Province, Pakistan

Riyaz Geelani was not happy to be going home. Mumbai was still too hot to suit him, but he had no choice. The heat had followed him to Pakistan, and the suggestion from Major Leghari that he solve the problem swiftly was, in fact, an order.

Could he have refused?

Perhaps, but that would mean the severance of his connections to the DISI first, and then the full weight of the government would fall upon his refuge. It behooved him to obey the major, when defiance stood to cost Geelani everything. And at the same time, if he could recoup his losses personally—or at least punish the men responsible, make an example of them to discourage future adversaries—it would boost Geelani's flagging reputation in Mumbai.

But how?

His first step, he decided, was to squeeze his contacts in the CBI, the Indian Police Service and National Investigation Agency, getting his money's worth from all of them at last. If they ignored him, there were ways to force their hand, whether it took intimidation or the threat of scandal if their links to G-troop were exposed. How many ranking officers would risk a term in the Arthur Road Jail with convicts they had put away, all yearning for the taste of sweet revenge?

Geelani supervised his soldiers loading up their vehicles for the drive back to Jinnah International Airport, and while they worked, he used the sat phone. Sayeed Zargar answered midway through its fourth ring.

"Namaste."

"I'm coming back ahead of schedule," Geelani said, skipping over salutations.

"Oh?" Was that a note of disappointment in his chief lieutenant's voice, or simply curiosity?

"Our problem, as you know, followed me here."

"And we've had quiet since you left," Zargar replied.

"What progress have you made with matters of identity?" Geelani asked.

"Referring to…?"

"The only matter that I left to you." He let a drop of acid ooze into his tone.

"Of course, sir. Unfortunately, there is still nothing to say about the foreigner. The other may be a rogue sergeant from the CBI."

"May be?"

"I can't be certain yet. Our major is investigating."

Arutla Yugandhar. He was a smirking prick, prone to exaggeration of his own importance, but he had provided valuable information in the past.

"All right. I'll deal with it when I return. Meanwhile, reach out to all our men in Maharashtra and across the country. Call them to Mumbai without delay, and no excuses. If they're not incarcerated or in the hospital, they must drop everything and rally to the cause, prepared to fight."

"What of our other operations?" Zargar asked.

"They wait," Geelani said. "Eradication of our enemies must be the top priority for every member of the family."

"I understand, sir."

"Also, alert our other friend at CBI headquarters. You can still find him, I take it?"

"Yes."

"Tell him to expect disturbances. His men should do their jobs, but not too energetically. I don't want any special interference while we're cleaning house."

"It will be done."

"And finally, I need a team to meet my plane," Geelani said. "Ten men should be enough, with vehicles for ten more that I'm bringing home."

"I'll see to it."

"I have no doubt."

Geelani cut the link without goodbyes, frowning. Zargar's whole tone and attitude was off-putting, sounding a faint alarm that made him wonder if his second in command was cultivating thoughts of mutiny. It would not be unusual. Geelani had himself deposed the man who introduced him to a life of profitable crime. Zargar, no doubt, harbored ambitions of his own.

I'll miss him, Geelani thought, with a bitter smile. But not for long.

Kutch District, Gujarat, India

MACK BOLAN HEARD the convoy coming well before the vehicles were visible. He glanced across the narrow forest road toward Baji Sharma, saw the sergeant looking back at him, and nodded confirmation that the engine sounds had registered. He shifted slightly in his place among the arching mangrove roots, raising the Milkor MGL and focusing its Armson OEG collimator sight with both eyes open, waiting for the lead vehicle to appear.

It was a newer model of his own Mahindra Scorpio SUV, mud-splashed like Bolan's, with five men inside. Behind it, twenty yards or so, the first of four next emerged into view, then another behind it. He waited until all four were visible, biding his time, confirming that the last car in line was another Mahindra with gunners on board.

All present and accounted for.

In front of him, the road ran arrow-straight for about two hundred yards. Plenty of room to let the convoy pick up speed, its point men gaining confidence, hoping they'd made it through the worst bit, with the border well behind them now. They would be focusing on Bhuj, and then Mumbai, aware of danger on their route but growing more relaxed with every mile they covered. Likely, some or all of them had made this trip before, with other contraband, whether narcotics, arms or human cargo packed inside their 2.5-ton trucks.

But this time, they were dealing with the Executioner.

He sighted on the lead Mahindra's grille and squeezed the Milkor's double-action trigger, sending a 40 mm high-explosive round to meet it head-on. The explosion sent a shock wave rippling through the mangrove trees on both sides of the road, while the Mahindra's front end crumpled, seeming to implode on impact. Its hood peeled back, a ball of fire erupting from beneath it as it slammed into the SUV's windshield. Bolan could not have said, just yet, whether the driver managed to survive the blast or not, but he had clearly lost control, because the Mahindra swerved and stalled out, sitting crossways in the middle of the narrow road.

Perfect.

For his next shot, he aimed beyond the trucks, all four of them intent on braking as their path was suddenly obstructed. Bolan framed the tail car in his sights, giving its driver credit as he slammed into Reverse and tried to back away, but he could not outrun the HE round hurtling to meet him, traveling 250 feet per second. By the time he shifted gears, Bolan's second grenade was airborne, on its way to impact with the target.

A second detonation rocked the mangrove forest, this one taking out the right-rear quadrant of the second SUV, popping its hatchback open, shearing off one wheel, rattling the backseat passengers like helpless crash-test dummies. The gas tank didn't blow immediately, but he knew it had to be ruptured, spilling fuel and fumes onto the roadway, waiting for a spark to set it off.

Between two mangled, smoking wrecks, the trucks were trapped, their guards dismounting, seeking cover as they recognized their peril. Some broke toward the tree line, others dropping out of sight behind—or underneath—their vehicles, all armed with automatic weapons.

Come and get it, Bolan thought, and focused once more on the Milkor's sight.

FAROUK AZIZ HAD let his mind drift, tired of scanning mangrove forests for a misplaced shadow or a hint of sudden movement that might indicate a lurking enemy. His point and tail cars, packed with G-troop riflemen who'd met the convoy at the border, were on watch for danger. There was very little he could do except sit back and try to stay awake while boredom lulled his senses, clock-watching to keep the convoy more or less on schedule as it rolled south toward Mumbai.

Watching the forest was, he knew, a futile exercise. An army could be hiding in the mangroves and he wouldn't know it until the shooting started. Armed guards, on a run like this one, were as much for show as actual defense. Their presence would discourage common bandits, who might otherwise attack and pillage trucks passing through their territory, but who would not risk a battle with determined, well-armed men.

They had another fifty miles to go, he reckoned, before pulling into Bhuj. The convoy would not stop there—or slow down, for that matter, unless a herd of goats or something equally insipid blocked their road—and it was not the sort of place where enemies would try an ambush. Far too many witnesses around, as well as Gujarat police. His guards knew well enough to keep their guns down, out of sight, while passing through the city to avoid official confrontations that were bound to end in killing.

After all, a bribe for passage through the streets could only stretch so far.

Aziz was thus distracted when the point car suddenly exploded, smoke and flames obscuring his vision of the road ahead. His driver hit the brake immediately, holding steady as the truck decelerated, then another blast went off somewhere behind him. Craning for a quick look in his wing mirror, Aziz saw the Mahindra Scorpio behind the last truck burning, stalled crosswise, blocking the road.

He cursed, snatching the AK-47 from between his knees with one hand, while the other raised the walkie-talkie from the seat beside him. Though no orders should be necessary, still he barked them out. "Find cover! Save the cargo!"

He had not heard the shots that wrecked the two Mahindra Scorpios, had seen no smoking trail that would direct him to an adversary with a rocket launcher. Could the road itself be mined? Of course, it could be, but as Aziz leaped from the truck, he did not think that was the case. The demolition of his point and tail cars had been too precise, for one thing. For another—

Anything he had in mind was wiped clean by the third explosion, ripping through the front end of the truck cab he had just evacuated, peppering Aziz's flank with red-hot shrapnel as he turned to run for cover. He howled in pain, stumbled and fell to one knee, almost lost his rifle but retained it with a force of will alone. Dragging one leg, he made it to the tailgate of the truck, where two guards from the cargo bay were crouched, scanning the tree line left and right for targets.

"Where's Vinod?" one of them asked Aziz, referring to their driver.

"Dead, for all I know," Aziz snarled through his pain. "You want him, go and find him."

"What's the order?" asked the man.

"Protect the load at any cost," Aziz replied, and limped around to find a vantage point from which he could return fire.

But toward whom? In which direction?

With three vehicles disabled and the road blocked, north and south, the convoy wasn't going anywhere. He could attempt to radio for reinforcements, try one of the two-ways in a truck that was not presently in flames, but Aziz wasn't sure that he could reach the outside world from where they sat besieged. If only he could—

Wait! The sat phone!

He could reach around the world with that, but he had left it in the truck's cab when he bailed out. Was it still intact, and could he reach it through the fire?

The only way to find out was to try.

"Cover me!" he told the riflemen, and with his last reserve of strength, Aziz lurched back into the line of fire.

BOLAN FIRED his fourth grenade—an incendiary round—at the last truck in line, punching through its canvas cargo cover, lighting up the load of tightly packed hashish. In seconds, tangy smoke was drifting through the mangroves, wafting over gunmen crouched behind their vehicles and looking for a target to engage.

Across the forest road, Sharma was firing short bursts from his AK-47, walking them along the east flank of the convoy, keeping heads down, drawing some return fire. His fire distracted the surviving convoy guards who couldn't get a fix on Bolan, since his Milkor MGL produced no muzzle-flash or smoke to help them spot him. If he took down any of the G-troop soldiers, that was icing on the cake.

Two trucks remained, with two live rounds remaining in the Milkor's cylinder. He walked it forward to the second truck in line and dropped another incendiary round through the canvas onto crates of hash, lighting what had to be the biggest single joint on record. He could hear the G-troop shooters coughing now, and knew the spreading flames would force them out of cover soon, on one side of the roadway or the other.

One more 40 mm round remained in the Milkor's cylinder, and Bolan fired it toward the middle truck in line. It was a high-explosive round this time, and Bolan put it through the cab's windshield, resistance from the glass alone enough to detonate its impact fuse. The flat roof of the cab peeled back, resembling the lid on a sardine can, while the blast wave took out the rear window, ripping through the cargo bay, spewing the slats of shattered crates and all their leafy contents from the tailgate.

Setting down the empty launcher, Bolan raised his INSAS autorifle, peering through its sights along the line of shattered, burning vehicles. They could have left the convoy as it was, its cargo going up in smoke, another lesson for Riyaz Geelani, but the G-troop soldiers who survived this firefight would be victimizing someone else the next day. Heroin and hash were only half the problem.

Bolan was intent on wiping out the enemy, along with all his contraband.

His sharp eyes picked out movement in the smoke before him, figures scuttling from the cover of one truck to reach another, edging closer to the front of the demolished convoy. Framing one mark in his rifle's rear sight, he fired a 3-round burst from fifty yards and saw the figure stutter-step before it dropped facedown into the road.

Behind the dead man, two more turned and ran toward the cover they'd just vacated, the middle man too slow to make it as another burst from Bolan's rifle stitched three holes along his spine and put him down. The third dropped flat and rolled under the truck, taking his chances with the fire above him, rather than the sniper at his back.

Behind the vehicles, beyond his line of sight, Bolan heard AK-47s firing, G-troop soldiers matching shot for shot with Sharma. The Executioner took a moment, opened up the Milkor's swing-out cylinder, and dumped its empty brass among the mangrove roots, reloading it with M576 buckshot rounds. Each canister held twenty double O pellets within a sabot cup, calculated to cover a 1.5-meter circle from forty yards out. By comparison, the standard 12-gauge buckshot round held only seven pellets, with its kill zone correspondingly reduced.

Before departing from his cover, Bolan shoulder-slung the INSAS rifle, muzzle down and safety on, clutching the Milkor in both hands. He didn't know if Sharma needed help or not, but they were in the fight together, so he'd lend a hand, regardless. The soldier hoped as he did it that his sidekick could identify him in the smoke and the confusion, without taking Bolan down.

SHARMA PULLED THE empty magazine from his Kalashnikov and dropped it, fumbling for another from his pocket. In the time it took him to reload, three of his enemies had surged from cover, scuttling forward to the shadow of a closer truck. He caught the last in line, about to reach that place of safety, and his snap shot raised a puff of crimson from the runner's hip.

Not dead, but badly injured—maybe incapacitated. Sharma cursed himself for being hasty with the shot, hoping the shock of impact from his 7.62 mm slug would keep the mobster down and out of action while he bled to death.

But if he showed his face again…

Sharma believed they might be winning, but the haze of smoke before him made it difficult to say for sure. The convoy, certainly, would go no farther, and its cargo would not reach Mumbai. As for the escorts, some of them were down, but others still had fight left in them.

And one was all it took to kill him, Sharma realized. Even a stray shot could accomplish that.

But if they got into the mangroves, worked their way around to flank him, Sharma knew that he might never see or hear them coming. Not until the fatal shot struck home and took him down.

Casting a nervous eye around him, Sharma noted shadows moving in the forest, knew that they were likely birds and monkeys fleeing from the firefight, but there was a chance of adversaries edging toward him through the woods, advancing stealthily. The possibility distracted him enough to let a couple of the shooters on the smoky road advance from one truck to the next, before he could stop either one of them.

Infuriated by his own distraction, Sharma wondered if all the hashish smoke was working on his brain somehow. He'd smoked the weed before, when he was younger, and he didn't have the old familiar giddy feeling now, but Sharma still thought that it might be having some effect.

There was more movement by the nearest blown-out truck, and this time when the shooters moved Sharma was ready for them. As the first emerged, a double-tap from Sharma's AK ripped into the gunman's chest, spraying the man behind him with a spout of blood from exit wounds. The second man recoiled, wiping the blood out of his eyes, and took the next shot through his forehead, spilling any final thoughts onto the road.

That kept the others under cover for a moment, but they wouldn't stay there long. Spare gasoline cans exploded in the middle truck, raising another burst of flame above the battleground. The fiery plume reminded Sharma of the flare stacks in Gujarat's natural gas fields, or those on the High Mumbai platforms offshore. Downrange, a running man appeared, his hair and clothes in flames, but he escaped into the mangrove marsh before Sharma could drop him with a mercy round.

Farther back along the line of blasted vehicles, Sharma heard voices calling back and forth. He could not make out their words, but they had to be organizing an attack on his position, whether from the front or through a fast, concerted rush into the forest, there to work their way around behind him. If they made it into cover, out of sight, Sharma supposed he would be forced to cut and run, or stand and fight, outnumbered and outgunned.

A shout rose from the pall of smoke, and half a dozen men or more broke cover, sprinting from the tree line. Sharma sprayed them with his AK-47, saw one fall, but then the rest were disappearing into shadows. Cursing at his slow reaction, Sharma hunkered down among the arching mangrove roots and braced himself to meet the next attack.

BOLAN MADE IT to the rear end of the stalled convoy in decent time, scanning between the vehicles as he proceeded in a search for living targets. None was visible, from which he gathered that the G-troop soldiers who survived were banking on a move to circle Sharma and eliminate him, then perhaps to double back on Bolan for a clean sweep. But they'd missed their chance in that regard, at least.

The Executioner was hunting them.

He crossed the road behind the tail car, glancing only for a second at the blackened corpses hunched inside it. The left-rear door was open, so he knew at least one of Riyaz Geelani's men had managed to escape the SUV before fire gutted its interior. Whether that one was fit to fight or not, he couldn't say.

But he would soon find out.

Once he had crossed the road, Bolan moved back into the trees, negotiating passage through the mangrove maze, watching for scaly swimmers in the knee-deep brackish water, while he simultaneously scanned ahead for human enemies. The short, erratic sputter of Kalashnikovs told him that he was headed in the right direction, toward the last point where he'd seen Sharma alive.

How long the sergeant would remain that way was anybody's guess.

He overtook the first two stragglers just about a minute later. One of them was wounded, hobbling, dragging his comrade through the water.

Taking them out would be an easy shot, one 40 mm buckshot round for both of them, but that would also tip the others to a big gun on their trail. Instead, Bolan went with his semiauto pistol, sound suppressor attached, and gave each of the lagging G-troop riflemen a new vent in their skulls, dropping the pair of them facedown with muffled splashes that were lost in the reports of gunfire up ahead.

The Executioner pressed on, skirting the bodies that would soon be meat for swimming scavengers, reduced after their lives of predatory violence to low men on the food chain. He left them in his wake, proceeding more aggressively now that he had the main force of their cronies roughly spotted, narrowing the gap.

Approaching from the rear, with Sharma still somewhere in front of him, Bolan had two priorities. The first: to kill as many of the G-troop shooters as he could before they turned on him. The second: make damn sure that Sharma didn't gun *him* down by accident, while firing at and through their enemies.

The Milkor MGL, he thought, would help with both concerns.

More gunmen visible before him now, high-stepping through the water, ducking under cover of the mangroves when a hostile AK-47 stuttered at them, farther still ahead. Bolan decided he was close enough to let his big gun speak, angling the Milkor's muzzle toward a group of three G-troopers twenty yards ahead and slightly to his left.

Its *pop* when Bolan fired was not impressive, but the storm of buckshot ripping into flesh and bone was nothing short of hellish. Bolan saw his targets come apart, collapse and sink. Before the bloody froth had time to spread, he'd pivoted and found another trio, sighted, fired and heard their dying screams.

The others—half a dozen, max—knew someone was behind them now. They turned, firing their autorifles, making Bolan duck and cover, but he came out on the far side of another giant mangrove, fired again and watched two more disintegrate in ruby mist. A couple of the shocked survivors broke and ran, but their escape route took them into Sharma's sights and they were chopped down in their tracks by his Kalashnikov.

"Two left!" Bolan called out, drawing their fire and dodging it, letting the nearest mangrove take the punishment. He doubled back, emerging where they least expected him, and fired again, the last two shooters splashing down in water that had once been greenish-brown, now taking on a brick-red hue.

"I'm coming in," he called to Sharma.

"Come ahead," the answer echoed back.

They met beside the last two fallen gunmen, one still thrashing weakly, trying not to drown before he bled out from his wounds. A silenced round from Bolan's pistol settled it, and him.

"Geelani won't be pleased," Sharma said, with a weary smile.

"Especially when we get finished in Mumbai," the Executioner replied.

CHAPTER FOURTEEN

Captain Patel could be persuasive when he needed to. His first call, in pursuance of his risky plan, had gone to Special Deputy Director Jai Bhagwan Sherawat. Despite what he believed to be suspicion on the part of his superior, Patel had spun a tale designed to feed Sherawat's curiosity, if it did not inspire his trust. Patel had finally learned the identity of the rogue officer who'd run amok on G-troop and believed he could arrange the maverick's apprehension. Still, he feared sharing the whole story with anyone but Sherawat, and only then when they could speak in utmost confidence.

Would it be possible for them to meet after hours, in Sherawat's office?

It would.

His next call, still in-house, was made to Captain Kapil Ram, at the Special Crime Branch. He'd told Ram that the special deputy director wished to speak with both of them, and that he'd asked Patel to pass the word because of difficulties in the big man's office with security. That naturally made Ram curious, but Patel told him Sherawat had not explained in any detail, simply warning Ram in strong terms not to call back asking questions.

Would the captain be available for meeting after hours? Of course, he would.

Now it was nearly time, and while Patel was fairly trembling with anxiety, he had a plan in mind that just might save his life—or end it, finally, before a firing squad.

Disposing of two mortal enemies at once was dangerous enough. Doing the job *inside* CBI headquarters increased the odds against success tremendously. It could be done, but only if he kept his wits about him, dealt with every detail and omitted nothing.

First, he stripped and double-checked the Walther P-22 he had removed from the evidence room, then reassembled it, attached its coupling and suppressor, loaded and replaced its 10-round magazine. While working on the gun, Patel wore latex gloves and wiped each surface thoroughly, inside and out, including each individual .22 long rifle cartridge he fed into the magazine. He'd leave the gloves on when he went to see the special deputy director, trusting that by the time Sherawat noticed, Patel would have control of the situation.

The pistol fit his normal shoulder holster, a horizontal model, open-ended nylon, which permitted the suppressor to protrude behind his armpit. When he put on his suit coat, a lump was visible, but Patel thought that if he left the coat unbuttoned, did not stop and dawdle on his way to meet with Sherawat, no one was likely to observe it. By the time the special deputy director had a chance to notice, Patel would have drawn the pistol, so it made no difference.

Speaking for Sherawat, he had instructed Captain Ram to go directly from his own office to their superior's, arriving precisely at 6:15 p.m. Like everyone who worked for Sherawat, Ram knew the deputy director was obsessed with punctuality, holding equal disdain both for early birds and those who were tardy. Ram would make sure to arrive precisely when instructed, even if he had to loiter in the outer hallway, killing time.

Perfect.

At 5:52 p.m., Patel left his office and walked to the elevator, gloved hands in his trouser pockets except when he pushed the buttons. No one met him in the hallway, and he had the elevator car all to himself. Sherawat's receptionist left work at 5:30 p.m., and her desk was vacant as Patel entered the outer office, moving quietly toward the open door of Sherawat's inner sanctum. He drew the silenced Walther as he neared that doorway, holding it against his thigh, knocking on the door frame with his left hand.

Sherawat looked up at him from paperwork, wearing his normal frown. His eyes flicked toward a large clock on the nearest wall. "You are two minutes early, Captain," he declared.

"I couldn't wait," Patel replied, and raised the Walther into view.

Sherawat blinked at him, but otherwise his face remained deadpan. "Is this some kind of idiotic joke, Patel?"

Instead of answering, Patel said, "Place your hands flat on the desktop. If they move from there, you die."

Somewhat surprisingly, the deputy director did as he was told. His frown had turned into a full-blown scowl. "I assume you've lost your mind," he said. "If any shred of sanity remains, hand me that gun immediately."

"So you can finish what your G-troop assassins started? I think not."

Sherawat missed a beat, then said, too late, "I don't know what you're talking about."

"Lies won't help you. The truth *may* save you, but I promise nothing. Are you ready to confess?"

"Confess *what?*"

"That you've sold your oath of office and your soul to be a lackey for Riyaz Geelani."

"Captain, I am warning you—"

Patel shushed him, cocking his head. "Be quiet, now," he ordered. "We have company."

He turned to face the doorway just as Captain Ram appeared, took in the scene and froze two steps across the threshold. "What is—?"

Patel fired two rounds into Ram's chest from a range of ten feet, maximum, then turned to cover Sherawat again before his hands could move. They both watched Ram's death throes and listened to the drumming of his heels, until he shivered one last time and then lay deathly still.

"Now, then," Patel told Sherawat. "I think there's something that you wish to say."

Bhuj Airport

BHARAT DESHPANDE WAS waiting as promised, his Gippsland GA8 Airvan gassed up and ready to go. The next leg of their trip being domestic, there should be no customs agents waiting when they landed in Mumbai, 360 miles due south, but Bolan never took an easy hop for granted. He'd be ready for whatever happened on arrival, and they had the better part of three hours to plan their next moves in Mumbai, while they were airborne.

Bolan was gambling that the loss of his drug convoy, coupled with another blitz on his home ground, would bring Geelani back to face his enemies. The heat they had applied in Pakistan should be enough to make authorities uneasy about sheltering Geelani, while the mounting losses would compel him to come back and fight or risk disgrace that was the kiss of death for any gangland godfather. Bringing him back to India and closing for the final showdown there, in turn, would have more impact on the rest of G-troop than eliminating him while he was hiding in the hills outside Karachi, far away.

Since takeoff, Sharma had been writing on a notepad, drawing up some kind of list. When they were thirty minutes out from Bhuj, he finished it and leaned across the aircraft's narrow center aisle toward Bolan, with the list in hand.

"I've thought about more targets," he explained. "We have done well, I think, but there are still more operations we can interfere with. One of them, a private bank, conceals a great deal of Geelani's cash. If we removed it…"

Bolan had to smile at that. "You want to rob a bank, now?"

Sharma shrugged. "I've seen the place, pretending that I wished to open an account. Of course, I was refused. They claim to deal only with individuals from certain trades. The story changes as required, so that a teacher walking in, for instance, will be told the bank is operated for the benefit of building contractors. A contractor might hear that it belongs to truck drivers. I had a chance to look around, however."

"And?"

"The guards are from Geelani's own security consortium, which also does private investigations—that is, blackmail—against public figures and celebrities. G-troop assassins dressed as make-believe police."

"But not off-duty cops?" Bolan asked.

Sharma shook his head emphatically. "Geelani would not trust police to guard his money. Some of them might try to take it for themselves. His soldiers know better."

"That might be worth a look-see," Bolan granted.

"There is probably more cash than we can carry," Sharma said. "But he will mourn the loss of every rupee."

"What else have you got?" Bolan inquired.

"A trucking company that handles toxic dumping," Sharma said. "The city's second-largest taxi fleet, legitimate on paper, but its drivers also transport drugs and prostitutes. Another gambling casino, this one in Andheri West. Something Geelani calls a 'breaking stable' for imported women who will occupy his brothels. A garage that deals in stolen vehicles. I think you call it a chop shop."

"You got it right," Bolan said. "That's some list."

"Enough to get us started, I believe."

"Enough to finish off Geelani, if we're lucky."

"And if not…" Sharma sat back and let the sentence trail away.

Bolan knew how the sergeant felt, ripped out of a career that felt secure and dropped into the middle of a private war with no way out, beyond the striking polar opposites of victory or death. He'd been a sergeant, too, with plans to make the military his career, when tragedy had torn his family apart and set him on a path of no return.

So that was life. You took what came and made the most of it, knowing that no one finished the race alive. You took the hurdles as they came and flattened those you couldn't negotiate by any other means.

There wasn't any manual on how to get it done.

The Executioner was writing his as he pressed on, one blood-spattered page at a time.

Chhatrapati Shivaji International Airport, Mumbai

SAYEED ZARGAR WAS nervous. Why deny it? In his mind, he had replayed his conversation with the Pakistani major time and time again, searching for hidden snares that might be laid to trap him. He could not imagine why Leghari would suggest a coup against Riyaz Geelani if he did not wish to see a change in G-troop's leadership, unless it was a test of Zargar's loyalty. But would Leghari join in the deception if Geelani had conceived the plan? It seemed a waste of time and energy for someone with the major's burden of responsibility.

Waiting on the tarmac for Geelani's private plane to finish taxiing along the shorter of the airport's two runways, Zargar attempted to compose himself. He'd brought four cars, as ordered, to receive Geelani and the bodyguards that he was bringing back from Pakistan, with extra men on hand in case their enemies were bold enough to stage a raid before they cleared the airport proper. Zargar, for his own part, was less worried about being shot by strangers than the fate that would be waiting for him if Geelani learned about his conversation with Leghari.

And if he already knew…then what?

To save himself, Zargar could blow the whistle on the Pakistani major, but to what result? If it had been a trap devised between Geelani and Leghari, any lie he told about rejecting the proposal would only enrage Geelani further. If the call *had been* a trap, then he—Zargar—had fallen headlong into it, and he was doomed.

Geelani's jet was off the runway now and rolling toward them on the taxiway, the shrill noise from its engines slowly winding down. Zargar stiffened his spine and squared his shoulders, making the most of his five-foot-six stature, putting on a face that mixed determination with a feigned relief at seeing his master return.

Meanwhile, his mind was churning with alternatives for taking out the boss.

It would be best for him, he had decided, if the blame should fall on someone else. Their unknown enemies made perfect scapegoats, but Zargar would have to watch his step in that regard. It would not do for him to kill Geelani and attempt to blame the faceless raiders, if they struck immediately after in Karachi or some other distant place.

Of course, by then Geelani would be dead, and if Zargar

could count on backing from Major Leghari, who would challenge him?

That question nagged at him. The answer: almost anyone, if he displayed a trace of weakness.

Now on top of everything, Zargar was forced to give Geelani more bad news. The word had come to him from Gujarat about the drug convoy. Geelani would have been airborne when the attack occurred. Hearing about the latest insult, and the massive loss of cash it represented, he was bound to be enraged. And, Zargar knew, the fact that *he* had no part in the new calamity might not protect him if Geelani felt an urge to kill the messenger.

In which case, the result would not be metaphorical.

Zargar had contemplated holding back the news until he had Geelani on the road home from the airport, thought perhaps he could ice the crime lord himself while they were rolling through the streets, but if Geelani had his watchdogs from Karachi in the car with them, the effort would be suicidal. Finally, he had decided to deliver the announcement on the taxiway, in broad daylight and full view of the airport's tower, hoping that Geelani would be less likely to kill him on the spot, in front of witnesses.

Less likely, but still not guaranteed.

The jet had stopped now, engines silent, and its wheels were being chocked as if the airport's staff was worried that a high wind might arise and send it rolling down the tarmac. Zargar waited for the door to open and the folding stairway to descend. A bodyguard or two would doubtless exit first, before Geelani showed his face.

Time dragged, as if the world around Zargar was all on film, and the projector had been switched to run in slow-motion. His heart, by contrast, beat so rapidly that he felt dizziness encroaching, until he forced himself to draw a

slow, deep breath and hold it, quieting his nerves by force
of will alone.

Another moment, and the worst would be behind him.

After that, he had a killing to arrange. An empire ready
for the taking.

Central Bureau of Investigation Headquarters, Mumbai

THE SPECIAL DEPUTY director stared into Patel's eyes, found
no mercy there, and glanced once more at Captain Ram's
limp corpse before he spoke again. "All right," he said.
"What is it that you wish to hear?"

"The truth," Patel replied. "All of it, from the day Geelani first corrupted you."

"Corrupted me?" Sherawat barked a ragged laugh. "You
think I was a saint before he came along?"

"At the beginning, then. Whoever turned you to a criminal."

Sherawat sighed, his shoulders slumped, but he was
careful not to move his hands from where they rested on
the desktop. Slowly, haltingly, he told the story of an up-
and-coming officer's decision that his salary would never
be enough to meet his needs, or those a younger wife imposed on him. He had begun by taking small payoffs, then
graduated to collaborating with one syndicate against its
rivals, earning money *and* advancement when the crime
lord of that day gave him information leading to spectacu-
lar arrests. Of course, they never fazed the gang that kept a
leash on Sherawat, but his superiors were satisfied with the
results in court—and with their share of his illicit bonuses.

In time, Geelani had deposed the mobster Sherawat was
working for, and they continued the arrangement. Sherawat received promotions through the ranks, until he finally ascended to the CBI's supreme position in Mumbai.

By then, in a position to decide which gangs received attention from police and which were left alone, he was a prized commodity—almost a member of the G-troop team in his own right. The tale he told would certainly imprison him as an accessory to countless felonies, if it were ever aired in court.

But that would never happen.

From the start, Patel had known that he could never use a word of Sherawat's confession without standing trial himself for homicide. A plea of self-defense would likely get him off the hook for the three shootings in Dharavi, but Kapil Ram's death was clear premeditated murder, under law. No matter if the captain was in league with criminals who wanted Patel dead.

But he had planned for that, as well.

The crime, he hoped, would not be laid at his doorstep.

When Sherawat completed his recital, silence stretched between them for a moment, and then the special deputy director said, "That's all. There is no more to say."

"It is enough," Patel replied.

He moved around the desk to stand at Sherawat's right side. The seated officer stared up at him and asked, "What now?"

"Nothing," Patel said as he brought the Walther's muzzle into skin-touch range and fired a single shot into Sherawat's temple.

The P-22 was an ideal assassin's weapon. It had no recoil to speak of, and its .22-caliber bullets rarely passed completely through a human skull. Instead, as in this case, they entered, then began to ricochet around inside the cranium, sometimes fragmenting in the process, turning gray matter into bloody Swiss cheese. Sherawat was probably dead before his forehead smacked the desktop between his splayed hands, but Patel checked his pulse nonetheless. He felt nothing underneath his probing fingertips.

All that remained, then, was to place the pistol into Sherawat's right hand, closing the still-pliable fingers around its cast polymer grip. They would stiffen in time, and even if the staged tableau failed to convince investigators absolutely, there was nothing in the office that should lead them to Patel.

He'd let them spin their wheels and ask their questions, turn headquarters upside down and inside out in search of answers. They would trace the murder weapon back to evidence storage, puzzling over Captain Ram's printed name in the logbook. When they finally discovered Major Yugandhar's body, the mystery would deepen. They would postulate conspiracies, chase each in turn, and in the process might discover—if, indeed, it was a secret—the connection of the three dead officers to G-troop. That might close the inquiry for fear of scandal, or it might result in some concerted action, at long last, against Riyaz Geelani.

Either way, unless he tipped his hand somehow through outright foolishness, Patel believed that he was in the clear.

Leaving the special deputy director's office, he took care to scan the corridor before emerging, walked past the elevator and descended to street level on the service stairs. Five minutes later, he was in his car, finally relaxing, peeling off the latex gloves and stuffing them into a pocket for later disposal.

Not certain, yet, if he was safe, at least Patel was satisfied to have his fate back in his own two hands.

Chhatrapati Shivaji International Airport, Mumbai

BOLAN WOUND UP paying Bharat Deshpande twice the sum they had agreed on, thereby guaranteeing that the pilot would be stricken with amnesia if police came asking questions in the next few hours. After that, Bolan supposed it wouldn't matter, either way. His time in India was winding down, the numbers falling in his head like the incessant ticking of a Doomsday clock, but there was still more work to do.

He would begin with Baji Sharma's latest list, raising sufficient hell for G-troop in Mumbai that no godfather worth his salt could fail to take the bait. Riyaz Geelani had to fight, or risk a loss of face so catastrophic that he would fall prey to every second-string pretender in the city—maybe even nationwide.

The Suzuki Liana was waiting where Bolan had left it, in long-term parking. He did a walk-around, saw nothing to suggest it had been tampered with since last he saw it, but he still maintained a healthy distance, Sharma at his side, when he unlocked its doors with the remote control. There was no blast, no ball of fire, so Bolan slid into the driver's seat and twisted the ignition key.

The final test.

A moment later they were rolling, paying the cashier, putting the airport's sprawl behind them, vanishing with other drivers into Mumbai's endless deluge of traffic. Bolan kept his eyes on the road and the Suzuki's mirrors, playing a defensive game against the kamikaze rush of motorcycles, minicars and overloaded buses, while his mind ran down the roster of potential targets.

They had missed closing time for Geelani's private bank, so that would have to wait until it opened the next morning, all things being equal. Like survival. Next up in his mind was the perverse facility Sharma had called Geelani's "breaking stable" for imported women snared by human trafficking. Bolan had no doubt what the *breaking* would involve—rape, torture, forced addiction to narcotics—and it sickened him. If he could crack that hellhole, punish those in charge and liberate its captives, that alone would be a victory of sorts.

Mumbai produced 33 percent of India's income tax revenue, 60 percent of the country's customs duty collection, 20 percent of its central excise collection, and 40 percent of its foreign trade. All that was on the record, without reckoning the profits from black-market trading and the underground economy that thrived in every major city of the world. Small wonder, then, that G-troop made the teeming, thriving city its headquarters, robbing rich and poor alike in countless ways.

Bolan had heard an old-school lawman say that he would tolerate one gang in any town, as long as they left "decent" citizens alone, but two gangs made things dangerous and ought to be suppressed. Bolan took the opposite view: *no* gang was good for anyone except the gangsters, and their crimes affected everyone, "decent" or otherwise. That was the credo that had set him on his lonely war against the Mafia, and G-troop's only difference, in Bolan's view, was its adoption of religious and political trappings.

Were homicidal fanatics truly religious? Bolan wasted no time pondering the question, which was meaningless to him. A felon's motives could be useful in determining his moves. Beyond that, Bolan didn't care if he—or she— was Christian, Muslim, Sikh, whatever. He had zero interest in a killer's history of child abuse or pampering, his mental illness or his topflight grades in school, his love of animals or hatred for his parents.

Mobsters were terrorists, by definition. Terrorists were predatory scum. The only language that they understood was violence, and Bolan spoke it fluently.

Another lesson for the human monsters was coming up.

CHAPTER FIFTEEN

Siddharth Nagar, Mumbai

Another night, another warehouse. This one stood on Worli Hill Road, sandwiched between two factories with stark, graffiti-scarred facades, closed now. Whatever they produced was manufactured during normal twelve-hour workdays, by employees earning less than minimum wage. The warehouse dealt in misery. It never closed, and no one could attach a price tag to the suffering it caused.

Riyaz Geelani's "breaking stable" was another target that required deft handling. Most of those inside it would be victims, trapped in different stages of enforced conditioning to serve Geelani and his pimps as human livestock, until their failing health and physical appearance rendered them unpalatable for the flesh trade. After that, dismissal from the captive ranks by one means or another, either buried in a shallow grave or dying on the heartless streets alone, used up, unrecognizable to families that mourned their disappearance.

Bolan seldom acted out of anger—knew, in fact, that yielding to emotion was a common soldier's downfall—but abuse of women and children sparked a fierce, slow-burning rage inside of him that only blood could quench.

They parked up range, along an access road between a railway line and the factory north of their target. Bolan was dressed to kill, the 40 mm Milkor launcher slung across his back, the INSAS autorifle in his hands. Beside him, Baji Sharma held his AK-47, with the Mini-Uzi underneath his right arm, its sling across his chest. They jogged through darkness past the silent factory to reach a fence surrounding G-troop's little patch of Hell on Earth, chain-link with coils of razor wire on top.

The topping didn't bother Bolan. Plying wire cutters, he opened up a flap at ground level and wriggled through, with Sharma close behind him. They made no attempt to hide the access hatch, since there were no lookouts in evidence, and any whom they met along the way were marked for death.

Beginning with the young guy Bolan saw emerging from the back door of the warehouse when they'd closed to twenty yards. He blinked at them, seemed stupefied by what he saw, then took the silenced round from Bolan's pistol through his forehead, dropping like a sack of dirty laundry to the garbage-littered ground. Behind his prostrate corpse, the door stood open, welcoming the Executioner inside.

The atmosphere of dread within that house of pain and sheer perversity was palpable. Somewhere ahead of Bolan, moaning issued from behind a padlocked door. Sobbing was audible from farther down the hall, mingled with mocking laughter. Over all, a show tune out of Bollywood jangled and jived from speakers mounted in the ceiling overhead. A burst from Bolan's autorifle shattered one of them and cut the laughter short, replaced it with the sound of scrambling feet and shouted warnings.

"Here we go," he said, raising the INSAS to his shoulder. They'd already talked about the risk of bullets penetrating walls and finding helpless targets on the other side. He trusted Sharma's marksmanship and his ability to judge a shot without losing his head.

Two half-dressed men spilled from a room on Bolan's right, halfway along the corridor. He caught one struggling with a pistol and the zipper on his pants, put two rounds through his sweaty chest, and was already tracking toward the other as the dying rapist fell. Sharma was on it with the AK-47, picking off the second guy with one clean shot that sheared off half his skull and left him gaping at his killers with the one eye he had left, before he dropped.

They moved on through the warehouse, which had been converted into something like a barracks, opening the doors they could, passing by those with padlocks on them for the moment. Halfway down the hall, another door popped open to disgorge a pair of figures locked in an embrace. One was a wild-eyed man, clutching a naked woman as a human shield, holding a pistol to her head. He shouted something Bolan didn't understand. Sharma was about to answer him when Bolan fired a single shot over the woman's shoulder, ending it. The corpse and sobbing captive fell together, Sharma rushing forward in a crouch to separate them, while Bolan watched his back.

That was the end of it, as far as fighting went. The four goons they had killed appeared to be the night shift at Riyaz Geelani's nigthmare factory. The rest came down to clearing rooms, blasting the padlocks off doors, telling the victims they found huddled in their cells that help was on the way. One room turned out to be a closet for supplies, ranging from whips and chains to normal cleaning products—and a can of red spray paint.

"You want to mark it?" Bolan asked.

"I do," Sharma replied, and took the can from Bolan. Moments later, he had sprayed the corridor's west wall with dripping letters four feet high.

"I recognize Geelani's name," Bolan observed, "but what's the rest of it?"

"A comment on his parentage," Sharma replied. "I should apologize to pigs and goats for the comparison."

"I think they'll let it go this time," Bolan said as they passed into the night.

A siren sounded as they walked back to their car, followed by yet another, and another. Flashing lights were visible in Bolan's rearview mirror as they pulled away, seeking another target in the neon night.

Malabar Hill, Mumbai

THE HOUSE NO longer felt like home. Riyaz Geelani moved through rooms where he had dined and entertained, schemed and conspired, made love after his fashion— and it all seemed alien to him somehow. The palace that had cost him so much to acquire, then renovate, felt like a stranger's house, no longer someplace where he could relax and be at peace.

There was a target on his back, invisible to normal eyes, but he could feel it like a fresh tattoo on tender flesh. There was no safety for him in Mumbai—or anywhere on Earth, it seemed—and would not be until he crushed his enemies, leaving their corpses in the street as an example to his would-be rivals in the city and across the country. Only thus could he restore Major Leghari's failing confidence and guarantee continuing support from Pakistan.

Without that vital link, what would become of him?

Geelani, like all other criminals, concerned himself primarily with Number One. And like successful mobsters everywhere, he had a sharp nose for betrayal. That might be too strong a term for the aroma he had picked up from Sayeed Zargar, but there was *something* in his chief lieutenant's attitude, behind his shifty eyes.

What was it?

Why not ask? Sayeed would lie, of course, if he was guilty. Still…

He'd been distracted at the airport, by the crushing news about his drug convoy. It was, if not a crippling loss, then certainly a major one. The tons of drugs, which he had paid for in advance, were gone forever, with his trucks, two SUVs and twenty-six more soldiers he could ill afford to lose. Beyond all that, the damage to Geelani's reputation was incalculable. He supposed Leghari had to have been informed by now, and would be reconsidering the future of his agency's collaboration with G-troop.

But if there was a traitor close to him, perhaps Sayeed Zargar himself, it might explain the troubles that had plagued Geelani for the past two days and counting.

Who had been in charge of grilling the suspected spy? *Sayeed.*

Who had coordinated efforts to recapture him and to identify his friend? *Sayeed.*

Who had been spared, thus far, while killers stalked Geelani from Mumbai to Pakistan and back again? *Sayeed.*

Who always brought bad news, these days, and could not solve the simplest problem for their crime family?

"Sayeed!" he bellowed from his office, through its open door. "Come here!"

Three long minutes later, there he was, a skulking figure on the threshold. "Yes, sir?"

"I want you to reach out," Geelani ordered, "to our major at the CBI. Yugandhar."

Barely audible, Sayeed replied, "He's disappeared, sir."

"What do you mean, he's disappeared?"

"Missing. No one can find him. They've begun a search, I understand."

"And you've just thought to tell me this?"

"I didn't think—"

"Go up the chain, then," Geelani said, interrupting him. "The deputy director. Call his private line and tell him that I wish to speak with him, immediately."

"As you wish."

Zargar was gone for ten long minutes, then returned, his face ashen as he stepped into Geelani's office.

"Well? Where's the telephone?"

"The deputy director cannot speak to you, sir."

"Cannot? Cannot! I want him on the phone *right now!*"

"He's dead. A suicide, they say, after he shot another officer at headquarters."

Riyaz Geelani felt the floor tilt underneath his feet. He stagger-walked around his desk and dropped into its swivel chair, a step or two before he might have fallen.

"Suicide? A murder-suicide?"

Zargar managed to nod and shrug at the same time. "It's what they say, sir. No doubt, they will investigate."

Geelani swore. "All right. The captain, then. Kapil Ram."

"I am sorry, Riyaz, but—"

"Sorry? Sorry for what? Just make the call!"

"I cannot. Captain Ram…he is the officer killed by Director Sherawat."

Geelani roared and bolted from his chair, rushing around his desk with both fists raised above his head. Zargar stood waiting for the storm to strike him down, his eyes closed, but something in his attitude compelled the crime lord to stop.

"Get out," Geelani ordered, finally. "Go on. You're useless to me. I'll take care of this myself."

Riyaz Geelani barely registered the closing of his office door.

Byculla, Mumbai

THE CHOP SHOP, known as Mumbai Motor Madness, stood on Hansraj Lane, in shadow of the A. Patil Flyover. That freeway flowed with traffic day and night. None of its harried, preoccupied drivers could see through the rooftops below, cloaked in darkness. None knew or cared what happened there.

Compared to Bolan's last stop on the hellfire trail, this target was innocuous. Its staff received an endless stream of cars and trucks from thieves, recycled some with new vehicle identification numbers for selected buyers and stripped the rest for parts. It was a thriving business which, at least in theory, harmed no one who had bothered to insure their vehicles. It was a G-troop moneymaker, to the estimated tune of six or seven million U.S. dollars yearly.

That made it worthy of the Executioner's attention. Anything to hit Riyaz Geelani where it hurt him most.

At half past nine o'clock, the place was busy. Bolan counted four men working on a slate-gray BMW sedan, three more dismantling a green Mahindra Scorpio. From where he stood in outer darkness, he could also see a small-ish, glassed-in office space, where one man sat behind a desk, conversing with another parked in front of it.

"I make it nine," he said, "if no one's in the john."

"The john?" Sharma inquired.

"The head, loo, water closet. Take your pick."

"Ah, yes."

"You say they're all G-troop?"

"They are. It guarantees their silence under paramilitary discipline."

And sealed their fate, as far as Bolan was concerned.

"Okay, gloves off," he said. "Let's go."

Bolan led with the Milkor MGL, launching a high-explosive round from thirty yards out. It sailed in through the chop shop's broad open door and hit the BMW nose-on, detonating with a crack of smoky thunder inside the garage. Two of the G-troop mechanics were instantly airborne, one striking the nearest wall in a spread-eagle crucifixion pose, another one somersaulting into collision with a tall tool chest on wheels. Two others simply vanished in the smoke and flames erupting from the shattered luxury sedan, but Bolan heard them screaming in the midst of the inferno.

His second HE canister was on its way before the first exploded, this one taking out the office cubicle. It may have detonated when it smashed the office window or on impact with the boss's desk. In either case, it had the same effect, delivering hellfire on target and obliterating two more of Riyaz Geelani's men. Killed instantly, or slowly dying in the wreckage, they were no longer a threat.

They had almost reached the shop, ten yards and closing, when he fired a third round, this one toward the partly stripped Mahindra Scorpio. The three mechanics working on it had already started running for their lives, straight into Sharma's line of fire, and his Kalashnikov was hacking pieces off them when Bolan's final HE round exploded, taking out the car that they'd been working on.

Then, it was over, and the only sounds remaining were the crackling of the hungry flames that spread from leaking gasoline tanks, and the endless hum of traffic passing overhead, along the A. Patil Flyover. Bolan didn't know if any of the drivers passing by up there had seen the short engagement, or if they were checking out the fire right now, reaching for cell phones to report it. He and Sharma had accomplished what they'd come to do, and it was time to go.

On to the next target in line, rattling Geelani's cage until the Mumbai mobster couldn't take it anymore and he was pushed into a corner. He would either come out fighting, then, or go to ground and hope the storm would pass him by. Whichever course he chose, Mack Bolan would be ready for him.

He was looking forward to the final confrontation, when Geelani's private army had been beaten down and broken up, ranks decimated, useless to the next godfather rising up the food chain. That there'd be another was unquestioned. Human predators, unlike some valuable species in the realm of nature, never faced extinction.

Bolan had to keep on killing them, one jackal at a time.

Girgaum Chowpatty, Mumbai

CAPTAIN VIVAK PATEL did not go home from CBI headquarters. There was still a decent chance, he realized, the G-troop gunmen might be waiting for him there, still acting on directions from the enemies he had eliminated. On the other hand, when members of the office cleaning crew found Sherawat and Ram, then called detectives to the scene, he did not wish to be sitting alone, at home.

Patel required an alibi.

The timing was not perfect, granted, but he headed for Chowpatty Beach, one of the top attractions in Mumbai for tourists and fun-loving locals alike. Accessible twenty-four hours a day, brightly lit after sundown, the beach was a magnet for families, young dating couples and insomniacs who hoped that walking on the sand or mingling with the crowds would ultimately tire them to the point of blessed sleep.

Patel parked his car along Marine Drive, near the bronze statue erected to Officer Tukaram Omble, the policeman who had captured Ajmal Kasab—last surviving terrorist from the attacks conducted on November 26, 2008—near that very spot.

Chowpatty Beach was crowded, as Patel expected. As he'd hoped. He moved among the masses, watching children at their pony rides, hearing the music and cries of mock terror from huge Ferris wheels. Chowpatty's air was not the freshest, nor its surf particularly clean, but it was free of litter thanks to the custodians on round-the-clock patrol, well lit and staffed with lifeguards day and night.

Patel sought out a pair of them and struck up idle conversation, making sure to introduce himself by name while learning theirs, flashing his badge and spinning tales of his assignment to review security procedures on the beach. They would remember him when he was hauled in for interrogation about Sherawat and Ram, confirming Patel's presence on the beach. The timing would not be precise, of course, but it was still better than nothing.

From the lifeguard stand, he moved on down the beach, past food stalls selling *aloo tikki, panipuri, bhelpuri,* and *pav bhaji.* Performing monkeys capered for the crowd and snatched their coins, beside a skeletal contortionist who made a pretzel of himself. Far down the beach, the lights and cameras of a film crew were recording some dramatic scene while hundreds of spectators stood by, gawking from the sidelines.

Surprised to find he had an appetite, Patel purchased a serving of *bhelpuri* and strolled on toward the movie shoot, devouring savory mouthfuls of the hot puffed rice and *sev* noodles mixed with potatoes, onions, *chaat masala* spice and chutney. He would buy a cola when he finished to cool his palate, but at the moment, he enjoyed the heat upon his tongue and coursing down his throat.

While walking through the crowd, Patel remained alert for any sign that he was being followed. It was possible that someone could have trailed him from headquarters to the beach, although he'd taken every feasible precaution to prevent it. He wore his Smith & Wesson M&P service pistol in its normal holster, on his belt, beneath a lightweight sport coat. The jacket would have made him stand out on the beach in daylight, but at night, with cool winds wafting inshore from the Arabian Sea, it was not out of place. In fact, except where Patel paused to introduce himself deliberately, no one had given him a second glance.

How long should he remain there, going through the motions of a man relaxing after one more normal day at work? Patel supposed he might start homeward around midnight, making sure to leave his car littered with evidence of time spent on the beach—his paper plate, a soft drink cup bearing the logo of its vendor, possibly a ticket stub from riding on the Ferris wheel. It wasn't much, in terms of evidence per se, but he'd left nothing to incriminate him at the double murder scene or at the site where he had killed Major Yugandhar earlier. Let the investigators try to build a case against him if they could, without exposing the corruption of the three dead officers.

And if he found G-troop assassins waiting for him at his flat? What then?

Worry about that if it happens, Patel thought.

He had already proved that they were not invincible, and an attempt upon his life might actually help his case, divert suspicion to Riyaz Geelani's syndicate.

Meanwhile, Patel decided, he would do his utmost to enjoy himself.

Why not, if it turned out to be his final night on earth?

Mulund West, Mumbai

JUMADI TRUCKING OPERATED from a spacious lot on Devi Dayal Road, in the Meghal Industrial Estate. While they were driving over to its site, Sharma explained the choice of names. Jumadi—also known to some as Dhumavathi—was a hermaphroditic Hindu deity who wore a crown of hissing snakes and was best known for vanquishing the cannibal demon Dhumasura, slayer of countless humans. Bolan didn't take the story seriously, but he caught the irony in that Jumadi Trucking made a fortune for Riyaz Geelani by illegally dumping toxic waste in close proximity to human habitation.

That kind of subversive pollution for profit was practiced worldwide, but had become a special scourge in India on several fronts. Some of it was accidental—the garbage, military waste and other jetsam of neighboring countries washing ashore on the Indian coastline—while European nations had also begun shipping poisonous, inflammable refuse to India in containers falsely labeled for recycled plastic or newsprint. India's own industries also produced their share of lethal byproducts, which firms like Jumadi Trucking were happy to dump around slums, rural hamlets or off in some nature preserve.

What did Geelani care about pollution, cancer, birth defects or the extinction of endangered species? Nothing, if a violation of the law put money in his pocket.

But this night, he was about to lose another hefty chunk of change.

Bolan and Sharma scouted the Jumadi lot and found a solitary watchman making lazy circuits of the property, checking the gate and fence approximately once per hour. When he'd gone back to his shack, the latest round completed, and returned to watching television, Bolan used his wire cutters to breach the fence out back and slipped inside. Sharma was at his shoulder when they rushed the guard shack, caught the lookout by surprise and punched his ticket with a silent round from Bolan's pistol.

After that, it was a turkey shoot. Jumadi Trucking had

a fleet of vehicles including two large tankers and three smaller ones, five dump trucks, two flatbeds and two road-weary cargo vans, lined up in tidy ranks that took up two-thirds of the property. A smallish office sat to one side, closed now, with a dim light burning somewhere in a back room, sitting idle overnight.

The company's last night.

Standing well back from the assembled trucks and vans, Bolan unleashed his Milkor MGL, firing incendiary rounds among the vehicles while Baji Sharma strafed their fuel tanks with his AK-47, 3- and 4-round bursts unleashing small cascades of gasoline to feed the spreading flames. Before the two weapons were empty, they had spread a searing lake of fire, more than one hundred feet across, that fed on fumes, on melting rubber tires and on the vehicles themselves. Dense smoke rose to the sky, more poison, bringing unintended tears to Bolan's smarting eyes, while heat from the expanding firestorm baked his face.

He left the small office intact, deliberately, trusting that its safe and filing cabinets would hold some evidence connecting G-troop to Jumadi Trucking. What police might do with that was up to them, but even if it only tickled the imagination of reporters in Mumbai, they would have struck a double blow against Geelani and his outlaw family. Each blow delivered would be felt, would resonate, and force Geelani that much closer to his breaking point.

How soon?

Bolan had never been a fortune-teller, but he had enough experience with terrorists and mobsters to predict reactions with a fair degree of accuracy. They preferred to play offense, and soon lost confidence when they were being hammered by aggressive adversaries, losing soldiers, property and profits to an enemy they couldn't corner and control. Worst of all was losing face, an injury that hit them where they lived, wounding their egos *and* making them vulnerable to attack by smaller jealous rivals.

On their jog back to the rental car, Bolan was thinking through his next strike, and the next one after that. The secret to a blitzkrieg was incessant forward motion, one relentless hit after another, until the enemy lost confidence and finally collapsed, or else rallied his final ounce of strength for a futile counterattack. On paper, the odds still favored G-troop, and it only took one shooter, one clean shot, to end the Executioner's campaign, but no one in Mumbai had dealt with anyone like Bolan in the past.

He wasn't finished yet, but he was getting there.

CHAPTER SIXTEEN

Malabar Hill, Mumbai

The plan had struck Riyaz Geelani in the middle of the night, as bad and worse news kept arriving via telephone. Sometime around midnight, trapped in a waking nightmare that appeared to have no resolution, he conceived the scheme that might, if he was lucky, salvage the remainder of his crime family.

Instead of waiting for his enemies to strike at will, adopting a reactive posture that had proven weak and ineffective, he would go on the attack. Granted, he did not know his foes by name, would not have recognized them if they passed him on the street, and could not find them to deliver anything resembling a death blow—but he *could* do something else. The thing that he did best.

Attack the so-called "innocents."

Geelani was Mumbai's "most wanted" fugitive, at least on paper, due to acts of random terrorism he had carried out for Major Ibrahim Leghari and his Pakistani paymasters. What better to divert police and media attention from his present difficulties, while impressing those who might decide that he was weak enough to challenge, than by lashing out once more against Mumbai itself?

His last attack had fallen during Maha Shivaratri. Now it was almost time for Holi, the Hindu festival of colors, also known to some as Phagwah or Dol Jatra. The festival celebrated spring's arrival, while commemorating the legendary incineration of the demoness Holika in a contest with her brother, Prahlada. During the festivities, celebrants sprinkled each other with perfumed water and smeared one another with brightly colored powders, representing the bounty of spring. At midnight, on the last full moon of Phalguna, bonfires of fallen leaves and dead wood simulate Holika's death.

This year, Geelani thought, he would provide a very different flame.

Excited now, he left his office, roaming through the mansion, shouting for Sayeed Zargar until his chief lieutenant suddenly appeared beside him, anxious looking, as if he had sprung from nowhere. Was he fidgeting, or was Geelani's own excitement skewing his perception?

Never mind.

"I have decided on what must be done," he told Zargar.

"Indeed, sir?"

Geelani hastily described his plan, inserting details as they came to him. He sketched the chaos he intended to create, the possibility that Hindus, once inflamed, would strike at Muslims, causing deeper rifts between the two hostile communities. The DISI would be pleased as well to see the campaign carried through at no expense to them.

"Have you informed them of your plan, sir?" Zargar inquired.

Geelani stared at Sayeed as if he had lost his mind. "You think I need *permission* to kill Hindus in Mumbai? You think Leghari and the others won't be *thrilled* to see those headlines? That they won't be *grateful* for us taking the initiative?"

"Perhaps, sir. But in the past, have not the plans originated on their side?"

Geelani felt his cheeks warming again, but with resentment now. "You think we are their puppets, only moving as directed? Do we not control our destinies, Sayeed?"

"Of course. I only meant—"

"I will *inform* Major Leghari of my plan. I will not go to him with hat in hand, pleading for his support. If he serves Allah ardently, he will embrace our offering with gratitude."

Zargar nodded, left with no choice but to agree.

"We're in agreement, then," Geelani said, not asking him. "The preparations must begin at once, for time is short. When they assemble and begin to sprinkle one other with their pagan ointments, we must be on hand to paint them red with blood."

"Sir, our men—"

"What of them?"

"I've dispersed them as you ordered, seeking out our enemies," Zargar replied.

"And you will leave them to it," Geelani said. "All that I require for what I have in mind is eight or nine committed soldiers. If you can't select them, I will do the job myself."

"Of course, sir, you may rely on me, as always."

"May I?"

Something flickered in the depths of Zargar's eyes before he bowed his head and said, "I swear it."

"Then be quick about it. Eight or nine, no more. And since the celebration ends with fire, we should accommodate the ritual."

"Sir?"

"Isn't it obvious? In Pakistan, the enemy employed a flamethrower against our poppy farm. Why not return the favor now, in honor of their festival?"

"I don't believe we have any, sir."

"I'm thinking of the M202A1 FLASH," Geelani said, displaying his familiarity with military hardware. "Shoulder-launched, four barrels loaded with triethylaluminum incendiary rockets. If we have none on hand, check the National Security Guard arsenal in Marol."

"I'll see to it."

"Be quick about it. Great things lie in store for us," Geelani said, "once we assert ourselves."

Nariman Point, Mumbai

DAYBREAK STRIPPED MUCH of the color from Mumbai, dousing the neon, switching off the headlights on bustling vehicles, casting a gray blanket over the city before full sunlight arrived to glint off chrome and mirrored glass. There was a lull of sorts in commerce—or as close as Mumbai ever came to one—before the city awoke to start another day.

Nariman Point was the city's premier business district and India's first recognized central business district, the throbbing financial heart of a great metropolis. It stood on land reclaimed from Back Bay, available for rent for a modest $2,500 per square foot. As of 2012, it ranked as the fourth most expensive office market in the world.

In short, it was the perfect place to tuck away a private bank that laundered dirty cash.

Such banks might operate at night, if an emergency arose for the owners, but they otherwise adhered to the city's leisurely banking schedule, open to walk-in customers between 10:00 a.m. and 3:00 p.m. That meant a wait for Bolan, since he didn't plan to crack the bank at night, defeating various alarms and dodging SWAT teams in the process.

To fill the time, he'd taken Baji Sharma on a visit to the Ranganatha Taxi Company—another of Riyaz Geelani's fronts named for a Hindu deity, in this case the resting form of Lord Vishnu. Bolan was mildly curious about Geelani, a devout and militant Muslim, naming companies after the gods and demons of a rival creed that he despised, but he supposed it finally came down to simple marketing.

There'd been no gods in evidence when they'd arrived at Ranganatha Taxi, turning half a dozen idle drivers out at gunpoint, leaving the dispatcher with a message for Geelani as they turned a dozen taxis into smoking scrap iron. And the message was simplicity itself: *You're running out of time.*

They'd stopped for breakfast at a coffee shop on Dinshaw Vacha Road, where Bolan ate a paneer sandwich, with a side order of *aloo poha,* rice with potatoes and green chilis. Washed down with strong black coffee, it filled him up and fired him up for their adventure in high finance.

In the background, while they ate, a television news program regaled the diner's patrons with a litany of violence that had erupted overnight. Police were not prepared to call it terrorism, though some links had been discovered to notorious crime lord Riyaz Geelani. In other news, the special deputy director of the CBI had killed one of the captains under his command and then committed suicide. A major from the agency was missing, present whereabouts unknown.

Sharma had listened closely to the latter item, visibly relieved when he discovered that the captain shot was not his own. Beyond that, he could offer nothing in the way of explanation for the killings, since he'd been away from headquarters for weeks on end.

They were outside the Narayana Trading Bank, when its doors opened for the day, each carrying an empty leather satchel they had purchased overnight. The lobby guard gave them some attitude, then backed off after Bolan asked to see the manager. That brought them to a pudgy, balding man who made up for his lack of hair on top by cultivating sideburns that connected with a stiffly waxed mustache. He introduced himself as Andaram Barooah and inquired about their business.

"We're withdrawing our entire account," Bolan replied.

That left the banker flummoxed. "I'm afraid there has been some mistake," he said. "I am acquainted personally with our various depositors, and yet…"

"Riyaz Geelani sent us," Sharma said.

The banker's eyebrows rose. "Indeed? You won't mind if I contact him at home to verify—"

"That won't be necessary," Bolan said, drawing his jacket open just enough to show the pistol holstered there.

"A robbery? If this is meant to be a joke—"

"See if Geelani's laughing when you tell him later," Bolan said. "Right now you need to fill these bags with cash. Stick to the big bills, nothing smaller than a thousand rupees."

"But—"

"You've stalled us long enough," Bolan said, then he caught a flicker in the banker's eyes, glancing across his shoulder.

Turning in a single fluid motion, pistol leaping to his hand, he caught the lobby guard advancing toward him with an awkward, semistealthy stride. The guy was reaching for a hidden weapon, but the single muted shot from Bolan's pistol stopped him, opening a keyhole in his forehead, snuffing out his life.

A teller squealed as the dead man collapsed and Sharma rushed to silence her and prevent her from triggering any alarms. The banker gaped at him, dumbstruck, until Bolan poked him with the sound suppressor and said, "The cash. Right now."

"Of c-c-course!" the banker stammered. "This way, if you please!"

High Street Phoenix Mall, Lower Patel, Mumbai

CAPTAIN VIVAK PATEL believed he understood, at last, the title of a novel he had read long years ago, by Thomas Wolfe: *You Can't Go Home Again.* He'd tried, in fact, after a long night on Chowpatty Beach, only to find a carload full of gunmen waiting on the street outside his flat. Not CBI, as he had half expected, but a clutch of G-troop goons.

So, here he was, on Senapati Bapat Marg, losing himself among the several thousand shoppers crowding High Street Phoenix Mall. The place had started life as Phoenix Mills, more than one hundred years ago, producing cotton textiles. After fire swept through the plant, back in the latter 1970s, its owners redeveloped it as a twenty-eight-story residential tower, gradually adding on a bowling alley, restaurants and nightclubs, and a major bank. Finally, in 2007, Shangri-La Hotels and Resorts had teamed with the Phoenix founding family to build a five-star hotel, followed in turn by ritzy shops that occupied the mall's justly famous Skyzone shopping space.

It was the perfect place for hiding in plain sight, if a person was on the dodge.

But how long could it last?

Patel had thought about returning to his office, waiting to be called in for interrogation, serving up his alibi and hoping for the best. But after seeing that his flat had been staked out by G-troop killers, it occurred to him that he would not be safe at headquarters or even in protective custody. He had drawn up a mental list of people he could trust, and it had not turned out to be a list at all.

One name. His sergeant, Baji Sharma.

What bitter—or delicious—irony that was! The man whom he had sent to infiltrate G-troop, who'd almost lost his life and then turned rogue, was now the only person in Mumbai who might be able to assist Patel.

In doing what? After examining his options, it appeared that he could only hope to live if he escaped the city, and perhaps from India itself.

Could Sharma help him? Would he even try? The possibility was tantalizing, partially supported by the strange alliance Sharma had developed with the unidentified American—or was he European?—who had joined him in his raids against Riyaz Geelani's syndicate. If he could plead his case to them, convince them to assist him, there might be a chance for Patel to move on, leave the disaster of his present life behind and start afresh.

He had some cash laid by, though not as much as a corrupt policeman would have saved. If he was cautious, he could check in and collect it from the bank that morning, have it ready if and when he found the opportunity to run. He'd leave in the clothes that he was wearing, and forget about the rest of his belongings. He owned nothing in the world that was worth dying for.

The problem, now, was how to get in touch with Sharma, when Patel had promised not to call again. Unless the sergeant still retained the cell phone they had spoken on before, his plan was doomed from the beginning. If that proved to be the case, Patel would take it as a sign and...what? Surrender? Find Geelani on his own and put a bullet in the gangster's head, before his bodyguards could open fire. Go out in a blaze of Bollywood glory.

Patel entered the mall's food court and found an empty

table well removed from the assorted take-out serving lines. He sat, back to a wall so no one could surprise him, opened up the prepaid cell phone he had purchased on arrival at the shopping center, hesitated with it in his hand and then began to tap out the number he had memorized for Baji Sharma.

If there was no answer, he could always try Plan B.

The phone rang twice, then a familiar voice responded. *"Namaste?"*

Malabar Hill, Mumbai

STEALING A MOMENT to himself was risky for Sayeed Zargar. He had obeyed Riyaz Geelani's order, calling back a handful of selected soldiers from their efforts to locate the enemies of G-troop in Mumbai, assigning them to plan the strike Geelani had commanded for the Holi festival, but now he had to warn Major Leghari of what he believed could be disaster in the making.

Not that the idea of killing more Hindus repulsed Sayeed; far from it. No, it was the thought of acting without sanction or support from DISI headquarters that made him think Geelani might have lost his mind. Leghari and his agency had sponsored each and every one of G-troop's terrorist attacks around Mumbai so far, and lashing out with no support from Pakistan—no place to run if it went wrong—impressed Zargar as something close to madness.

He was calling from a bathroom in the mansion, with the door locked, standing in the shower with its frosted glass door closed, hearing the phone ring in Islamabad, a thousand miles away. If he was overheard by chance, in spite of his precautions...

"Salaam," the major's voice cut in on Zargar's racing thoughts.

"Hello! This is—"

"No names." Leghari cut him off. "I recognize your voice."

"I need to warn you of a difficulty, sir."

"Why are you whispering?"

"Security. I am at *his* house."

"Very well. Proceed."

Zargar rushed through a brief description of Geelani's plan, remembering to quote his boasts of independence from Major Leghari and his agency's support, making his case in no uncertain terms. There was a risk, he understood, that DISI headquarters might welcome the attack, although they had not planned it. If that proved to be the case—

"And he means to go ahead with this...how soon, again?"

"The day after tomorrow, sir."

Leghari swore profusely, surprising Zargar with the outburst.

Regaining his composure in an instant, he said, "It seems that he's forgotten my instructions."

"Or ignores them," Zargar said, twisting the knife.

"Worse yet."

"If you would like me to eliminate the problem..."

"Don't be hasty. There is time for me to reach you, yet, before he ruins everything."

Zargar was taken by surprise at that. "You're coming here, sir?"

"It seems I have no choice. Hold on." The line hummed for a full half minute, Zargar trembling from the fear that he would be discovered, and then Leghari's voice came back. "I will be there this afternoon, connecting through Karachi. PIA Flight 274."

"Should I be there to meet the plane?" Zargar inquired.

"Too dangerous," Leghari said. "I would prefer to let my visit come as a surprise."

"Of course, sir," Zargar replied, trying to mask his own relief. "Just as you say."

"I shall be coming with assistance. Be prepared to find a resolution for our difficulty."

"I am ready."

"In the meantime, go along with the existing plan, but stop short of initiating any action."

"As you wish, sir."

Then a *click,* and he was gone. Sayeed closed his cell phone, returned it to his pocket as he stepped out of the shower. He flushed the toilet, just in case someone was passing by to hear it, and went on to wash his hands. Emerging from the bathroom, he found no one in the hall, but did not feel the least bit foolish.

It was life or death, the game he begun behind Riyaz Geelani's back, and it would only end when one of them was dead. Now that he had Major Leghari on his side, Zargar felt that his chances had improved tremendously, but victory was still not guaranteed. One clumsy slipup could defeat him, wipe him off the map. From now until Leghari landed in Mumbai, Zargar had to be on guard and give no indication of his planned revolt against Geelani.

Where would he be this time tomorrow? Either in command of G-troop, on the run or decomposing in a shallow grave. Major Leghari's personal support was critical, but in his present mental state, Geelani might lash out at both of them. It would be no great consolation, then, to know that agents from Islamabad would ultimately take him down.

What good would that be to the late Sayeed Zargar?

He had to be prepared for anything, be ready to strike first if it appeared Geelani was about to spring a trap.

And afterward—if he was still alive—there would be time enough to measure his rewards.

Khar West, Mumbai

"NAMASTE?"

"Sergeant! Are you in Mumbai?"

The voice, the question, came as a surprise to Baji Sharma. "Captain?"

"I was worried that I might not reach you," Vivak Patel said.

Sharma felt Matt Cooper watching him as he replied, "You weren't supposed to call again and put yourself at risk."

"It is too late to think of that," Patel said. "Possibly, you've heard about the deputy director's murder-suicide?"

"I have. And Major Yugandhar has disappeared, they say."

"They'll get to him eventually," Patel answered, cryptically. "It seems that all of them were working for Geelani."

"You've confirmed it?"

"From their own lips," Patel said.

Sharma began to understand. "Where are you, Captain?"

"Shopping," Patel answered, with a snort of laughter. "It's supposed to be relaxing."

Sharma glanced at Cooper and took a chance, asking his captain, "Is there some way I can help you?"

Patel was silent for a moment, then replied, "The only hope I see is getting out of India."

"Where would you go?"

"Away. There's been no time to think that far ahead."

"And are you ready now?"

"Not quite. I could be in an hour. Maybe less."

"Hold on." Sharma turned to the tall American. "My captain," he explained.

"I gathered that," Cooper said.

"The news we saw, about the deputy director of the CBI? He is involved with that, somehow."

"And?"

"Is it possible for us—for *you*—to help him flee the country?"

Cooper considered it, frowning. "I'd have to make some calls. No promises right now."

"How long?" Sharma asked.

"Thirty minutes, say, to find out if it's feasible. To make it work, I couldn't say. It won't depend on me."

"You'll try, though?"

Cooper returned his glance and asked the same thing that he had last time. "You trust him not to set us up?"

"I do."

"Okay. I'll try."

Sharma lifted the cell phone to his ear again. "Captain?"

"I'm here."

"Give me your number and I'll call back. Half an hour, more or less."

He listened, memorized the number Patel gave him, said goodbye and cut the link.

"I'll need some details," Cooper suggested.

"After the attempt to kill him in Dharavi, it appears that he identified some officers collaborating with Gee-lani. Now they've been eliminated."

"He did that?"

"He didn't say, exactly. But I think so, yes."

"So, now he's on the run?"

"Or should be. From his tone, I think he is resigned to anything that happens next."

"And he wouldn't sell you out to save himself?"

"It wouldn't help him anyway, if my suspicions are correct. Granted, there's only been one execution of a prisoner condemned since 1995, but he would not survive in prison with Geelani and the guards against him."

"All right," Cooper replied. "I'll see what I can do, but as I said, no promises. We're strictly off the books here, and it's probable nobody wants to get involved with any part of it."

"I understand."

Cooper drove another block, then pulled into the parking lot beside a Chinese restaurant, no customers this early in the day. He switched off the Suzuki's engine, took the sat phone from beneath his seat, tapped in a string of numbers and began to speak almost immediately. Sharma had no choice but to eavesdrop on Cooper's side of the conversation, gaining precious little from it as he spoke in neutral tones, explaining details of the situation to some person on the other end. At last, he said, "Okay… I'll try that… No… That's right… He understands… Later."

Sharma waited, half afraid to ask the verdict.

"I've got someone running interference with the U.S. consulate," Cooper said, "here in Mumbai. Don't get your hopes up. Taking in a refugee is one thing, but a cop-killer…"

"Of course. The scandal," Sharma said.

"The phrase I got was 'a disaster for our international relations.' On the other hand, if there was something in the pot that could relate to national security, you never know."

"As in a tie to Pakistan?" Sharma suggested.

"Possibly."

"We know Geelani operates with their state Directorate for Inter-Services Intelligence, the agency that helped conceal bin Laden from America."

"Something to think about," Cooper said, and brought

their rental's engine back to life. "It wouldn't hurt to keep your fingers crossed."

"Or say a prayer?"

"Not my department," Cooper replied, and took them back onto the street.

"When should we know?"

"The phone rings, or it doesn't. If they haven't called in half an hour, it's no-go."

Sharma glanced at his watch and willed the hands to move before it was too late.

CHAPTER SEVENTEEN

Pali Hill, Mumbai

They had not traveled far before the callback came on Bolan's sat phone. Hal Brognola would have passed the number on to someone at the U.S. Consulate, located in G-Block of the Bandra Kurla Complex, Bandra East. The voice addressing Bolan was not one he'd heard before, almost atonal, handling a job that no one else had wanted, starting off with lies.

"Rick Armstrong," the stranger said. "Who am I talking to?"

"Matt Cooper."

"You've got a package for me?"

"If you're willing to accept it."

"That's the question, isn't it? I don't mind a surprise from time to time, but if you try to stick me with a booby prize, I'll throw it back. We clear?"

"Crystal," Bolan said.

"Okay, then. We need to make arrangements for the meet and greet. A neutral place. You have a spot in mind?"

"I haven't thought that far ahead."

"All right. Where are you now, in broad terms?"

"Pali Hill," Bolan replied.

"You have the package with you?"

"No. I wasn't sure if we'd be hearing back from you or not."

"Well, here we are. How soon can you retrieve it?"

"Hard to say. We'll have to make another call, then set the meet."

"Uh-huh." Armstrong didn't sound impressed. "I've got a number for you. Do you have something to write with?"

"Go."

The caller rattled off eight digits, Bolan memorizing them and repeating them for confirmation.

"That's a prepaid cell," Armstrong informed him. "One hour from now, I pitch it down a storm drain and we're done."

"I hear you."

"Great. I like a neutral place for introductions. What I'm thinking of is fairly close to you. A dog park, on the ocean there, off Carter Road. Just north of it, they've got some kind of temple standing out over the water, on a causeway. You can't miss it."

"Dog park," Bolan echoed. "Does it have a name?"

"None that I've ever heard. Watch for the sign."

"I'll reach out for the package," Bolan said.

"One hour, max," Armstrong reminded him. "You don't call me, I won't be calling you. We never spoke in that case. Got it?"

"Understood." Same old, same old. Deniability was everything.

"Okay," Armstrong said, and the line went dead.

Bolan switched off the sat phone, told Sharma the caller's terms, explaining that they had a narrow window and no backup if they missed the opportunity.

"This man is from the CIA?" Sharma asked.

"That, or something similar."

"And he may still reject Captain Patel after they meet?"

"His call," Bolan replied. "At least your captain has a shot."

"And if he cannot reach this park in time?"

"Case closed."

"I'll call him now," Sharma said as he palmed his cell phone, thumbing digits. Seconds later, he was speaking Hindi on the line, relaying terms of Armstrong's deal, answering questions where he could. It was all incomprehensible to Bolan, but he noted Sharma nodding as he spoke and hoped, for his sake, that his captain found a way to play along.

If not…well, there was only so much he could do to help a cop who jumped the rails, killed three of his associates and then went into hiding. Bolan understood life on the lam, but going back there wasn't something that he planned to do. If Patel chose to make his break alone, then he was well and truly on his own.

Sharma signed off a moment later and announced, "He'll meet us there. He's leaving now."

"How long before he's at the park?" Bolan inquired.

"Allowing for the traffic, he believes it should take forty minutes, more or less."

"Okay. I'll call Armstrong and tell him that we're in."

The prepaid cell rang once before the now-familiar voice replied, "Thrill me."

"It's set," Bolan advised him. "The package is in transit now. Its ETA is forty minutes, give or take."

"Hot damn. I need to roll, then. See you."

And again, dead air.

So far, so good, Bolan thought. And immediately hoped he hadn't jinxed the deal.

Malabar Hill, Mumbai

THE LAP OF LUXURY was chafing at Sayeed Zargar. He had begun to wish that he could slip away and disappear, but there was far too much at stake for him to cut and run. His whole life was invested in G-troop and service to Riyaz Geelani. If the crime family dissolved, he would have nothing left except outstanding warrants forcing him to spend the rest of his existence as a hunted fugitive. But, on the other hand, if he cemented an alliance of his own with Ibrahim Leghari and his agency, allowing him to fill Geelani's shoes, his future could be bright and lucrative.

Assuming he survived the next few days.

He still had enemies to crush—at least a pair of them, still unidentified—while he was simultaneously dealing with Geelani and the loyalists who were bound to stand behind him to defeat a challenge from within the organization. Zargar knew soldiers who would likely join him in his bid for leadership, though he had never dared to broach the subject with them openly. Now time was short, and he would have to nail down their allegiance very soon, before he made a move that would be irrevocable.

And in the midst of planning palace revolution, he also had to orchestrate a terrorist attack on Hindus for the Holi festival. Perhaps Major Leghari, when he came, could talk Geelani out of what Zargar regarded as a mad, impulsive act that would rebound against them in ways Geelani had not considered. They were weakened at the moment, reeling from the various attacks they'd suffered. Sparking further public rage against G-troop in such an atmosphere seemed like insanity, particularly when they'd lost three of their highest-ranking allies with the CBI.

Zargar glanced nervously at his wristwatch. He still had nearly four hours to wait before Major Leghari landed in Mumbai, perhaps to rescue him.

Or would the Pakistani's presence only make things worse?

Riyaz Geelani, in his present state of mind, was unpredictable. His plan to strike at Holi celebrants without the DISI's aid or sanction indicated that he had forgotten why G-troop had undertaken terrorist assaults on Hindus in the first place. It had been a paying proposition, both in terms of cash and refuge outside India when heat was focused on the crime family. By risking—possibly destroying—that alliance, he placed everyone at risk. For what? To thumb his nose at fellow Muslims in Islamabad?

Despite his personal misgivings, Zargar forged ahead with plans for the attack, Geelani breathing down his neck. Two of his handpicked soldiers had acquired an M202A1 FLASH—short for flame assault shoulder weapon— a four-tubed rocket launcher manufactured in America, designed to fire 66 mm incendiary rockets fitted with tri-ethylaluminum warheads that burn at 2,192 degrees Fahrenheit. A boy could operate the launcher, with a minimal amount of training, and its impact would be devastating on a crowd.

Zargar was mulling over grisly images of charred and twitching bodies when Geelani suddenly burst in on him, raving, shouting curses. "Those rotten bastards!"

"What has happened?" Zardar asked him, almost cringing.

"The Narayana Trading Bank!" Geelani spit, as if that answered everything.

"Well? What about it?"

"It's been robbed! Two men. One white, one Indian. They took forty-two *million* rupees!"

Zargar did the calculation in his head: around three-quarters of a million U.S. dollars gone.

"The same men?"

"Yes! Who else? And still you cannot find them!"

He shifted it to Zargar's shoulders now, assuming no responsibility.

Three hours and counting remained until Leghari's touchdown in Mumbai. Once more, Sayeed Zargar stood wishing, hopelessly, that he could find a time machine before it was too late to save himself.

Ambedkar Nagar, Mumbai

VIVAK PATEL, NO longer "Captain" in his mind or heart, was making decent time. He knew the dog park where the meeting was supposed to take place, wedged between Carter Road and a seaside mangrove marsh, northwest of the neighborhood Naivedya. He could have traveled there by bus, but still preferred to drive his own car while he could.

Along the way, he'd stopped to close his one and only bank account, relieved that it had only taken fifteen minutes, more or less. There wasn't much to say about the relatively small withdrawal—553,000 rupees, or about $10,000—though the teller had pretended he was sad to lose Patel's business.

Perhaps he really was. Who knew? Who cared?

The money, paid out in one-thousand-rupee notes, padded the pockets of his suit coat and its matching trousers, making him feel overstuffed and awkward as he sat behind the steering wheel. It wouldn't slow him much if he had to run, but walking from the bank back to his car, Patel had felt that everyone he passed was staring at him, sizing up the odds of stealing his life savings by brute force.

The real weight that he carried was his pistol, and the knowledge that he'd killed several men within a single day. Broadcasts over the scanner in his car had not, so far, included any bulletins to have him stopped, hauled in for questioning or charged with any crime. Indeed, if anyone was looking for him—or aware that he'd dropped out of sight—it seemed to be a well-kept secret from his former comrades at the CBI.

How would his meeting at the dog park change things for Patel? So far, he only knew that Sergeant Sharma would be there, accompanied by one or more Americans. The U.S. Consulate might grant him sanctuary, or it might decide against him. Either way, it meant a drastic change in life for ex-captain Vivak Patel.

Acceptance would, presumably, result in his covert removal from the country to some distant place where he would serve his newfound saviors until they tired of him or he had nothing more to offer them. Beyond that, there was only mystery, surmise, a fog that rendered future days invisible. Rejection, on the other hand, meant being dumped back onto Mumbai's streets without a friend to call his own, inevitably being hunted down and killed by G-troop goons.

How many more could he take with him, if it came to that? His Smith & Wesson M&P held one round in its chamber, seventeen remaining it its fully loaded magazine. A second magazine was tucked inside one of Patel's pockets, beside a wad of thousand-rupee notes. Thirty-five shots, if he lived to expend them—and if each one scored a kill, miraculously, he could set a one-man record for mass killing in Mumbai.

Some great achievement for a man who once had pledged his life to upholding the law.

And it all came down to this: a squalid death or vanishing into oblivion, his life reduced to lurid momentary headlines or a nagging question mark.

In either case, he'd leave no family to speak of, and no friends that he could trust in light of what he'd learned about the CBI. Alive or dead, Patel would be forgotten soon enough—unless he went to work for the Americans some-

how and found another way to strike back at the men who
had corrupted everything he once held sacred under law.

With that in mind, he pressed on toward the meeting
and whatever lay in store for him beyond it.

Carter Road, Mumbai

THE SEASIDE HIGHWAY ran north-south between Jogger's Park
on the south and Hanuman Nagar on the north—1.9 miles
of four-lane traffic with ocean views, dog park, a walker's
promenade, assorted restaurants and shops along the way,
all adding up to a prime daylight hangout.

Bolan made a double drive-by, up and down the avenue
with Sharma riding shotgun, watching out for any hint of
an ambush in place. Nothing stood out, but the promenade
could have been crawling with G-troop commandos, others chowing down in this or that café. And if the CBI had
tapped in to the meet somehow—particularly if Sharma
was wrong about his captain, and Patel was working on a
setup of his own—the oceanfront could turn into a bloody
free-for-all in nothing flat.

And where was the ephemeral Rick Armstrong? Never
mind the name that sounded like he'd cribbed it from a
1950s comic strip. The guy was likely CIA—or maybe
DIA, a long shot there—and even though he did his best
to sound straightforward, everyone from that milieu was
schooled in double-talk, backstabbing and betrayal. Bolan
had no chance to vet him, but until Armstrong had taken
custody of Sharma's former boss, the Executioner didn't
intend to trust him any further than a rifle shot could reach.

"I'll have you covered to a point," he promised Sharma,
"but you'll have to watch your step. I can imagine three,
four different ways this meet could go south on you if you
let your guard down."

"You don't trust Captain Patel."

"I have to *know* someone before I trust him. Same with Armstrong. Either one could try to set you up, and either one could have a tail he doesn't know about. If anything goes wrong, take care of Number One—that's *you*—and double back on me. I'll cover your retreat the best I can."

"And Patel?"

"Let's wait and see."

Sharma fell silent after that, waiting for Bolan to deposit him as they'd agreed, a hundred yards south of the dog park. Any further conversation was superfluous, and Bolan didn't want to agitate the sergeant's mind when clarity of thought was paramount.

As soon as Sharma left the car and started walking north, Bolan pulled back into the flow of traffic and continued southward, looking for a place to stop where he could watch the meeting from a distance, weighing in if trouble reared its head.

He found it, pulled into the parking lot outside a smallish restaurant whose signs touted Authentic Mexican Food. It was the first supposed Latino place he'd spotted in Mumbai, and Bolan noted that the kitchen help collected near the back door, smoking cigarettes, all seemed to be Chinese.

Go figure.

None of them appeared to notice Bolan as he parked, removed binoculars from the Suzuki's glove compartment and focused on the dog park to the north. For all he knew, they might be used to strangers idling in the car park, taking in the sights. Until the moment one or more of them approached him, Bolan put them out of mind.

Up range, he spotted Sharma entering the dog park, standing out because he'd brought no pet along, but there were others on the benches there who had apparently turned out to watch dogs run and play, without the per-

sonal responsibility of caring for an animal at home. Once
Sharma found a seat off to himself, Bolan began to watch
out for the other players. He was at a disadvantage since
he'd never met Patel or Armstrong, but he compensated
for that deficit by watching everyone who sidled within
striking range of Sharma on his lonely bench.

It made a crowded killing ground, and Bolan hoped it
wouldn't turn into a slaughterhouse.

BAJI SHARMA SAT and watched dogs frolicking across the
grass in front of him, some yipping, others so devoted to
their exercise that not a sound escaped them. He had never
owned a pet of any kind, but recognized the bond some
people forged with animals. In other circumstances, he
would have been pleased to simply sit and watch them,
but his time was short, and Sharma knew his life was riding on the line.

He did not fear betrayal by Captain Patel, but the American who was supposed to meet them still remained an unknown quantity. Cooper did not trust him fully, if at all,
and there was still a chance that one or both men might be
followed to the park by someone else—G-troop, perhaps
the CBI—without their knowledge. Sharma was prepared
to fight if necessary, with his pistol and the Mini-Uzi slung
beneath his lightweight jacket on a shoulder strap, but if it
came to that among civilians in broad daylight, he could
not predict the outcome.

Eight long minutes after sitting down, he saw Captain
Patel approaching, walking like a man who half expected
each person that he met to strike at him. His face looked
drawn and haggard, but his suit was—well, not rumpled,
in the normal sense, but almost *overstuffed,* as if he'd padded it somehow to make himself look heavier. He fixed on

Sharma, forced a smile as he approached and sat down on the bench to Sharma's left.

"Where is your friend?" he asked.

"Nearby," Sharma replied. "We're waiting for the agent from his consulate."

Patel nodded at that, and then began a restless rocking motion that reminded Sharma of some drug addicts he'd seen, when they were anxious for a fix.

"You took precautions against being followed?" Sharma asked to break the silence.

Patel bobbed his head again. "I thought that there was someone, for a while. A blue car. But I lost them. Yes, I'm almost sure of it."

"Almost?"

"I'm not a fool, Sergeant!"

"But if—"

"Who's this?"

A white man, nearly six feet tall, with sandy hair the breeze had disarranged, was moving toward the bench they shared. Like Sharma and Patel, he had no dog in tow. Sharma stayed where he was, one hand inside his jacket, and addressed the stranger.

"Mr. Armstrong?"

"Guilty. You're the sergeant, I presume?"

"I am."

Turning to face Patel then, Armstrong said, "And you must be the walk-in."

Patel frowned at that. "Walk-in?"

"We used to say 'defector,' but the Cold War's over, so they tell me, and it wouldn't really fit our situation anyway, now would it?"

"You are from the embassy?"

"The consulate," Armstrong corrected him. "Our

embassy is in New Delhi. You weren't followed here, by any chance?"

"I've asked him that," Sharma said.

"And the answer was…?"

"I don't believe so," Patel replied.

"Wish you could be a bit more definite on that, old son," Armstrong replied. "Still—"

When his head exploded, Sharma saw the dead man's lips still moving, forming words that never made it from his vocal cords to open air. Blood spattered both men seated on the bench, proving that the shot had come from somewhere farther east, toward Carter Road. Sharma rolled over backward, off the bench, using its bulk as cover while he drew the Mini-Uzi from beneath his jacket. Patel hit the grass beside him, cursing as he fumbled for a hidden weapon of his own.

"Not followed?" Sharma growled. *"Not followed?"*

"How do I—"

Whatever else the captain meant to say was lost, as bullets started chipping divots in the concrete bench that shielded them, whining around their heads like angry hornets with a taste for blood.

BOLAN WAS READY when the shooting started, but he didn't see it coming. There was too much traffic flowing past on Carter Road—vehicular, pedestrian, canine—for him to spot the shooters gliding into the approach. The first shot gave him focus with its impact, echo and the physical response of innocent bystanders, but that didn't help the consular official he'd known only by the cover name of Rick Armstrong.

That first shot was a killer, dropping Armstrong in his tracks, while Sharma and his captain both got doused with blood. They managed to find cover of a sort, and Bolan left them to it, trusting Sharma with the fallback while he spied the shooter—one of them, at least—and raised his INSAS rifle to his shoulder.

The range was something like one hundred yards, less than one-quarter of the rifle's advertised effective range. As Bolan lined the shooter up, his mark was firing with a handgun toward the bench where Sharma and Patel had gone to ground. Away to either side of the attacker, and beyond him, other men were hauling hardware out of hiding, rushing in to join the fun.

Bolan squeezed off a round that closed the gap in one-tenth of a second, drilling through the lead shooter's sternum, then tumbling inside him, fragmenting to take out his heart and aorta, with parts of both lungs. He was dead on his feet, shocked as hell from the look on his face, then collapsed in a heap as his buddies stood wondering what had gone wrong.

Number two on Bolan's hit list tried to spot the sniper who had killed his friend, but didn't manage it. The second round from Bolan's INSAS pierced his cheek, a half inch from the left side of his nose, and took out a saucer-size chunk from the back of his skull. A woman screamed at that, belatedly, while people and their dogs ran back and forth across the killing zone, shouting and barking, some diving for cover, others leaping across the grass.

He had a fleeting glimpse of Sharma and Patel in motion, running his way, while the five or six surviving gunmen closed around them. They were G-troop, from the look of them, some firing now without regard to passersby or leaping canines. Bolan hit one with a 5.56 mm shocker in midstride, slamming him over backward as if he'd collided with an invisible wall. The gunman shivered out the final seconds of his life, but Bolan didn't watch it happen, tracking on to find another target while he still had time.

Say three, at least, were still firing after Sharma and Patel, when one of them got lucky. A slug from somewhere drilled Patel below one shoulder blade, ripping vital organs as it caromed off a rib and doubled back to nick his spine. He dropped facedown, already dying as he hit the turf, unable to respond coherently as Sharma tried to get him up and moving. Seconds later he was gone, and it was only Sharma running toward the parking lot where Bolan crouched inside their rental car, scanning the battleground.

His next shot was an unintended two-fer, punching through one target's upper chest, erupting from his back to blind the gunner coming up behind him with a spray of blood, hot metal shards and bone chips. Nothing fatal for the second guy in line, but he went down, his feet tangled, and stayed there as the Executioner tracked on to find the final G-troop soldier still afoot.

The man was bellowing in rage and firing wildly at Sharma, the jerking motions of his gun hand almost guaranteeing that he'd miss. A final round from Bolan's rifle hurtled through the open, roaring mouth and silencing the shooter forever.

Sharma reached the car ten seconds later, piling in while Bolan gunned the engine and got out of there. The Chinese kitchen staff had vanished back inside the restaurant, and Bolan found a hole in traffic, revving south on Carter Road with chaos in his rearview and a world of hurt ahead.

CHAPTER EIGHTEEN

Chhatrapati Shivaji International Airport, Mumbai

Major Ibrahim Leghari gave the customs agent his false passport, answering the questions that were posed to him with a genuine smile on his face. He enjoyed outwitting fools, and there was nothing in his travel paperwork—or in the passports carried by his two companions, checking through with different clerks—that should arouse suspicion. While the clerk who dealt with him displayed the usual inbred contempt for Pakistanis, he did nothing that would spark an incident.

Leghari and his men had checked no luggage through on their departure from Islamabad. Each had a satchel with a change of clothes, some reading matter for the flight, all perfectly innocuous. Their other gear was waiting for them in a car outside the terminal, driven by one of the DISI's long-term agents in place. Three pistols and two Uzi submachine guns, all with sound suppressors and spare magazines.

Major Leghari always liked to be prepared.

And he was pleased to find that his instructions to Sayeed Zargar had been obeyed. No one from G-troop was on hand to greet them, indicating that he had a good chance to surprise Riyaz Geelani when he turned up at the mobster's home. What happened after that was still a matter that remained to be decided, but Leghari was prepared to dress Geelani down in no uncertain terms for planning an attack without the DISI's full approval in advance.

Who did the miserable little thug imagine that he was, in fact? How long would he survive without support from Pakistan? Without the drugs and weapons furnished to him by Leghari and his agency? Geelani's arrogance was staggering, although by now, it came as no surprise.

The waiting car was a Tata Indigo XL, described in advertisements as a "stretch limousine," but in truth a luxury sedan that bore no resemblance to the foreign imports seen delivering stars and directors to Bollywood red-carpet premieres. Still, there was ample room inside it for Leghari, his two bodyguards and their driver, all settled into seats upholstered with fine European leather. They ignored the cars audio-video gear as they left the airport complex and merged with traffic on the Western Express Highway, rolling southward toward Malabar Hill.

Leghari and his two companions used the travel time to double-check their weapons, making sure that each was fully loaded and had live rounds in their chambers, with suppressors firmly fastened to their threaded muzzles. He was hoping to conduct his business without bloodshed, but Leghari knew how rapidly discussion could become an argument, and escalate from there to killing. If and when that happened, he intended to survive the confrontation and emerge victorious.

Which would depend, at least in part, on his alliance with Sayeed Zargar. Could Geelani's lieutenant keep G-troop's soldiers in line while deposing his longtime superior? If so, the transition would be a smooth one. If not, well, Leghari had to think about survival if and when the showdown came. He could acquire new allies for his country's covert war with India, but only if he was alive and free to do so. Dying in Mumbai, or being thrown in prison there, would mark the end of any future he might have with Pakistan, much less advancing through the DISI's ranks to ultimate command.

When they'd finished checking out the guns, Leghari slipped out of his jacket and put on the shoulder holster that had been provided with his pistol—a SIG Sauer P 226, chambered for .40-caliber S&W rounds. That gave him sixteen shots without reloading, if he couldn't reach one of the Uzis in the case of an emergency, with each of his guards packing identical firepower. Their holsters were cut to accommodate suppressors, and Leghari didn't care if the outline of his suit revealed that he was armed.

In fact, he preferred it that way.

He did not want Riyaz Geelani thinking that he had three helpless Pakistanis on his doorstep when Leghari turned up to surprise him. It was not designed as provocation, but a necessary show of force—and a reminder that G-troop's relationship with Pakistan was predicated on obedience to orders issued from Islamabad. Without that understanding, there could be no partnership.

It would be chaos, with the world turned upside down.

Leghari had no plan in mind beyond confronting Geelani and scuttling his unsanctioned plan for new attacks during the Holi festival. Geelani's choice would be a simple one: scrub the attack or stand in clear defiance of Leghari and DISI headquarters. The first course would prolong his life, at least a little, but Leghari thought the Mumbai mobster might be psychologically unable to back down.

In which case, he would have to die. And after that...

The prospect troubled Leghari but also excited him. His last combat experience lay years behind him now, and he looked forward to discovering if he still had the skill, the courage, to survive.

Bandra West, Mumbai

"Sorry about your friend," Bolan said as they traveled east on Hill Road, lost in traffic flowing toward downtown Mumbai.

"He knew the risk," Sharma replied while staring out the window to his left.

"No way to tell if he was followed, or if Armstrong led them to us, but they looked like G-troop, either way."

"I should not have agreed to meet him," Sharma said.

"Don't put that on yourself," Bolan replied. "One thing I'm positive about, the shooters didn't follow us."

Sharma was nodding, still not buying it. "He was my friend," the sergeant said.

"We've all lost friends and family. Comes with the territory," Bolan stated.

"When does it end?"

"If I find out, I'll let you know. Meanwhile, put blame where it belongs."

"Geelani."

"And whoever's backing him."

"When can we rid ourselves of him?"

"He's next in line," Bolan replied.

His sat-phone call to Hal Brognola, setting up the consular connection, had been brief but still informative. Brognola's eyes at Stony Man confirmed Riyaz Geelani's flight back from Karachi to Mumbai, arriving shortly before Bolan's own return from Pakistan. Bolan had planned to move against him after they had taken out their final slate of targets in Mumbai, but Sharma's former boss had stalled that plan with his attempt to gain asylum.

All in vain.

So, when the sat phone rang again, Bolan was apprehensive, but he took it. It was Brognola on the line again, as gruff as ever, telling him, "Thought you could use an update on the players. Mark them in your program."

"Who's the latest?" Bolan asked him.

"Pakistan International Airlines just landed its biweekly flight from Karachi. We've got a lookout running facial recognition software in conjunction with their customs branch, reporting to our consulate. I heard what happened to the guy they sent to meet you, and it's got them agitated, as you can imagine."

"Understandable," Bolan said.

"Anyway, they *think*—and it's provisional—that DISI had a man aboard the flight this afternoon. He *might* be Major Ibrahim Leghari. Ring a bell?"

"I hear you." Bolan remembered the name from his briefing back at the Farm.

"Word to the wise. They could be wrong, of course, but if it *is* Leghari…"

"Two birds, one stone," Bolan said.

"Something to think about."

"I appreciate the heads-up."

"Stay frosty, eh?"

"The only way to fly," Bolan replied, and cut the link.

"What now?" Sharma asked, sounding worried.

"Do you recognize the name Leghari?"

"Certainly. Geelani's contact from the DISI."

"There's a chance that he's in town."

"Here? In Mumbai?"

"Fresh off the plane," Bolan said.

"That can only mean a meeting."

"And an opportunity for us."

"You think Geelani called for help?"

"Or else Leghari thinks he's losing it," Bolan replied. "I'd call it fifty-fifty, either way."

If Pakistan was losing confidence in G-troop, that could mean a new alliance in the making with some other syndicate, starting from scratch, negating most of Bolan's work around Mumbai and in Karachi. Punishing an act of terrorism was appropriate, but it would serve no other function if another network of fanatics instantly replaced the old one.

On the other hand, if they could cut the DISI's link to Muslim gangsters in Mumbai, if only for a little while, and maybe make it too expensive for them to resume…

Log that as wishful thinking—but that didn't mean it wasn't worth a try.

"We move against Geelani's house, then?" Sharma asked.

"Scout it first," Bolan said. "Check out the defenses. Start with aerial photography and go from there."

They could accomplish part of that with Google Earth, charting the house and grounds. For real-time satellite surveillance he would have to speak with Brognola again, but even then they'd only have an estimate of numbers on the ground and wouldn't know, for instance, if Geelani had a mob of reinforcements waiting for them in his basement at the mansion. Some of that could only be discovered by a soldier on the scene, and if it blew up in their faces—well, by that time it would be too late to change their minds.

THE EXECUTIONER HAD never fought a "safe" war, sending troops, smart bombs and laser-guided missiles out to do the dirty work, while he directed movements from a bunker miles behind the firing line. He took the point, often alone, and followed through until the bitter, bloody end.

How bitter would the end be in Mumbai?

He was about to find out for himself.

Malabar Hill, Mumbai

"WHAT DO YOU mean, they got away?"

Sayeed Zargar was close to screaming, but he kept his voice down with a force of will that made his temples throb.

His caller—and the lone survivor of a trap that should have solved his problems in a single stroke—replied, "They had a sniper standing by, sir. We killed two of them, but the others slipped away. I could not follow them alone. Police were coming, and—"

"You ran away," Zargar shot back at him, his voice dripping with contempt.

"I had no choice! Rahul instructed me to watch and to report."

"So now you tell me that the pair we wanted most have once again escaped. And can you tell me where they've gone?"

"No, sir."

"Useless. What of the two your brothers managed to eliminate?"

"The one they followed was a captain from the CBI, Vivak Patel. Major Yugandhar cast suspicion on him prior to disappearing."

"I know about him. And the other?"

"An American. I have no name yet, but he drove a car with diplomatic plates."

"The consulate?" Just when Zargar thought that the news could get no worse, it took another turn to amplify his misery.

"I think so."

"Your new task—your *only* task—is to identify the dead American. You understand?"

"Of course, sir."

"And if you fail, Raavi, do not return."

Zargar hung up before his shaken soldier could respond, feeling his stomach cramp at the idea of telling Geelani what had happened now. Another failed bid to eliminate or capture G-troop's mortal enemies, revealing an apparent link between the violence his family had suffered and the cursed U.S. government.

Zargar wished that Geelani kept a stash of liquor in the house, something to calm his nerves before they spoke again, although it was forbidden by their faith. Now he would have to face another raging outburst of Geelani's wrath, and hope—

The walkie-talkie on his belt, beneath his jacket, hissed with static, then resolved itself into a voice he recognized. One of the sentries on the gate that barred access to the estate was calling. The interruption was an irritant in Zargar's present mood, but he would deal with it. A brief diversion, prior to troubling Geelani with the latest news.

"What is it?"

"We have visitors, sir. They say they've traveled from Karachi."

Yes! This might be his salvation.

"Send them to the house," he ordered.

"Yes, sir."

Zargar walked to the front door, opened it and stepped onto the mansion's porch, watching the black Tata Indigo XL approach. His stomach knotted painfully, dreading the confrontation that was coming, even as he hoped that it would leave him in command of G-troop and its far-flung operations. Failing that, Zargar knew that his life might be snuffed out within the hour. Even granting that, however, he still felt that it was worth the risk. Thinking of the alternative, standing behind Geelani while he picked a killing quarrel with their longtime friends in Pakistan, he understood that it was really no alternative at all.

The black sedan rolled to a halt and began disgorging passengers. There were four men, including Major Leghari who was leading them as they approached the house, and Zargar saw that all of them were armed. He did not question how they'd managed that, knowing the agency had men and stockpiles of equipment throughout all of India. If it should come to open war someday—

"Sayeed!" Leghari greeted him, smiling, his hand extended.

Zargar shook it gratefully, saying, "It's good to see you, Major."

"Is our friend aware that I am here?"

"Not yet," Zargar replied. "I fear it slipped my mind, sir."

"Just as well," Leghari said. "His first reaction should be interesting."

"There has been more bad news. More raids. He's badly out of sorts."

"Let's see if we can pacify him, shall we?"

They met Geelani just emerging from his study, calling out, "Sayeed! There's someone at the gate! See who—"

He stopped and gaped, his eyes flicking back and forth between Leghari and Zargar. It took a moment for Geelani to find his voice again, and then he asked, "What have we here?"

"I've come to help you in your time of need," Major Leghari said. "Shall we begin?"

"Looks like Geelani has some company," said Bolan.

"It's a rented car," Sharma observed. "You see the decal on the bumper?"

"For a special visitor, let's say."

"Leghari!"

"That would be my guess."

They'd driven past the mansion once, then circled back in time to see a black sedan approach the gate, turn in, then get the nod to enter while they watched. It hadn't taken long—one of the lookouts on his walkie-talkie for instructions from the house—before he nodded to his partner and they rolled the gate aside. Bolan parked on the street, a short block farther on, watching the gate and sentries in his rearview mirror.

He already knew that was the only means of entry to Riyaz Geelani's property, unless they scaled the wall or found some way to drop out of the sky. Like many other walled estates around Mumbai, this one featured broken glass embedded in concrete atop its high surrounding wall. The shards were less obtrusive than a coil of razor wire, would still cut deep, but on the other hand, they couldn't be electrified.

Bolan had penetrated walled estates before, on numerous occasions, from his war against the U.S. Mafia to compounds scattered far and wide around the globe. Experience had taught him that, while penetration might be difficult, escape when he had finished with a strike could also prove extremely difficult. Even if he had dealt with all the enemies inside, that kind of mopping up took time— and reinforcements—cops or otherwise—could use that time to ring the place and cut off his retreat.

He couldn't hang back at a distance, potting targets with the Vidhwansak bolt-action rifle, in a neighborhood like this. There was no sniper's roost to let him fire over Geelani's glass-topped wall, and even if there had been, Bolan's ranking targets would be somewhere in the mansion, safe from prying eyes—or telescopic sights. Attacking here meant going in on foot, fighting past soldiers they would have no chance to count or locate in advance, then penetrating the big house and maybe fighting room-to-room until they found Geelani and Leghari.

If they found them.

Bolan didn't mind long odds; in fact, defying them was something of a specialty for him. He hated flying blind, though, without any clue as to the numbers he'd be facing once he dropped inside that wall, the possibility of dogs patroling, booby traps throughout the grounds and who knew what else waiting for him as the afternoon began its slide toward evening. Still, if the situation offered no alternative…

"We ought to wait for nightfall," Bolan said. He eyed the sky and said, "Two hours, give or take."

No one had passed their car yet, either driving or on foot, which didn't mean the neighbors had not noticed them. Rich folks were protective of their high-priced turf and kept a close eye on the streets—or their employees did, alert for any sign of would-be looters checking out the neighborhood. Police were also more responsive to a phone call from the "right" address than from a working-class abode or shantytown.

"We cannot spend the whole time here," Sharma said, speaking from a cop's experience.

"I'll go around the block again," Bolan replied. "Come back the other way and find a spot down there. Keep doing that at fifteen-minute intervals and break it up."

It wasn't perfect, but at least they wouldn't trouble any single neighbor of Geelani's by parking at their curb for an extended length of time. Better than nothing, and he didn't want to leave the area entirely, just in case—

"What's this?" he asked, his eyes locked on to the rear-view mirror.

Sharma used his wing mirror to check it out. Behind them, at Geelani's place, the gate was opening again. They waited for a moment, and an SUV came out, immediately followed by another, then the black sedan they'd seen pull in as they arrived. Three more Mahindra Scorpios brought up the rear, making a six-car caravan that turned away from Bolan's rented ride and rolled off in the opposite direction, northbound.

"Looks like the party pulled up stakes," Bolan said.

"And we follow them?" Sharma asked.

Bolan was already turning the Suzuki's key as he replied, "It's like you read my mind."

"YOU'RE LEAVING?" LEGHARI asked as he stood before Riyaz Geelani, staring at a pair of suitcases that stood together in the foyer.

"We were not expecting you," Geelani said, as if that were an answer to his question.

"And the bags?" Leghari pressed him.

"There have been more serious developments," Geelani grudgingly admitted. "I've decided that my compound in the country would be more secure."

"It's lucky that I did not miss you, I suppose," Leghari said. "It would have been a disappointment, after flying all this way."

Geelani frowned at that, his eyes shifting back and forth between Leghari and Sayeed Zargar, standing beside him. "If I had been told that you were coming, Major—"

"I preferred to drop in unannounced," Leghari said. "Something held over from my army days, perhaps. Surprise inspections, eh?"

"I did not know that we were subject to *inspections,*" said Geelani.

"No, of course not. Please forgive my careless turn of

phrase. But there is something that we need to talk about. It's urgent, and I did not trust the telephone."

"Perhaps you'd like to join me at the compound?" Geelani asked. "It is both relaxing and secure, I can assure you."

Glancing at his watch, Leghari asked, "How far away is that?"

"We can be there within two hours," Geelani said. "Perhaps a little less."

It hardly mattered to Leghari now. The next commercial flight from Mumbai to Karachi was a full three days away. "All right," he said resignedly. "Why not?"

Despite the forced smile on Geelani's face, Leghari could not tell if his unwitting host was relieved or put off by his agreement to the change of scene. Geelani nodded, made the proper noises, but Leghari sensed his presence had increased the gangster's agitation.

As, in fact, it should have done, given his plan to launch a new campaign behind the man's back.

"Sayeed," Geelani said, "you'll help with the arrangements. Quickly, now!"

"Of course, sir."

Geelani's second in command rushed off to do as he was told, his backward glance telling Leghari that the swift evacuation came as a surprise to him. Was the crime lord reacting to some imminent, specific threat, or was he giving way to panic?

"This retreat of yours…"

"It's safe, I can assure you," Geelani said, interrupting him. "And I keep a helicopter there, which can take you to the airport when our business is completed."

"As to that, Riyaz—"

"Excuse me for a moment while I get my people organized," Geelani said, and scuttled off before Leghari could complete his thought.

"Be wary," he advised his men, when they were left alone. "He seems erratic."

"I could deal with him," one of Leghari's bodyguards, Chaudhry Dar, replied.

"Not yet," the major said. "I need to find out what he's set in motion first, and whether we can stop it."

He cared nothing for the lives of Hindus, much less the disruption of their childish festival, but new attacks, coming so soon after the last, might well rebound against the DISI and Islamabad. On previous occasions, they had let investigations run their course, with nothing proved against the agency in spite of public accusations, then resumed the campaign of subversion after months had passed, lulling their targets into complacency. Leghari did not want the world's eyes focused on Mumbai for a protracted period of time, examining connections between G-troop and its foreign sponsors. It was better, in his mind, to move against Riyaz Geelani privately, replace him with a more compliant leader, and then proceed from there.

Five minutes passed before Geelani and Zargar returned, and in the meantime, vehicles were pulling up into the driveway at the mansion's front. Leghari heard them idling, heard men talking as they gathered, ready to depart. As soon as G-troop's leaders had rejoined them, he suggested, "You should ride with us, Riyaz. We can begin discussion of our business while we travel."

Leghari thought Geelani blanched at that, shooting a sidelong glance at his lieutenant, who stood silent, his face deadpan. At last, after overlong hesitation, Geelani replied, "Of course, if that's your wish."

"It is," Leghari said.

"Sayeed will take my place in the lead vehicle," Geelani

stated. Then, to his second in command, he added, "Make sure they do not lose their way."

"Of course, sir."

Leghari thought there might have been an undercurrent in Geelani's words, perhaps suggesting that he knew Zargar himself had tipped Geelani's hand and brought Leghari to his doorstep, uninvited. At the moment, as they walked back to their cars, that possibility was not Leghari's primary concern. He worried more about the events Geelani had already set in motion.

That, and getting through the night alive.

CHAPTER NINETEEN

Leaving Mumbai

Bolan trailed Riyaz Geelani's caravan north from Malabar Hill on Dr. Annie Besant Road, then picked up G. M. Bhosale Marg northbound, until his quarry led him east along Pandurang Budkhar Marg to catch the Elphinstone Flyover, once again northbound.

"Any idea where they're going?" Bolan asked as they began to leave the city's sprawl behind.

"Geelani owns more property outside Mumbai," Sharma replied. "I have not seen it personally, but there is supposed to be a camp of sorts, near the district border between Thane and Ahmednagar. Agents of the CBI looked for him there when he was first declared a fugitive, before the search became a weak charade. From information I've received, it's similar to his compound outside Karachi."

"Would he take Leghari there?"

"It's possible, if they had something to discuss or plan, and he is frightened of remaining in Mumbai," Sharma said.

Bolan knew a rural site could work to their advantage, but he'd have to scope it out before he started making plans. The good news was Leghari's presence with Geelani's team, placing the DISI major within Bolan's reach at last. If he could take Leghari out and leave his body with Geelani's, it would prove a case that had been speculative in the past, concerning Pakistan's involvement in the terrorist attacks around Mumbai and throughout India.

Would that change anything, in terms of troubled international dynamics?

Bolan doubted it, but taking out the DISI's go-to guy for contact with Islamic terrorists in India should, at the very least, slow the incidence of raids across the border—until Geelani was replaced. By then, there was at least an outside chance that pressure from the international community would make Islamabad think twice about state-sponsored terrorism as a tool of foreign policy.

Bolan had long since learned to count on little where diplomacy and long-winded debates came into play. His way of dealing with a problem was reserved for certain situations where all else had failed, from routine law enforcement to collaborations between nations.

Like today.

"I estimate a force of twenty men, at least," Sharma said as they ran a quarter mile behind Geelani's convoy, tracking the six black cars from a distance. They resembled a funeral procession, lacking the hearse, and Bolan was on board with the analogy.

"We'll have to see who's waiting for them at the other end," he answered. "Could be two, three times as many as they're taking out of town."

"Will we proceed in that case?" Sharma seemed to know the answer, even as he asked the question.

"You mean, as opposed to giving them a pass?" Bolan replied. "I'm going in regardless. No hard feelings if you've hit your limit."

Sharma shook his head. "No, no," he said. "I've come too far for that, and there is nothing to go back for."

Bolan knew that feeling, and he knew that it would pass. "Don't write your life off just because it's looking bleak right now," he said. "No one's expecting you to make this a career."

"Is there another choice?"

"Relocate," Bolan said. "Start over. I know people who can likely help you, once the smoke clears."

"In America?"

"Not necessarily. You'd have to work it out with them."

"Leave everything behind?"

"You just got finished telling me there's nothing left," Bolan reminded him.

"I need more time to think," the sergeant answered, weary-voiced.

"Take all you need. At least, until we find out where we're going."

They rode in silence after that, trailing Geelani's convoy from a mile behind, then more like two, as traffic thinned outside the suburbs of Mumbai. Bolan resisted the impulse to run up behind his targets, preferring not to let them spot him in their mirrors if he could avoid it. Long-haul truckers passed him, running interference without knowing it, and Bolan took advantage of their slipstreams, keeping pace without pursuing in the normal sense.

As for Baji Sharma's soul-searching, he put it out of mind completely. Only Sharma could decide upon the course that suited him. Bolan had long since chosen *his,* and there could be no turning back. His war was everlasting, and his course directly forward, toward the enemy.

It was the only way he knew to play the game.

National Highway 3, Maharashtra, India

SAYEED ZARGAR KNEW where he was going, but still could not say what awaited him there. His nervousness was not assuaged by thoughts of Major Leghari and Riyaz Gee-

lani riding together in the convoy's middle car, while he
led the procession north and eastward.

Would they come to terms, despite Leghari's plan to
cut Geelani out and cede control of G-troop to Zargar?
Would the major decide it was better to deal with the devil
he knew than Geelani's untested second in command?
And if he did, would he betray Sayeed to keep his own
hands clean? Perhaps inform Geelani that Zargar, and not
Leghari, had proposed the change in leadership?

If that transpired, Zargar knew that he was as good as
dead. None of the soldiers he had spoken to in confidence
would back him when they saw the plan had been aborted
and that rebels would be purged. Zargar would stand alone
in that case, his life expectancy measured in seconds.

National Highway 3 was one of India's major roadways,
with four paved lanes connecting Mumbai to Agra, in Uttar
Pradesh, 740 miles to the northwest. Geelani's convoy was
not traveling that far—would not leave Maharashtra State,
in fact, before the six vehicles reached their destination.
Having made the trip at least a dozen times before, Zargar
could have recited the names of each town and village they
passed through from memory: Kalyan, Khadaoli, Vasind,
Shahapur, Khardi. In some, the people stopped along the
road and stared; others were large and populous enough
that no one gave the passing vehicles a second glance.

Zargar had never liked Geelani's rural hideaway. He had
been city born and raised, amid the clamor and tumult of
daily urban life, and had a deep mistrust of nature in the
wild. The city had its dangers, certainly—erratic drivers,
hostile gangs, police—but they were nothing in comparison to tigers, crocodiles and cobras. You could see a lorry
or a taxi coming, maybe leap out of the way before it ran
you down. But if a leopard dragged you off into the bush...

Enough! he thought. There was plenty to worry about as

it was, without imagining a host of forest creatures standing by to pounce on him and gnaw flesh from his bones. All things considered, if Leghari sold him out, a leopard or a crocodile would be more merciful than anything Riyaz Geelani might devise to punish traitors in his ranks.

Zargar breathed slowly, deeply, trying to relax. If he was going to be sold out by Leghari, then he had to assume the deed had already been done. Geelani would ignore him until they had reached the compound, then command his soldiers to seize Zargar—but it would not be that simple. Zargar was armed with a Brügger & Thomet MP9 machine pistol, used by both the army and Mumbai police. It was a compact weapon, just under twelve inches long with its stock folded, chambered for 9 mm Parabellum rounds. With a cyclic rate of fire logged at nine hundred rounds per minute, the MP9 could empty a 30-round transparent box magazine in just two seconds flat.

If and when Geelani gave the order for his men to seize Zargar, the Mumbai crime lord would get a rude surprise.

Perhaps Major Leghari, too.

And if Zargar was cut down after that, what difference did it make? At least his death would be a quick one, rather than the days of agony Geelani might prefer. If he could not cheat death, at least Zargar would leave his bloody mark.

On the other hand, Zargar still hoped Leghari would hold true to their agreement, that Geelani would begin to rant and rave about his plans for bloodshed at the Holi festival and prove himself unstable. If the Pakistani major kept his word and gave the signal for Zargar to take Geelani out, Zargar would not indulge in any sadism or make an effort to humiliate his former boss. A simple head shot ought to be sufficient, and a shallow grave.

Zargar would have to wait and see, but one thing now was crystal clear to him. Whatever Major Ibrahim Leghari

might decide, their drive into the hinterlands of Maharashtra would be someone's one-way trip to death.

Khardi, Maharashtra, India

"IT WILL NOT BE much farther, now," Sharma announced
as they pulled into Khardi, a resort town famous for its
scenic hiking trails among the Sahyadri Mountains and
three nearby lakes—Bhatsa, Tansa and Vaitarna. Tourism
was the city's economic lifeline, catering particularly to
overstressed residents of Mumbai, and the government of
Maharashtra had protected its environment by declaring
Khardi a No Chemical Zone, from which polluting industries were permanently banned.

Sharma did not relate those facts to Matthew Cooper as
they passed through the town, stopping for gas at a Hin-
dustan Petroleum station before they moved on. Geelani's
convoy had outdistanced them, but that was not a problem
now since they had acquired a GPS fix on the mobster's
country hideaway, still thirty miles or so ahead of them.

Satellite photographs revealed the compound's layout,
accessed by a narrow road that left National Highway 3
ten miles before they reached Igatpuri, on the border between Thane and Nashik District. They could chart the
path of their approach to G-troop's stronghold from the
photos, but could not predict how many soldiers would be
waiting for them on arrival or what kind of weapons they
would have at their disposal.

Still, for Cooper, it seemed to be enough.

Sharma waited until they cleared the city limits, then
began to double-check his weapons, making ready for the
battle that would finish his campaign against Riyaz Geelani, one way or another. The turn his life had taken still
astounded him, but he had nearly managed to stop worry-

ing about what lay ahead of him, during the next few hours, drawing strength from Cooper's inherent confidence.

Nearly.

The Suzuki Liana slowed for a turn, twenty-five miles north and east of Khardi. Cooper left the headlights on for two more miles, then doused them, using only fog lights for the next three, rolling slowly through the dark thereafter. They were favored with the wan light of a half moon overhead, and the access road—while never paved—was well enough maintained to keep the small sedan from scraping bottom or rattling itself to pieces on potholes.

Once off the highway, they could only estimate the distance left to travel, looking for a place to stash the car before proceeding toward Geelani's camp on foot. Sanjay Gandhi National Park lay behind them, more open country ahead, but still wooded, with sharp-edged kunai grass growing up to six feet tall, its blood-red leaves seeming almost black by moonlight. Cooper picked out a place to take the car off-road, slowly and cautiously, alert for any hint of sinking into soft earth, and killed the engine when they were concealed by tall kunai from any other drivers who might pass along the road.

It was a warm night, humid, nothing strange in that for India. Sharma stood by the car, breathed in the night air for a moment, well aware that these could be the last moments of peace and quiet in his life. Within the hour, he might well be dead—and all for what? He was not sure that anyone would understand, or even care, but nonetheless, he felt as if he had accomplished something in the past two days.

Redeemed himself, perhaps, after a life of marking time. Of seeing evil thrive, despite his own halfhearted bids to intervene.

They suited up by moonlight, Cooper packing his 40 mm

Milkor launcher, INSAS rifle and his sidearm. Baji Sharma took the AK-47, Mini-Uzi and his pistol. They divided the remaining stock of hand grenades, clipping their spoons to belts, pockets, wherever they could be secured. A breeze rustled the tall grass, whispering around them, bringing the unwelcome thought of ghosts to Sharma's mind.

Why not?

His faith taught that every person had two bodies, the *gross* and the *subtle*. When a life was ended prematurely, the deceased remained on Earth in ethereal form—a ghost—until a new physical body was available for habitation. Cut off from life's pleasures, disembodied spirits were supposed to suffer greatly, as their senses still survived without any means of gratification. That belief explained the prevalence of cremation among Hindus, to prevent frustrated spirits from returning to the bodies that were stolen from them by untimely death.

How many vengeful spirits had Sharma created since Matt Cooper had saved him from slaughter by G-troop? He had not bothered counting, but there were enough to haunt him, certainly. And if he died himself this night, would he be doomed to roam these woodlands until he was born again? Would he remember any part of this life, in the next?

"Ready?" Bolan's voice cut through his reverie.

"Ready," Sharma confirmed, pushing the ghosts away. He followed the big American into the tall grass, moving eastward, toward whatever fate awaited them.

MAJOR LEGHARI HAD not told Riyaz Geelani that he was aware of the Mumbai gangster's plans to strike at Hindu Holi celebrants. During his flight, he had considered different angles of attack to solve the problem, and decided on a moderate approach to start. During the drive from

Mumbai to Geelani's rural hideaway, he'd kept the conversation turned toward generalities, including future plans the DISI had in mind for destabilizing India. Their counterfeiting was proceeding well, but he had mused that any further mass attacks should be postponed until the autumn, possibly the celebration of Dussehra in October, or Diwali in November.

As he spoke, Leghari had observed Geelani fidgeting, biting his lower lip, his hands restless in his lap. He had thought the gangster might blurt out his scheme, but Geelani managed to restrain himself and gave no hint of his intentions during their protracted journey. Seeing that, Leghari had made up his mind.

Geelani had to go.

With that decided, it remained only to pick the time and place. Geelani was surrounded by Leghari's men inside the T Indigo XL, but five carloads of G-troop soldiers still surrounded them. It would be risky, at the very least, to reach the compound with Geelani dead. Leghari was not sure whether Sayeed Zargar could take control in time to stop a firefight which, admittedly, would result in the annihilation of himself and his small entourage.

Better to wait until they reached the camp, he thought, and work it out in private with Zargar. For all he knew, there might be some procedure G-troop had in place for challenging a leader who had clearly lost his mind. Leghari needed time to speak with Zargar and marshal his forces, forestalling reprisal by any die-hard Geelani loyalists. It could be done, he thought, without risking the ultimate self-sacrifice.

Loyal Muslim that he was, Major Leghari never felt the urge for martyrdom.

The compound's glow was visible before they reached it, security lights ablaze in the forest. Leghari thought the lights were, in themselves, a testimony to Geelani's infiltration and corruption of the state police and central agencies. If officers had truly been pursuing one of India's "most wanted" criminals, they should have had no difficulty finding him, either at home in Mumbai or camped out in the hinterlands of Maharashtra. Somehow, he was overlooked—or, in the worst case, warned of an impending raid, allowing his escape to Pakistan.

Leghari wondered, idly, what would happen when Riyaz Geelani disappeared for real. Would they accept Sayeed Zargar as his replacement, as the grand charade went on? His best guess was that those entrusted with enforcement of the law would pocket cash, no matter who delivered it. Their promise to protect and serve had always been conditional—with paltry salaries and the dangers they encountered when they came to grips with well-armed criminals, and they would take the easy, profitable course whenever possible.

Leghari was prepared to bet his life on that.

Or, rather, he would bet Sayeed Zargar's.

The gates were opening in front of them, the convoy rolling through, past guards with automatic weapons in their hands and pistols on their hips. A few saluted, greeting their commander. Others moved among the compound's prefab buildings, executing duties or idling away their free time. Leghari counted thirty soldiers, then quit counting, with his bodyguards outnumbered by twenty to one.

His survival would depend upon Sayeed Zargar, a prospect that did not exactly thrill the major. Still, he was a decent judge of character—or lack thereof—and was convinced that Zargar was a slave to personal ambition. He had chafed under Geelani's thumb for years, wishing that he could seize control and run the syndicate *his* way, maintaining the alliance with Leghari's agency while grow-ing fabulously rich besides. Make it Z-troop, perhaps, in honor of himself.

In strict Islamic terms, Zargar would be condemned for criminal activity, but politics and war made strange bed-fellows. If service to his faith and nation forced Leghari to rub shoulders with the earth's worst scum, so be it. He believed that Allah understood and would be pleased to make allowances.

The gates were closing now, behind the convoy's final SUV. The lead car, with Sayeed Zargar inside it, had al-ready stopped and was unloading passengers. Leghari met the level gaze of his two bodyguards, tried to project a sense of calm as the limousine braked to a halt. Beside him, Geelani had started to fidget once more, clearly anx-ious to exit the car.

Leghari smiled and nodded to his men before they stepped into the glaring light.

BOLAN AND BAJI SHARMA walked a half mile through the forest and kunai grass under moonlight until they could pick out the artificial blaze that emanated from Riyaz Gee-lani's compound. Spotlights meant the camp had to have at least one generator, since no power lines extended to the site from Khardi. Something to consider when he started spotting targets, with an eye toward causing chaos for the home team.

But they had to get there, first.

It wasn't a long hike from where they had left the Su-zuki, or physically challenging, but Bolan had to watch his step. Most of the region's deadly snakes were relatively small, incapable of biting through a boot or pant leg, but king cobras—thankfully a rarity in Maharashtra—could rise high enough to strike a grown man in the chest or throat. Given their circumstances and their distance from the nearest hospital, a bite like that would literally be the kiss of death.

Aside from creepy crawlers, Bolan's primary concern was lookouts posted on approaches to the compound, and booby traps Geelani might have salted through the woods around his hideaway. Deadfalls, trip-wired grenades, pits filled with sharpened stakes—the possibilities were virtually endless, with the tall kunai grass camouflaging any man-made obstacles that G-troop might have laid to stop intruders. Moonlight helped a little, but it didn't reach the ground among the kunai roots or pierce the shadows cast by looming trees.

So, easy does it was the rule, making for slow but steady progress through the woods. Ahead of them, the compound's glow beckoned, and when they'd closed within two hundred yards or so, they started picking up on sounds from the encampment. Voices, and an engine puttering along—perhaps the very generator Bolan had in mind to incapacitate. He slowed his pace still further as they neared the lights, and stopped entirely at a range of fifty yards from the compound's surrounding fence.

It was chain-link, surmounted by barbed wire, with no concession to aesthetics out here in the middle of the forest. Bolan spied a single lookout tower, at the northwest corner of the compound, with its crow's nest looming twenty feet above the forest floor. The tower had its own spotlight, dark now, with room beneath its peaked roof for a pair of guards watching in opposite directions. Not a bad setup, but at the moment, those stationed on high would not be seeing much of anything beyond the camp's own glow of light. He could approach within a dozen paces of the fence and stand in darkness, as it was. Without the generator, sentries in the tower would have no significant advantage over any soldiers on the ground.

Crouching at the edge of darkness, Bolan scanned the camp and saw Riyaz Geelani standing near one of the prefab bungalows with several other men. The nearest on his left, without a doubt, was Major Ibrahim Leghari, pride of Pakistan's DISI. Sayeed Zargar, Geelani's number two, was standing back a pace, watching his boss engage in some kind of discussion with the major. Body language told him something had Zargar on edge, while Mumbai's reigning crime lord was trying to drive home some point Leghari wasn't buying.

Better yet.

Dissension in the camp could only work in Bolan's favor when the fur began to fly. Catching Leghari in the compound was a bonus, any way he looked at it, but if the opposition was divided, falling out at odds with one another, that was the icing on the cake.

He turned to Sharma, whispered, "Stay here while I scout the perimeter. I should be back in twenty minutes, give or take."

A nod acknowledged the instruction, his companion fixed on watching G-troop's leaders huddle with their Pakistani handler. Bolan eased away from him and started moving clockwise, traveling along the camp's perimeter while staying just outside the range of light within the camp. He picked out targets as he went: the motor pool, communications hut, the generator he'd been looking for, the mess hall where it seemed a meal was being served, a building that he took for the command post, barracks and assorted tents to house the rank and file.

Sentries patrolled along the fence, but they were few and far between. Despite their quick evacuation from

Mumbai, his adversaries seemed to think that they were safe here in the wilderness.

Mack Bolan meant to prove them wrong.

CHAPTER TWENTY

Thane District, Maharashtra

The compound's mess hall was preparing supper, a stew, but now Riyaz Geelani had begun to smell a rat. Major Leghari had been talking all the way out from Mumbai, dancing around some point he hoped to make, perhaps intending for Geelani to jump in and help him with specific questions. But Geelani would not play the major's game. Only half listening most of the time, nodding when it seemed appropriate, he'd registered Leghari's main points, recognized a trend, but chose not to engage the Pakistani in debate.

But now, surrounded by his own men, on familiar ground, he could no longer hold his tongue. "You mention Holi. Why, specifically?" he asked.

Leghari shrugged without conviction. "I supposed the celebrations on that day might be a tempting target," he replied. "But I—and my superiors—believe that fresh attacks so soon after the last would be...let us say, premature and ill-advised."

Geelani shot a sidelong glance toward Sayeed Zargar, feeling furious heat in his cheeks. "You've been talking to someone about this idea?" he demanded.

"A supposition, as I said," Leghari answered, feigning innocence. "Simply offering advice."

"If I were paranoid, I might think someone close to me

was bent on undermining my authority," Geelani said, feeling Zargar's eyes on his face. "I do not suffer traitors in the family."

"*If* you were paranoid," Leghari said. "But since you're not—"

"Nor am I blind," Geelani said. "I see what's going on here, an—"

The rattling *crump* of an explosion sounded from the far side of the compound, and the camp went dark, as if someone had thrown a master switch to kill all lights. Instinctively, Geelani took a long step backward, putting space between himself, Leghari and Zargar, as he gritted, "What have you done?"

"Nothing!" Leghari answered back. "You heard—"

A second blast sent shock waves rippling through the compound, with a burst of flame to mark its source. Part of Geelani's mind absorbed the fact that his communications hut was gone, and that the first explosion had to have taken out the generator.

Instantly, the other pieces tumbled into place for him. Leghari's knowledge of a plan known only to himself, Sayeed and a small group of handpicked commandos. This was their attempt to seize control of G-troop and the empire he had built—although, admittedly, he saw no gain for them in blacking out the camp or detonating its connections to the outside world.

No matter. Action was required, and he was equal to the task.

Geelani whipped out a pistol from underneath his jacket, thankful that the Glock 19 he carried had no safety switch to bother with, besides the trigger safety that required only an index finger's simple squeeze. He squeezed it now, one 9 mm Parabellum bullet each for Sayeed and

Leghari, the shots ringing in the darkness, and then Geelani turned and bolted for his nearby quarters.

He kept other equipment there for just such an emergency: a Taiwanese T91 assault rifle, chambered for 5.56 mm NATO rounds; a Benelli M4 Super 90 semiautomatic shotgun; a half-dozen Indian-made Shivalik fragmentation grenades; and a hard-plate reinforced ballistic vest in the universal camouflage pattern favored by U.S. and British troops. If he could only make it that far…

A third explosion echoed through the camp, just as Geelani stumbled up the steps to reach his quarters, elevated three feet off the ground like other structures in the compound. At the same moment precisely, something sizzled past his left ear, almost close enough to singe Geelani, as it struck the door frame just in front of him.

A bullet? Shrapnel? He could not have said, and didn't care. The unlocked door opened immediately, and he lurched inside, then slammed it shut behind him. Poor protection, but at least it bought him time to cross the blacked-out room and reach the cabinet where he stored his weapons and his body armor.

It was somewhat awkward, putting on the vest, switching his Glock from hand to hand, afraid to put it down as he stood facing toward the door and single window. Firelight from the compound limned Geelani's face, but offered only poor illumination of the scene outside. One thing: he knew that it would be reflected off the window's glass, frustrating anyone who might be peering in at him, while they appeared in silhouette.

He finished fastening the vest, holstered his Glock, snatched the T91 from its rack and confirmed that its 30-round box magazine was loaded. Geelani tugged the charging handle, chambering a NATO round, and set the four-position fire-selector switch by feel for 3-round bursts.

Snatching grenades with his left hand, he clipped them to loops on his tactical vest. Only the shotgun remained, and Geelani grabbed it, slinging it over his neck and left shoulder.

Thus prepared for anything—except the fear that clenched his stomach like an ice-cold fist—Geelani turned and started for the door.

BLOWING THE GENERATOR first was a no-brainer. With a single HE round from his Milkor MGL, Bolan blacked out the compound and bought the time he needed to cut a low flap in the camp's chain-link fence. A moment later, he was on the inside, angling toward the commo hut, lobbing his second 40 mm thunderbolt.

Its blast was music to his ears.

Soldiers could only prep themselves so much for total chaos. Drill sergeants could bellow at them to expect the unexpected, but in practice the idea was meaningless. No one, even a raving paranoiac, could prepare for every possible catastrophe. And criminals, by definition, were not truly soldiers. Bottom-lining it, they're felons for the simple reason that they couldn't obey the rules or cleave to discipline. They might be grim, ferocious fighters, but their fatal flaw was looking out for Number One above all else.

That's why Riyaz Geelani's troops began to run around like headless chickens when the lights went out, shouting across the camp when silence was the way to go, forgetting their assigned positions if they had any, firing at shadows in the night outside the wire.

Not looking for the enemy within.

After the commo hut, Bolan's third HE round went to the compound's solitary lookout tower. It was blacked out, too, but shooters in the tower had a better chance of spotting him or Baji Sharma on the ground, and Bolan couldn't risk it. When his 40 mm round exploded in the crow's nest, two men somersaulted into space and hit the ground like sacks of garbage, lying still and shattered on the ground.

The compound was alive with muzzle-flashes now, some of the automatic weapons firing tracer rounds that streaked into the night like supercharged fireflies. No one had spotted Bolan yet, and the Executioner in his turn couldn't have said if Sharma was inside the fence yet, or if so, precisely where he'd gone. They had a plan, sure, but plans tended to fall apart in combat, and they'd both have to be careful about wasting each other on the killing ground.

Beyond that, everybody else was good to go.

Targets had been prioritized—Geelani, Zargar and Leghari, taking out the leadership. There were no hapless hostages inside the compound. Every one of G-troop's men who died this night was one less causing pain and suffering tomorrow, next week or next year.

No quarter. Scorched earth all the way.

Bolan picked out a central spot and fired the last three rounds from his revolving launcher at the mess hall and the nearest barracks. Prefab structures didn't offer much resistance to a high-explosive charge traveling 250 feet per second and detonating on impact. Each blast left its target crumpled, twisted and in flames, as if someone had called an air strike on a village made of tinfoil.

And the men inside them—those who had survived the blasts—were screaming as they fried.

Bolan reloaded on the run, still free and clear as far as G-troop opposition was concerned. The Milkor had no muzzle-flash, and its report was muffled, like the popping of a champagne cork amid the compound's shouts and screams and gunfire. With his next six rounds, he targeted Riyaz Geelani's motor pool, the vehicles lined up as if for his convenience on the camp's south side. He walked six HE rounds from one end of the lineup to the other, left to right, and then moved on before the final detonation rocked the night.

But it was Hell on Earth among those cars and trucks and SUVs, with spreading lakes of gasoline in flames and acrid smoke fouling the air. The bad news: fire meant light, and it would now be easier for Bolan's enemies to spot him as he moved around the compound, leaving devastation in his wake. And easier for them to pick out Baji Sharma, too.

The good news: G-troop's gunmen wore no uniforms per se. The first thing to betray him would be Bolan's size; the next, his pigment. Sharma might be luckier in that regard, but there were still long odds against them.

Getting better all the time, but it remained a deadly game.

And this time, Bolan was all-in.

RIYAZ GEELANI CLEARED the steps of his command post seconds before it exploded behind him, pitching him face-down into the dirt. His flak vest saved him from a crippling injury, but shallow shrapnel wounds burned up and down the backs of both legs, with the worst in his left buttocks. Reaching back, Geelani found a hot piece of aluminum protruding from the cheek there, cursing as he yanked it free.

It hurt to stand, but lying where he was meant dying there. Geelani struggled to his feet, felt fresh blood coursing down his wounded legs and soaking through his trousers, but his legs still functioned as he put more ground between himself and the smoking ruins of his quarters. All around him, gunfire cracked and stuttered through the blacked-out camp, his men running pell-mell in all directions, shouting questions, imprecations, incoherent cries of outrage.

What had happened to Leghari and Sayeed? Neither was lying on the ground outside his quarters when Geelani had emerged, and it had been impossible for him to check for bloodstains on the ground. Not dead, apparently, but had he wounded either one of them? Were they hunting him right now? Was the attack part of a plan cooked up between them?

No, that made no sense. Sayeed, if he'd turned traitor, still would not try to annihilate the men he needed to support him, once Geelani was removed from leadership of G-troop, though Leghari might. More likely, it was still the same two bastards who had been plaguing him these past two days. The pair had followed him somehow, their method hardly mattered, and were doing everything within their power to destroy him.

Could Geelani stop them? Might he have the pleasure, even in his dying moment, of annihilating one or both of them?

He would never know unless he tried.

And first, he needed help. Geelani started shouting through the darkness at his men, calling for order, bent on rallying his troops. First one, and then another, joined him, half a dozen gathered to receive instructions, seeming grateful to have found him—when the motor pool erupted into flame and thunder. Leaping tongues of fire rose toward the treetops, while the shrapnel from exploding vehicles hissed through the smoky air. Part of a fender struck one runner in the face and sheared off half his skull, leaving the semiheadless body to lurch on for several strides and then collapse.

Geelani turned and found that two of the men who had joined him moments earlier were missing, vanished into shadows when the vehicles exploded. Two more seemed about to bolt, but Geelani snapped at them, holding them in line. His anger seemed to strengthen them, the function of a leader in adversity.

"Rally the others!" he commanded. "If you see Sayeed, bring him to me. Also Leghari. He has brought this down on us!"

That was stretching it, but it motivated them to find the Pakistani and his bodyguards. What fools they were, to plot against Geelani and believe they could depose him on his own ground, with an army at his beck and call. As for his future dealings with Islamabad, Geelani would consider that the next day, if he was alive to see it.

This night he was engaged in fighting for his life.

The light from burning vehicles was fading now, the gasoline from their fuel tanks mostly consumed. A pall of greasy smoke obscured the half moon overhead and blotted out the stars that had been clearly visible moments earlier. The scent of gunpowder mingled with those of high explosives, gasoline and roasting flesh, a heady mix that proved almost intoxicating to Riyaz Geelani.

He had always loved the thrill of violence, the smell of war.

The first men he had rallied were returning now with others, several of them wounded but responding to their master's call. None yet had found Leghari or Zargar, but they were still within his reach. The gates were closed and guarded; there was no way out for those who had betrayed Riyaz Geelani.

He would find them yet, and when he did, his vengeance would be terrible.

BAJI SHARMA WAITED for the first explosion, blacking out the compound, then cut through the chain-link fence as

Cooper had done on his side, wriggling through the flap as all hell broke loose in the camp. He snagged one foot and had to kick it free, then rose to one knee as a sound of running footsteps closed upon him from his right.

Spinning in that direction, Sharma saw one of Geelani's lookouts racing toward him—toward the action, rather, seemingly unconscious of the danger right in front of him. A 3-round burst from Sharma's AK-47 stopped the runner in his tracks and dropped him thrashing on the turf beside the fence, cut down with no idea how death had found him in the dark.

Before the corpse stopped twitching, Sharma shifted his position, scuttling toward a nearby building that he took to be a barracks. With its windows open, he could hear men scrabbling for their clothes and weapons, startled out of sleep perhaps, or just undressing for the night when they were called to fight by gunfire and explosions. Sharma pressed his back against the nearest wall, unclipped one of the grenades and pulled its pin, then lobbed the bomb through the open window just above his head.

Before it blew, Sharma was moving once again, ducking around the corner, diving headlong to the ground. The blast came seconds later, shrapnel punching holes through thin aluminum siding, startled voices replaced by ragged cries of pain. In front of him, the barracks door burst open and a line of shadow figures started spilling out.

He cut them down with short precision bursts of 7.62 mm fire, the steel-cored slugs ripping flesh and shattering bone at 2,600 feet per second. Some of the dying might have known what hit them, but it didn't help. They fell regardless, gutted, bleeding out, with no real hope of fighting back. Sharma was on his feet and moving past them in another heartbeat, ducking through the open barracks doorway to survey the room beyond, just as the motor pool exploded into soaring flames.

That light enabled him to scan the barracks, more or less, seeking survivors. He found two men moving, barely, but the blood fanned out around them told Sharma that they weren't long for the world. He'd killed them, and it did not trouble him. They had invited this on themselves, and he reserved his sympathy for those they'd victimized on orders from Riyaz Geelani.

Who, as far as Sharma knew, was still alive and well somewhere inside the camp.

A situation that he planned to remedy as soon as possible.

Retreating from the slaughterhouse, Sharma emerged onto a firelit battleground. He spent a moment in the barracks doorway, checking out the field and spotting targets, knowing he had to move before engaging them or risk being penned up inside the prefab building with the men he'd lately killed. He hopped down from the top step, landing in a crouch, and broke off to his left, moving in the direction of what once had been the compound's rolling stock, all twisted steel and smoking wreckage now.

But not abandoned yet.

Several of Geelani's men still moved around the burning hulks that had been working vehicles just moments earlier, as if expecting to find one of them still operational. Their silhouettes against the flames made clear targets for Sharma, aiming his Kalashnikov from thirty feet and squeezing off with grim determination, one mark at a time.

The first man dropped, another at his side half turning toward a fallen comrade when the second boattail bullet smashed into his skull. He made a yelping sound as he collapsed, first to his knees, then pitching forward on his face beside the other dying mobster. Sharma was already turning toward a third man when the others turned to face his muzzle-flashes, but he held his ground and worked his way along the line with three more rounds.

Three solid hits.

He could not say if all the men he'd shot were dying, but he knew that they were down and out of action, badly wounded at the very least. Designed to yaw through flesh, the AK slugs inflicted massive damage even in the absence of an instant mortal wound, leaving the stricken enemies to bleed while shock set it, with no medics at hand to rescue them.

Reloading as he rose, Sharma retreated from the flaming junk pile of the compound's motor pool and went in search of other prey. Riyaz Geelani, if he should present himself. Perhaps Sayeed Zargar or Ibrahim Leghari. Any one of them would be a prize, but he would take what he could get.

The bloody night was young. The hunt went on.

MACK BOLAN SPOTTED Baji Sharma quite by chance. He was across the compound when a barrack blew, the muffled sound of a grenade inside it, and a handful of Geelani's men came stumbling through its open doorway. When an AK-47 started chopping at them, dropping one after another, Bolan knew where Sharma was, but had no way to signal him across the killing ground. It was enough, for now, to have a rough fix on his ally while they hunted independently, both of them generally working clockwise through the camp, as they'd agreed while scouting the perimeter.

Beyond that, Bolan knew that it could go to hell within a heartbeat, nothing certain in the midst of battle, absolutely nothing guaranteed besides an escalating body count.

He was adding to it on his own, the Milkor launcher slung across his back now, while he tracked fresh targets with his INSAS rifle. Running men in semidarkness weren't the easiest targets to drop, but Bolan's long experience was an advantage few of his opponents from the Mumbai underworld could rival. Even those who'd joined G-troop directly from military service would be rusty, since the army's last active engagement had occurred along the Bangladesh border, back in 2001.

Rusty, and long since accustomed to dealing with victims who didn't fight back.

A double shock, when suddenly confronted by the Executioner.

Bolan had his rifle's fire-selector switch for 3-round bursts, allowing him—at least in theory—to drop ten adversaries with a standard 30-round load. It didn't always work that way, of course, but Bolan was an old hand when it came to making each shot count.

Two runners crossed his field of vision to the left-front, angling from the ruins of the mess hall toward the fence. Unclear on what they had in mind, he took the shot regardless, leading the front man by a yard and squeezing off, the INSAS spitting its three rounds downrange to catch him in midstride. The guy went down with arms outflung and plowed the green turf with his face, unmoving once he'd settled on the grass.

His buddy saw it happen, tried to change directions, but he'd already run out of time. The second burst from Bolan's weapon spun him like a whirling Dervish, tangling up his feet and dumping him a few feet from the first corpse. Dead or dying, it was all the same. Another pawn swept off the board, while Bolan went on hunting for the king.

He'd lost track of Geelani, going in, after the camp went dark. Bolan supposed there was a chance he'd dropped the Mumbai crime lord already—in what he took to be the

command post possibly, or when he blew the commo hut—
but he would take nothing for granted. Even if Geelani was
among the fallen, that still left Sayeed Zargar and Ibrahim Leghari to be dealt with. This time, he was cutting off
the viper's several heads and making damned sure that it
didn't spring to life again.

At least, until the DISI found another pack of jackals
willing to play ball.

How long would that take? Bolan didn't know, and
didn't have the time to speculate. There would be multiple investigations when the smoke cleared, headlines
flashed around the world, earnest debates in diplomatic
circles. Pakistan might learn a lesson from the carnage—
and, if not, he might return someday to teach the same
lesson again.

This night, this battle was enough for any warrior.

Bolan saw four G-troopers ahead of him and saved his
ammunition, baseballing a frag grenade into their midst
before they registered an enemy's approach. The blast il-
luminated the shooters, its shrapnel cutting through them,
turning them to bloody rags and tatters where they stood.
Not bad, as deaths in battle went.

Bolan had seen much worse, and doubtless would again.

Geelani's people knew that there were enemies among
them now, not merely snipers somewhere in the dark, beyond the camp's perimeter. That knowledge clearly rattled some of them, provoking random shots at shadows
in the compound, mostly misses, but a clean hit here and
there. Bolan accommodated those reactions by remaining
under cover where he could, and moving swiftly where he
was compelled to travel over open ground. When weapons
turned his way, he answered them with short bursts from

the INSAS rifle, teaching his opponents the importance of precision fire.

A lesson those receiving it would not live to apply.

He moved on, still hunting through the devastation for bigger game.

CHAPTER TWENTY-ONE

Riyaz Geelani's first wild shot into the darkness had grazed Major Leghari's neck, etching a line of white-hot pain beneath his jawline on the right and clipping off his earlobe. He had reeled and twisted from the blinding muzzle-flash, falling to hands and knees before the mobster fired again. Sayeed Zargar had cried out that time, yelping like an animal, a sound that might be rooted in surprise, pain, outrage or some mixture of all three.

Leghari had not waited for another shot. He'd scrambled clear, lunged into darkness like a frightened quadruped and then collapsed, as more explosions shook the compound, scattering Geelani's men, demolishing the Mumbai mobster's private bungalow nearby.

And where were *his* three bodyguards? Leghari did not look for them at once. Instead, he checked his wound, determined that it was not critical, then drew his SIG Sauer P 226 from its shoulder holster and thumbed off its manual safety. He stayed low as gunfire rattled through the camp, likely Geelani's soldiers firing at thin air or at each other. Explosions aside, Leghari had seen nothing to indicate invaders on the property, but he was ready for them now.

Ready to pay Geelani back for the attempt to kill him.

First, though, he was anxious to retrieve his men. Leghari took a chance, calling their names, then shouting out commands in Urdu, hoping they would pick out his voice from the Hindi babble of Geelani's soldiers. If they did not answer soon, he would proceed without them. Try to reach their car, perhaps, and—

Even as his thought took shape, his so-called limousine and all the other cars lined up together on the camp's southern perimeter began exploding like a string of giant firecrackers. Amid that thunder, barely audible, Leghari recognized the *pop-pop* of a repeating grenade launcher laying down fire on the cars, but he could not spot its shooter in the dark. One of Geelani's phantom enemies, no doubt, arriving just in time to keep Leghari from concluding his business with G-troop.

Or making it easy?

A figure loomed beside him, from the shadows. Leghari raised his pistol, then made out the face of Gohar Noorani, one of the two agents who had flown with him to Mumbai. Noorani had one of the Uzis in his hands, and close behind him, with the other, came Asif Mashriqi.

"Where is our driver?" Leghari demanded, forgetting the other man's name.

Noorani shrugged and said, "We lost him, sir. Along with the car."

"So I see." Leghari pressed a hand against his aching neck and held it up for them to see the bloody palm by firelight. "This is from our host. We need to find him. Finish him."

"He may be dead already," Mashriqi said, peering toward the blasted ruin of Geelani's prefab quarters-cum-command post.

"I'll believe it when I see his body. Until then, assume he's still alive and well."

Both agents nodded, almost simultaneously. They would do as they were told regardless of the risks involved. That much, Leghari took for granted. Neither one had ever disappointed him before in situations where the stakes were life and death.

They could escape from G-troop's camp and make their way back to the nearest town. Once there, they could obtain a vehicle and drive back to Mumbai, departing on the next flight to Karachi as if nothing untoward had happened during their brief holiday.

But first, they would eliminate Riyaz Geelani. That was paramount. Leghari had intended to remove the mobster as it was, but now that mission had become a personal concern. Geelani's rash attempt to kill Leghari indicated that the thug had lost his mind, and might well try again if he survived the night. He was a danger to Leghari and his agency—to all of Pakistan, in fact—while he remained alive.

But he *would not* survive the night. Whether Leghari had the pleasure of eliminating him, or if Geelani's unknown enemies were fortunate enough to strike the killing blow, it mattered not. The major would not leave until he had proof that Geelani was a dead man—or had seen the whole damned camp obliterated first.

Proof positive. Was that so much to ask?

The trick, Leghari recognized, would be to find that evidence and still get out alive.

Night-fighting was a specialty. Some units train for weeks or months to tackle a specific target in the dark, when uniforms and faces were obscured. Eliminate the uniforms, and things got even worse—unless your side was limited to one or two combatants in a free-fire zone.

Like now.

MACK BOLAN HAD to watch for Baji Sharma as he moved around Riyaz Geelani's compound, but the other people present—all of them, without exception—were his enemies. He didn't have to think about civilians, hostages or any other neutrals. Anything on two legs was fair game.

And they were going down.

He didn't count the bodies as they fell—had never made a point of keeping score, in fact, even when "wanted" posters issued by the FBI in Washington had linked him to a thousand mafiosi slain in phase one of his endless private war. That number might have been inflated, or it could have been conservative. The only bottom line for Bolan was elimination of his enemies, wherever and whenever he encountered them.

He saw three of Geelani's shooters duck into a prefab building smaller than some of the others, larger than the shed that had contained the compound's generator, and he moved in that direction, hoping he could bag a triple. Bolan still had twenty yards to go when his intended targets reemerged, all lugging larger weapons than they'd carried going in. One had a light machine gun, probably one of the IMI Negevs issued to Indian infantry, belt-fed with 5.56 mm NATO ammunition. The other two were lugging RPGs, though how they planned to use them without killing their own men was anybody's guess.

Bolan didn't feel like waiting to find out.

He shot the leader of the trio, dropping his body in the path of his surprised companions. Both immediately shouldered their rocket launchers, scanning desperately for a target that would make a high-explosive shot worthwhile. As soon as one of them took two long paces forward, Bolan saw his opening and took his shot.

The 3-round burst from Bolan's INSAS rifle stitched across his target's abdomen, a kill, but not immediately. As he fell, the shooter still had time to fire his rocket—and consume the guy behind him with the searing back-blast from his launcher. Bolan ducked the 85 mm single-stage projectile as it rattled overhead, and heard the backup shooter screaming as he toppled over backward, all in flames. His own launcher went off before he hit the ground, projectile soaring skyward, off and gone into the forest, while the second back-blast finished him for good.

The building they'd ducked into for their weapons had to be the compound's arsenal. Before his other enemies could reach it, Bolan rose and sprinted forward, palmed one of his frag grenades and yanked its pin, lobbing the bomb through the open doorway to the armory. He turned and hit the deck then, counting off four seconds before the place went up in a concussive series of explosions, with an undertone of ammo cooking off. Hot rounds snapped overhead as Bolan crawled away and out of range, leaving G-troopers to absorb the damage from their own stock-pile of hardware.

Some kind of poetic justice, he supposed, if such things mattered in the real world.

His ears were ringing as he cleared ground zero, moving toward the camp's northern perimeter. That course brought Bolan circling back toward what he'd taken for Geelani's quarters and command post, smoking rubble now, but still a starting point for his attempt to find the Mumbai crime lord, alive or dead.

By now, Geelani's compound felt and smelled like every other battleground where Bolan had faced odds that others might have deemed impossible. He'd never bought that self-defeating point of view, though there'd been times when he'd retreated, in the interest of coming back to fight another day.

But not this night.

This night, right here and now, was do or die.

He circled toward the compound's gate, checking to satisfy himself that it was shut and latched, no one escap-

ing through it to the forest. Two of Geelani's men were
still on duty there, both looking nervous with good reason, but they hadn't broken yet, and Bolan left them to it.
They would let Geelani pass, of course, if he turned up.
Same with Zargar, and probably Leghari, though the Pakistani might meet some resistance. Bolan's job, now, was to
make sure none of his prime targets reached the gate alive.

Through smoke and fire, the hunt went on.

SAYEED ZARGAR SUSPECTED he was dying. He'd been standing no more than three paces from Riyaz Geelani when the
lights went out, a thunderous explosion shocking him, and
then Riyaz had lost his mind, drawing a pistol, firing first
at Major Ibrahim Leghari, then at Sayeed. Zargar had no
idea whether the Pakistani had been hit, and frankly had no
interest in finding out. His own wound—in his right side,
underneath his ribs—was all that he could think about.

The wound, and getting out of camp alive, by any means
available.

The shock of being shot had not prevented him from
running, powered by adrenaline, until he reached the
cover of a nearby barracks building, where he'd crouched
in shadow, back against the wall, to check the damage he
had suffered.

There was pain, of course, though not as much as he'd
expected from a bullet wound. Perhaps the worst of it still
lay in store for him, replacing momentary numbness with
a bone-deep agony. If so, Zargar supposed that he had to
use his time wisely, not lingering until the damage crippled
him. A cautious probe with bloody fingertips told him the
shot was through-and-through, no bones involved, but it
was bleeding copiously. He did not detect the spurting of
a severed artery, but had no way of knowing whether he
was bleeding out internally.

To hell with it.

If that turned out to be the case, he would be dead in minutes, and it would not matter what he did. With that in mind, the only thing Zargar *could do* was patch the wound, after a fashion, then attempt to flee the scene, escape to someplace where he'd find a doctor—better yet, a hospital—to help him.

Problem: while a couple of the men in camp had trained as medics during military service, any thought of finding them this night, amid the shooting and continuing explosions, was a wild-eyed fantasy. Beyond that, to his certain knowledge, there was no physician closer than the town of Khardi, roughly forty-eight kilometers from his location. Walking there would kill him, and since all vehicles in the compound had been blown to hell and gone by their attackers, Zargar reckoned that he was as good as dead.

What course of action, then, remained for him?

Die fighting, like a man.

With what? He had the pistol he had carried with him from Mumbai, a good Beretta 92, which gave him fifteen shots—plus one to end his misery if he began to suffer too much pain. The Koran strictly forbade suicide, to be sure, but Zargar had little patience with the details of his faith, despite the fact that he had been at war, ostensibly on its behalf, for years.

Warriors engaged in battle because there were battles going on. What other raison d'être did they have, beyond slaying their enemies?

Zargar had three foes he was certain of inside the compound. Two would be the bastards who had hammered G-troop so relentlessly in recent days, still unidentified, the motive for their sudden, devastating raids unknown. There was a chance that he could meet one or the other, if he lurched around the camp until he dropped, but he did not like the odds.

His other enemy was Riyaz Geelani, one man he could recognize on sight, whose madness spelled the end of living for Sayeed Zargar.

Riyaz it was.

He would expend whatever strength remained to him seeking Geelani and, if possible, repay him for his murderous treachery. Blast the twisted, scheming thoughts out of his skull.

If he could only move.

Zargar struggled to rise, keeping his back pressed tight against the barracks wall, leaving a viscous smear of blood along the way. When he was on his feet once more, he pushed off from the wall, tottered a bit, then found his footing. He could do this if he took it slowly, step by step. If no one blundered into him and knocked him down, or shot him in the frenzy of confusion that had gripped the compound.

He could walk, albeit slowly and with difficulty, and would know Riyaz Geelani when he saw him, even in the reeking, smoky darkness. And the next time they stood face-to-face would be the last, for one of them.

Perhaps for both.

BAJI SHARMA FOUND the camp's latrine by smell, the inescapable smell that remained despite employing quicklime to dissolve accumulated waste material and quell its stench to some extent. It would have been too complicated and expensive to install a proper septic system, or to service trucked-in portable uits, so G-troop's labor force had dug a trench, then placed a prefab structure over it, exhaust fans powered by the compound's generator—which, of course, had now been blown to smithereens.

In normal times, Geelani's men would make use of the latrine as necessary and avoid it otherwise, located as it was on the far east side of the compound, but this night was not a normal time. Sharma had seen four men duck into the latrine, trying to hide there, and had thought it was another barracks until his nostrils told him otherwise.

So be it. He was not in a discriminating mood, as far as targets were concerned.

Sharma had two grenades left as he neared the building, coming up on its south side. Thanks to its function, there were open windows all around, with thin mesh screens in place to help keep flies outside. Setting his AK-47 on the ground, he drew a pocketknife and opened it, reached overhead and ran its three-inch blade along the nearest windowsill, then up one side, leaving the screen partly detached. There was no gunfire in return, presumably because the racket from the camp prevented anyone inside from hearing the soft *hiss* his knife made slicing through the flimsy screen.

Next, Sharma unclipped a grenade, withdrew its safety pin and clutched the orb in his left hand, with its spoon secure in place. He stooped, retrieved his rifle, then reached up to lob the grenade in through the flap he had created, turning simultaneously and retreating from the prefab structure in a sprint.

Five seconds later, with a whopping *bang,* the feces literally hit the fan. Sharp cries of pain echoed from inside the latrine, as shrapnel ripped through flesh, bone and aluminum. The frag grenade's shock wave carried a noxious odor with it, curdling Sharma's stomach as he hugged the turf, watching and waiting for survivors to evacuate the latrine.

The first man out was staggering, hunched over, clutching at his abdomen. Sharma lined up the AK's sights and shot him through the head, dropping the wounded figure in his tracks. A second came out running, more or less, wiping wet muck out of his eyes with one hand, brandishing a compact submachine gun in the other, spraying slugs across the camp with no attempt to aim.

Sharma flinched involuntarily, although aware that those incoming slugs were passing six to eight feet overhead, but then recovered and responded with a double-tap that punched the gunman over sideways, kicking as he fell. It wasn't what he'd call a clean kill, but it *was* a kill, and Sharma didn't feel like wasting any further ammunition on a dying man.

Rather then rise immediately, just in case his muzzle-flashes had been spotted by an enemy, he rolled a few yards to his left, then pushed up to a crouching posture, sweeping left and right with his Kalashnikov. No one immediately challenged him, so Sharma rose and put the reeking house of death and waste behind him, angling toward the tents Geelani had assembled for his men who could not find a bed inside the prefab barracks.

Most of them were flattened now, trampled by gunmen rushing back and forth through camp, or by the impact of explosions. Those he found still standing were unoccupied, since canvas offered no protection from incoming fire. A pair of legs protruded from one flattened tent, inert and unresponsive when he paused to kick one of the dusty boots, and then moved on.

Another corpse.

But there were still enough live targets on their feet and moving, firing single shots or automatic bursts around the camp, to keep him busy, checking each in turn to verify that it was not Matt Cooper before he squeezed the AK-47's trigger. One down, two down, three—

But as the third man fell, he also fired off half his submachine gun's magazine, a rattling, flashing spiral, dying index finger clenched around the trigger with no thought of aiming. One slug grazed Sharma's right thigh, high and inside, before another sliced into his groin.

He fell, breath driven from his lungs on impact, the Kalashnikov wedged underneath him, bruising ribs. The sudden pain surprised him, left him weak and gasping. Worse, when he tried standing up, his legs refused to function.

Sobbing out profanity, using his arms alone, Sharma began to drag his weapon and his body toward the center of Riyaz Geelani's camp.

BOLAN HAD SWITCHED back to the Milkor MGL after a quick reload with half a dozen 40 mm buckshot rounds. Call it a one-gauge shotgun, more or less, although the measurement was not precise. Optimum killing range, a little over forty yards, which served his purpose well enough.

By Bolan's calculation, he and Sharma had eliminated roughly half Geelani's armed defenders since they started hammering the compound. That still left another twenty-odd, at least, assuming that their estimate had been correct to start with. If it was mistaken, high or low, they still had shooters on the prowl, alive and well, despite the hail of slugs and shrapnel that had scourged the camp.

What better way to thin the herd than with the mother of all scatterguns?

Traveling clockwise through the compound, Bolan had completed two-thirds of a circuit on the camp's perimeter, leaving a trail of ruin in his wake. Sharma should be somewhere ahead of or behind him—all a matter of perspective—wreaking havoc of his own. Bolan still hadn't seen Riyaz Geelani or his ranking cohorts since the lights went out, but logic told him that his quarry had to be somewhere in the killing pen.

Press on.

Ahead, two figures lunged across the shadowscape, immediately marked in Bolan's mind as enemies since Sharma would have been alone. He swung the Milkor their way, sighted quickly and blasted the runners with twenty-four pellets of buckshot. Behind them, dying firelight lit a haze of crimson mist as both men hit the ground, riddled. Again, the Milkor's relatively subtle *pop* was lost amid the crack and rattle of surrounding gunfire.

To his left, a prefab building stood apparently undamaged. One of G-troop's shooters had contrived to mount its roof somehow, and he had spotted Bolan from the last shot, firing at him from the high ground. It was close, but no cigar, as Bolan tumbled through a shoulder-roll and came up with the Milkor leveled at his enemy. A trigger stroke, and suddenly the enemy was airborne, squealing out his last breath as he vaulted backward, out of sight and out of mind.

Four rounds remained in the launcher's cylinder.

He used the next one on a pair of shooters coming from the general direction of the compound's gate. From hiding, Bolan watched them run a few yards, crouch, then run a few yards more. He didn't know where they were going, and it made no difference. Next time they stopped and hit their knees, he solved the problem for them with a blast that dropped them together in a bloody heap.

Almost too easy. Bolan wanted bigger game, but he'd seen nothing of Geelani or the other ranking targets since he'd blown the generators, blacking out the compound. It had been the right move for the operation, and he wasn't second-guessing it, but part of him now wondered if he could have dropped the leaders first—a buckshot round, for instance—*then* destroyed the generator with an HE charge and let the rest play out.

Spilt milk. No tears.

He moved on, circling inexorably back toward where he'd made his entry to the compound. Bolan reached a smallish shed and checked inside it, just in case one of Geelani's goons was hiding there, hoping to spring out and surprise him. What he found, instead, were propane tanks, at least a dozen of the twenty-pound variety, presumably stockpiled for use in what had been the camp's mess hall. Seizing the opportunity, he primed a grenade and tossed it in among the tanks, then turned and sprinted clear before it blew, counting the numbers as he ran.

On *five,* he hit the turf and hugged it, while the night erupted into flame behind him once again. The shed's roof shot skyward, riding on a fireball that ascended fifty feet, at least, to light the underside of scudding clouds. Using its light to scan the camp from where he lay, Bolan spied a familiar face and vaulted to his feet in hot pursuit.

CHAPTER TWENTY-TWO

Baji Sharma's pain had faded, which he took to be a bad sign. He was cold, despite the warm and muggy night, an overt sign of shock. He knew what that meant: blood withdrawing from capillary beds of body tissue in an effort to preserve the vital organs, lowering blood pressure and releasing hormones from the adrenal glands in an attempt to raise the heart rate. At the same time, yet another hormone was released, constricting veins in a bid to retain body fluids.

Sharma knew the symptoms of shock from his military training and his time at the police academy. He knew the different kinds of shock, and recognized his own as hemorrhagic, caused by loss of blood from open wounds. Nothing his body tried to do to save itself would help as long as he was bleeding out. He only had a short time left—minutes, perhaps—and did not plan to waste a single one of them.

Not when a target he'd been searching for all night suddenly loomed in front of him.

It was Sayeed Zargar, and from the way he moved— hunched low, clutching his side—Sharma determined that he had to be wounded, too. Not fatally, perhaps, but that could easily be remedied.

Rather than simply shoot Zargar from where he lay, Sharma began the painful task of struggling to his feet, using his AK-47 as a crutch of sorts. The effort cost him dearly, fresh blood pulsing from the wound below his belt,

one leg nearly refusing to support him, but he found a point
of balance nonetheless and raised the automatic rifle to his
shoulder as he called out to his enemy.

"Sayeed Zargar!"

Geelani's chief lieutenant halted in his shambling progress, turning first his head toward Sharma, then limping
around until he faced his adversary more directly.

"Are you one of them?" he asked, his voice grating as
if he had gone for days without a drink of water.

Sharma knew what he meant. Proudly, the sergeant answered back, "I am."

"But *why?*" There was a hint of anguish in the wounded
mobster's voice.

"Because you set yourself above the law," Sharma replied. "Because you killed my friend."

"What friend?" Zargar was visibly confused.

"Vivak Patel. I doubt you even knew his name."

"The captain, eh? From CBI?" Zargar was smiling now.
"I ordered that myself. You've come to the right place if
you are looking for revenge."

"I came for justice," Sharma said.

"And what is that? Where do you find it?"

"Here and now," Sharma replied—and squeezed the
trigger of his AK-47, blasting half a dozen boattail rounds
through Zargar's chest within a second, lifting the dead
man completely off his feet. Geelani's second in command
sprawled on his back, while Sharma crumpled to his knees,
threw out one arm to keep himself from falling on his face.

Though fading rapidly, he was not finished yet. Two
major targets might still be at large, and Matthew Cooper
was somewhere in the compound, fighting for his life. If
nothing else, before he finally collapsed, Sharma wanted
to tell his friend of short acquaintance that he had eradicated one of G-troop's leaders. If nothing else, and even

if it took his dying breath, he could assure Cooper that he had not failed.

That was a matter of importance to him, even as he felt his life's blood draining from his body. In the time remaining to him, Sharma still had work to do. As long as he could move, draw breath and hold his weapon steady, he would fight. Let others judge whether his life was a success or failure, whether he had been a hero, fool or something in between the two extremes.

Weakening by the moment, by the step, he struggled on.

RIYAZ GEELANI SAW three men advancing toward him through the smoky darkness. All were armed, and while he could not see their faces yet, he sensed familiarity in how their leader held himself, the way he moved. There was no question in Geelani's mind that he'd seen all of them before—a logical assumption since they were inside his private compound, and his enemies, as far as he could tell from the accumulated evidence, numbered no more than two.

His soldiers? It was possible, and yet…

He had already emptied his T91 assault rifle, firing at shadows and imaginary interlopers as he moved around the camp, switching to the Benelli M4 shotgun in its place. The men he'd sent to gather reinforcements had apparently deserted him, or maybe they'd been killed before they could complete their mission. Either way, Geelani was alone once more, frightened and furious in equal measure, pressing on because he had no other choice.

He might be able to escape—but then what? With his army decimated and the DISI turned against him, what options remained? His lone hope, and slim one, lay in taking out the men who had betrayed him, proving to the world that even in extreme adversity, he still fought back and triumphed in the face of overwhelming odds. If he succeeded there, Geelani thought there was a possibility of rallying G-troop's survivors, supplementing them with new recruits, fighting his way back to the pinnacle of power that he'd long enjoyed.

But what of Pakistan? Collaboration with the DISI was a relatively new aspect of life for G-troop. He could do without it—or, perhaps, convince the agency's directors that it had been rash of them to side with Ibrahim Leghari and attempt to break Geelani's hold over Mumbai. Whatever, he would need to find Leghari first and deal with him.

And now, as if by magic, there he was!

Geelani recognized the major he had tried to kill a short time earlier, flanked by the bodyguards whose names he had not bothered to absorb. Before they could react to his appearance in their path, he had them covered with the shotgun, index finger twitching on the weapon's trigger.

"So, Riyaz," Leghari said. "You see, I am not dead."

"Neither am I."

"You thought I meant to kill you?" the major asked.

Watching for a move by either of the Pakistani bodyguards, Geelani said, "It hardly matters now."

"Perhaps you're right," Leghari acknowledged. And was about to add some other comment, possibly a whispered order to his gunmen, when they all ran out of time.

Geelani opened fire from twenty feet, riding the semi-auto shotgun's recoil, squeezing the trigger as rapidly as possible, sweeping the muzzle left to right and back again. Loaded with seven rounds, the 12-gauge emptied in a second and a half, his mutilated targets surrendering to the draw of gravity.

Geelani did not bother checking for a pulse on any of the three. Hits to the head and chest from sixty-three double O pellets were fatal, full stop. A close-up look would show him leaking brains and ravaged faces that a mother would not recognize. Why waste the time?

Regretting that he had not pocketed more ammunition for the shotgun while he'd had the chance, Geelani dropped it where he stood and drew his Glock 19 with two rounds missing from its magazine. That pistol, and the grenades clipped to his armored vest, were all the weapons that remained to him, unless he picked up more along his way.

To where?

In search of other enemies. Sayeed Zargar, for one, and the two nameless bastards who had done their best to spoil his life.

If they believed that they were finished with him, they had made a critical mistake.

BOLAN WAS CLOSING in behind Major Leghari and his flankers when they stopped short in the southeast quadrant of the compound, confronting someone who'd emerged out of the battle haze to intercept them. Bolan couldn't see around Leghari and his men to make an ID on the guy who'd blocked their path, but they were talking to him, back and forth in Hindi, unintelligible to the Executioner.

Their conversation didn't last long. Two or three exchanges, then the man he couldn't see cut loose with what had to be a semiautomatic shotgun, cutting down Leghari and his sidekicks in a storm of buckshot pellets. Some of those flew past the crumpling targets, headed straight for Bolan as he dropped and rolled, hearing the lead balls rustle overhead. He felt—imagined?—a warm sprinkling from their passage, maybe blood falling from some that had already passed through flesh and brains before they reached him.

Red rain coming down.

By the time he raised his head, the fellow with the scatter

gun had dropped it and was running off in the direction of the compound's gate. He held a pistol now, his upper body bulked out by some kind of garment that could be a combat vest, and Bolan wondered if he was imagining Riyaz Geelani's profile as the shooter fled.

Not likely.

Bolan rose and started after G-troop's founder, worried when the shadows swallowed up his quarry. Did Geelani know that he was being followed? Had he veered off course to lay another trap? Again, not likely, but the Executioner had not survived this long by taking anything for granted on a killing day.

Three rounds remained in the Milkor's cylinder. He had fed the INSAS autorifle a fresh magazine before he swapped it for the launcher. He could deal with anything Geelani tried—unless he dropped his guard and let the Mumbai mobster spring an ambush on him by surprise. Bolan was tough, resilient, all of that and more, but he had never been the "superman" that some reporters sketched in print before his staged death threw them off his trail.

Superior in skill and stamina, without a doubt, but not immortal.

One of the corpses sprawled before him suddenly sprang upright, howling, brandishing a knife the size of a short sword. Without breaking stride, Bolan gave his assailant a round in the face, obliterating skull and all with a 40 mm buckshot charge that had no chance to spread beyond a palm's width prior to impact. Running through the spray of blood—no doubt about the red rain, this time— Bolan left the headless body standing in his wake, knees buckling slowly as its muscles gave up waiting for a message from the brain he'd vaporized.

Where was Riyaz Geelani? Somewhere up ahead? Had he veered off to the left or right? Was he aware of the pursuit in progress, or was he proceeding on some strange, erratic course derived from instinct?

Two buckshot rounds remaining. Bolan could have fired at random, hoped he hit Geelani, *anybody,* but he didn't favor wasting energy or ammunition. He would wait until a target was presented, then would strike before it had another chance to slip away from him.

If he could find Geelani.

If he hadn't lost his chance for good, this time.

DAZED AND GROWING weaker by the moment, Baji Sharma found that he had lost his way somehow. Instead of circling clockwise through the compound as intended, he had either doubled back at some point, or had crossed the camp instead of following its fenced perimeter. In either case, he recognized the prefab building now before him as the barracks he had earlier cleared out with a grenade and automatic rifle fire. The corpses huddled by its doorstep were like old, familiar friends.

Disgusted with himself, Sharma limped past them, trailing blood, and sat on the steps, his legs going limp in front of him. He doubted that he would be able to stand up again, and found the thought of dying where he sat oddly…disinteresting. It almost bored him now, as he leaned back against the door frame, with his AK-47 braced across his lap. His trousers, soaked with blood, made little squelching sounds as he adjusted his position on the steps.

It was enough. His race was run. He still had two full magazines to feed the folding-stock Kalashnikov, together with his pistol and a couple of grenades. He would be pleased to blaze away at any targets passing in front of him, but as far as mounting a pursuit around the compound, Sharma knew that he was finished.

Where was Cooper? Alive or dead? He would not bet

against the tall American, but there were still at least a dozen shadow figures drifting here and there around the camp like wraiths, hunting or trying to avoid a hunter. It was odd, he thought, how they remained instead of fleeing from the compound. Was it loyalty? Fear of Riyaz Geelani? Possibly an atavistic craving for revenge?

Or were they simply lost, like him?

One of those figures was approaching Sharma now. Not Cooper; he knew that from the gunman's slouching posture. Shifting on the steps, Sharma raised his left knee to brace his rifle as he covered the advancing shadow-shape. He had his finger on the AK-47's trigger but resisted firing for the moment, interested suddenly in making out the features of the man he was about to kill—or who would finish him.

And Sharma almost laughed aloud as he made out the face of Mumbai's crime lord.

"We meet at last," he called out, almost cheerfully.

"And who are you?" Geelani asked.

"You would not know my name," Sharma replied. "Your men have tried to kill me several times."

"One of the infiltrators?"

"At your service."

Through clenched teeth, Geelani told him, "I congratulate you on your fighting spirit. And your friend? Where is he?"

"Busy elsewhere, I suppose," Sharma said, as another burst of automatic fire rattled across the camp. "I'm sorry that you missed him."

"I shall make do with what Allah has presented to me."

Shiva help me, Sharma thought, as he began to raise the sagging muzzle of his AK-47. It had gained weight, somehow, dragging on his arms and shoulders as Geelani

raised a pistol from his side and slammed a bullet into
Sharma's chest.

The impact bounced him off the barracks door frame,
and he slithered down the wooden steps, his rifle slipping
from his fingers. Sprawled on his left side, waiting for the
pain to register, he had a dizzy sideways view of legs and
feet advancing toward him, stopping within arm's reach,
if his arms had still possessed the strength to move.

Riyaz Geelani knelt before him, peering into Sharma's
eyes. "That wasn't difficult," he said. "I don't see what the
fuss was all about." He waited, possibly saw Sharma's lips
move silently. "No answer, then? Shall I leave you to it?"

Sharma felt the muzzle of Geelani's pistol pressed
against his forehead. It was warm.

Just like a mother's good-night kiss.

MACK BOLAN HEARD two pistol shots, well spaced, the second muffled, and he moved in that direction. Why? He'd
found the shotgun that Geelani dropped, figured his target
could be down to fighting with a sidearm now—but it was
more than that. The last two shots had sounded like an execution, with a coup de grâce, and Bolan couldn't picture
anybody else from G-troop taking time for that, when they
could better use their time evacuating Hell.

Bolan had spotted several G-troopers making for the
gate, and he'd backed off of his resolve to kill them after
all, preferring to pursue Riyaz Geelani. Now, just when
he had begun to think he might have blown it, pistol shots
refocused him. He got a fix after the second shot, picked
up his pace, advancing swiftly toward the spot where he
was reasonably sure the sounds had come from.

Two men huddled in the door yard of a barracks that
had suffered only minor damage, maybe shrapnel from
within, and one short strafing at the northwest corner.

One man, Bolan saw, was out of it, the other rising from a crouch beside him, handgun dangling at his side. A few more steps, and Bolan recognized the face of Baji Sharma, masked by blood, distorted from within by pressure from a close-range gunshot to the head, but still a semblance of the man he'd known and fought beside over the past two days.

"Geelani!" Bolan called out to the other man, the one he'd hunted since arriving in Mumbai.

The crime lord turned to face him, startling Bolan with a crooked smile. "You found me after all," he said. "Your friend hoped we would meet."

"Looks like he got his wish," Bolan replied, watching the mobster's gun hand.

"This is like one of your movies, yes? *Gunfight at the O.C. Corral?*"

"O.K. Corral," Bolan corrected him—and fired his Milkor from the hip before Geelani had a chance to raise his pistol. Impact from the 40 mm buckshot round lifted the mobster off his feet and slammed him back against the barracks wall, spread-eagle, and before he slipped away, the last round from the launcher pinned him there, painting a crimson splash across the pale aluminum siding.

Dropping the empty weapon, Bolan moved to kneel beside his fallen comrade, checking for a pulse although he knew the exercise was futile. Head wounds were not always fatal, but the sergeant's massive blood loss, plus a bullet to the chest *and* a point-blank shot through his left temple, had eradicated any sign of life.

The sound of running footsteps at his back distracted Bolan. In a single fluid move, he dropped the INSAS rifle from its shoulder sling and pivoted to meet a pair of shooters closing on him from behind. Whether they'd seen their leader die or simply happened on the scene by chance did not concern him. Coldly and efficiently, he fired two

3-round bursts that put the shooters down and left them thrashing spastically until the last spark shivered out of them and they were done.

Then it was time to go.

He set down the rifle and hoisted Sharma's corpse over his shoulder in a fireman's carry, then retrieved his weapon before straightening to stand erect. The trick of carrying another human was to move and stay in motion, let momentum do at least a portion of the work.

And leave no fallen comrade on the field.

He didn't know when the authorities would reach Geelani's compound—or, in fact, if they *would* come. For all he knew, there might have been some backup plan in case of a disaster, that would bring G-troop survivors and collaborators in to sweep and sanitize the battleground. Riyaz Geelani might be one of those durable desperadoes like Jesse James or Billy the Kid, whose death was disputed by closet admirers, elevating him to the status of an invincible urban legend.

Whatever.

Bolan knew that he was dead, along with Ibrahim Leghari. If Sayeed Zargar had managed to escape, so be it. He would have to build the outfit up from scratch, without his Pakistani sponsor to assist him. And if he was lying dead somewhere around the compound, why, so much the better.

The compound's gate was open and unguarded when he reached it. Bolan watched for shooters lurking in the shadows, but the ones who'd managed to survive—however few there were—had obviously used their energy escaping while they had the chance. Still, he was wary as he started on the hike back to the hidden rental car, holding his autorifle ready as he carried Baji Sharma through the fields of clinging kunai grass.

The plan, as far as he had formed one in his mind, was to deposit Sharma's body near a hospital and phone it in to the authorities. Whatever happened after that was out of Bolan's hands, and wouldn't matter much to Sharma. If there was an afterlife of any kind, the gutsy officer would be there, working on his next great mystery. If not…well, what the hell?

In Bolan's world, a soldier did his duty without any promise of reward, in this world or some other. Warriors carried on because they could, because they recognized their contract with a so-called civilized society. They kept on fighting until the issue was resolved by victory or death—and sometimes both.

Sharma had played his hand out to the bitter end.

Mack Bolan still had other hands to play.

EPILOGUE

Iberia Airlines Flight 4709, Mumbai to London

Bolan missed the funeral, but watched a snippet of it live on CNN, using his laptop. It was big news for Mumbai, five officers of the Central Bureau of Investigation found slain within twenty-four hours and buried together with the police equivalent of full military honors. Talking heads regaled their audience with the traumatic loss of Special Deputy Director Jai Bhagwan Sherawat, Major Arutla Yugandhar, Captains Vivak Patel and Kapil Ram, and Sergeant Baji Sharma. Graveside speeches hailed all five as fallen heroes, speculating that their killers had been terrorists, most likely bankrolled from Islamabad.

As for the battle at Riyaz Geelani's camp, authorities were claiming that they'd crushed a nest of smugglers thought to be involved in the narcotics trade. More details would be broadcast at a later date, after the dead were all identified and evidence had been subjected to analysis by experts at Mumbai's Central Forensic Science Laboratory, operated by the Indian Ministry of Home Affairs. The study was expected to require at least eight weeks.

The sat phone buzzed as Bolan switched off his laptop. "So, you're homeward bound?" Hal Brognola asked.

"Looks like it," Bolan said.

"Sorry about your friend."

"He knew the odds."

"I see they're spinning it for all they're worth."

"What else is new?"

"No mention of Geelani or the other big shots, yet."

"Why waste a first-rate bogeyman?" Bolan asked.

"That's one way to handle it. Beef up appropriations if they lay the whole thing off on him, and pound the drum for sanctions against Pakistan."

"Does that surprise you?" Bolan asked.

"Nothing does, these days. Now, if I woke up and the gray was gone out of my hair..."

"They've got a rinse for that," Bolan advised.

"I heard. Thing is, I can't afford to turn the ladies on like that, you know?"

"Must be a burden."

"I'm just saying."

"I've got a layover in London," Bolan interjected. "Should be Stateside by the day after tomorrow, latest."

"See you then," Brognola said. "We've got a couple things you might look in to, if you're up for it."

"I can't wait," Bolan told his oldest living friend.

"Stay frosty, eh?"

"The only way to fly," the Executioner confirmed, and killed the link.

And he *was* looking forward to the next job. Something he could talk all day and night about, but never make civilians understand.

A warrior fought because he could.

The Executioner was blitzing on.

* * * * *

The
Don Pendleton's
Executioner®
BREAKOUT

A secret syndicate profits by freeing ruthless criminals...

When notorious killers and drug lords break out of a maximum-security penitentiary, it soon becomes clear that these weren't escapes; they were highly organized rescues. A covert organization is selling prison "insurance," promising to bust criminals out of jail for a hefty price. With the justice system in shambles, Mack Bolan steps in as an undercover rival insurance salesman, hiring his own team of con men. But he'll need more than his war skills to destroy the operation's kingpin.

GOLD EAGLE®

Available February, wherever books and ebooks are sold.

GEX423